Peter Buckman wa: publishing and is no

still working. In between he was a full-time writer, producing books, plays, scripts for films, television and radio, articles and reviews. *The Pumpernickel Mysteries* are his first crime series, and feature a quartet of characters in their seventies (including the dog) who are still working, still learning, and still enjoying life with all its problems. Peter and his wife Rosie have lived in the same Oxfordshire village for over fifty years: they have two daughters, two grandchildren, and a black cockerpoo called, amazingly, Pumpernickel.

The Pumpernickel Mysteries

Dead Early
Dead Honest

Dead Rich
Dead Famous
Dead Unpopular
Dead Religious

DEAD HONEST

Peter Buckman

WORD OF MOUTH BOOKS

ISBN: 978-1-0683333-1-6

Cover design by Nick Castle.

Published by Word of Mouth Books.

WORD OF MOUTH BOOKS

One

Felix's fury with his grandfather didn't evaporate when he found him dead at his desk. It turned into disbelief, then grief, then guilt.

He managed to hold it together through an inquest, which was inconclusive, and a memorial service in Westminster Hall, where the Prime Minister led the tributes. The PM described Sidney Playfair as a MP of the highest integrity, which was a diplomatic expression to disguise his loathing and contempt for a man who had resigned from his own front bench on a matter of principle.

The glamorous Lady Maxine Ensor, who always looked good in black, called Sidney a worthy opponent, though she had sworn the House of Lords would shred his Accountability Bill, which would have penalized politicians who broke their promises.

A junior member of the royal family said the King mourned the loss of a man who would have revolutionised politics; a popular comedian joked that he wasn't surprised that security was so tight, because if a bomb removed all the politicians present, the country's problems would be solved at a stroke.

Some commentators said this was in poor taste, but it aroused appreciative murmurs and some bitter laughter from the many members of the public who attended. Hundreds of thousands of them had marched in support of Sidney's campaign to hold politicians to account, and many muttered suspiciously about his death, which occurred the day before he'd hoped to see his bill get its Second Reading in the Commons.

After the memorial Felix returned to Oxford to resume his studies, and promptly had a nervous breakdown. He attempted to kill himself with paracetamol and whisky; his friends found him comatose and covered in vomit. He was confined in the Warneford Hospital and kept on suicide watch. All he would say was that Sidney's death was his fault. He refused to explain why.

~ ~ ~

Pumpernickel barked when he bounded into the office a week after Sidney's funeral, and saw the state of it.

He'd gone ahead of Leo up the stairs to their second-floor rooms in the narrow Soho house perfumed with Chinese spices from the grocery on the ground floor, with his master puffing a bit behind. They were both about the same age – ten in dog years, early seventies in human – and both considered themselves fit, though Leo maintained he was entitled to get a bit breathless when exerting himself, it was a sign everything was still working. Which it was, mostly, and though his hearing wasn't as sharp as it used to be, he no longer needed glasses to read the subtitles he turned on when watching TV. You win some, you lose some. He still hated his hearing aids and insisted they made things worse. Marion, his partner for the last five years, said he had to be patient. Which had never been one of his virtues.

The main office looked alright, dominated by the desk that was slightly too large for the space, but which had been a bargain at the second-hand furniture warehouse in Peckham that threw in an almost-new leather orthopaedic chair with levers whose function Leo had never worked out. The Arsenal mug of pens and pencils, the metal tray of papers awaiting filing, the flat-screen monitor, cordless keyboard, and compact printer were all in place by the window whose glass was dusty and frame slightly rotten, but which still afforded a clear view of the room on the opposite side of the street where mature people in colourful Lycra were twisting themselves into impossible yoga positions. The framed prints on the walls were undisturbed, including the Warhol of Marilyn Monroe given to Leo by a grateful client, which hid a safe he scarcely used, as so much was digital these days. The three padded visitors' chairs were in their usual place on the faded Persian carpet, another bargain whose stains were hidden beneath the desk, the legal books on the shelves were untouched, and Pumpernickel's dog basket, with its tattered blanket and selection of chews, was where it always was, between the desk and the door.

It was the smaller office that looked as if it had been hit by a snowstorm . Filing cabinets had been torn open and their entrails spilled all over the floor. The drawers had been pulled out of the compact desk that Leo's secretary Marjorie had used for years until she died. You couldn't see the lino on the floor for papers and folders. The only thing left untouched was the table under the skylight that held a tray on which was a coffee maker and several porcelain mugs the cleaning lady always left upside down.

Leo said, 'What the—' and Pumpernickel barked again.

'Maybe that boy who came in yesterday?' Leo suggested, looking around, not knowing where to start. 'You know, the ex-con, Malcolm something, wanted help with his girlfriend who's an illegal. You were a bit wary of him, remember?' Pumpernickel growled.

Leo bent down with a grunt to grab the nearest sheaf of papers. 'He was a fidget, that's for sure,' he continued. 'Couldn't sit still for a moment, and he wouldn't take no for an answer. Is it my fault he can't get anywhere with the Home Office? But why take it out on us? And I didn't even charge him!'

He glanced at the papers in his hand while picking his way to the coffee machine. The dog, undecided how to help, sat down in the doorway between the two offices. A preoccupied Leo stepped over him, holding the steel coffee pot he was going to fill with fresh water from the kitchen on the floor below. He managed this while still reading the papers in his hand.

'The Conigsby case,' he said. 'Why did I waste such eloquence on a *momser* like that, eh, Pumpy? God, I was good in those days!'

He looked down at the dog. 'You're supposed to say, "You still are,",' he said. As Pumpernickel remained silent, Leo dropped the papers back on the floor and went out. Left on his own, Pumpernickel wandered further into the room and started sniffing around in that zigzag fashion that looks haphazard but indicated he'd picked up a scent. When Leo returned several minutes later, the dog was sitting on an open folder, looking pleased with himself.

'I've talked to Mr Chi,' Leo said, 'and it wasn't the boy at all.' He put the coffee pot on its stand, fitted it with a filter paper, added six scoops of ground coffee, decaffeinated continental roast, and switched the machine on. Pumpernickel wrinkled his nostrils and gave a short bark of encouragement.

'Yes, well, Mr Chi said this woman arrived just as he was opening, and begged him to let her come up here because she wanted to leave me a surprise birthday present. Except my birthday's in August, and her gift was to turn us over!' The dog growled.

'So Mr Chi didn't see her leave, and when I asked what she looked like, he said we all look the same. What else can I tell you? I filled your water bowl, by the way.'

He poured himself a mug of coffee, which he took black, ran his hand through the curly white hair that he allowed to grow down his neck to compensate for it retreating from his forehead, and sat in the little office chair Marjorie had used. He looked around with resignation.

'Lucky we don't have a busy morning,' he said. 'And if you look on the bright side – like when do I do anything else? – I've been meaning to have a clear-out. Marjorie was a bit anal when it came to retaining things—'

Pumpernickel whined. 'It's OK,' Leo continued, 'I wasn't criticizing. She was terrific, and she was with me for longer than I've had you. She kept everything organized, but you know what? If she was so good with computers, how come we've still got all this?' He waved his hand around the blizzard surrounding them.

Pumpernickel yelped. 'Alright, I don't trust computers either,' Leo said, 'but what choice do you have these days? People make notes on their phones! Does anyone use a fountain pen, let alone know how to fill one? Yet when all those satellites crash into each other, or the sun has one of its magnetic storms, the whole damn internet is going to go down, and it'll be back to pen and paper. Or pencil.'

The dog lifted his head and barked. Leo frowned at him while sipping his coffee. 'You don't have to make such a noise,' he said. 'You can disagree with me politely, you know what I'm saying? We've both had a bit of a shock here, but there's no need to make a big drama out of it.'

Pumpernickel got off the folder he'd been sitting on, and made a noise at the back of his throat that was between a yelp and a growl. He looked from Leo to the folder, and back again, then cocked his head to one side. Leo put his mug down. 'What?' he asked. 'What have you got?' He levered himself upright without grunting too heavily, and went over to the dog, who encouraged him with another throaty noise. Leo picked up the folder, and sniffed it.

'What's that smell? Is that why you're making such a fuss?' he asked. In response he got a brief bark. Leo patted him on the head, and read the name on the tab.

'Nancy Chen. What about her? Rings a vague bell, but you know what? I think my memory's slowing down a little. I mentioned this to Marion, and she says it's because there's so much stuff stored away in our ageing brains, you can't always get to it as quickly as you'd like. In court it's not a problem, or not yet, but when you throw a name at me out of the blue...'

He bent down and picked up some of the papers scattered around Nancy Chen's folder. 'OK,' he said, glancing through them, 'so she had a problem with her insurance, and her mortgage, and with the Home Office, but who didn't? Why would Marjorie file all this stuff, when Nancy Chen must be...Wait a minute! I remember now! She gave me some papers to keep before she was killed in a skiing accident or something! And her boyfriend, or ex-boyfriend, came round asking if I had the letters he wrote to her. That's right! He was getting married, and he didn't want his letters to fall into the wrong hands, or some such *bupkis*. I told him they would be the property of the person they were addressed to, and he wasn't pleased. But they're not here, are they?' He hunted among the litter, then suddenly straightened up.

'The safe!' he said. 'Maybe that's where they are! Not the letters – I don't remember her giving me any letters – but whatever she gave me to look after before she went skiing. That must be, what, twenty years ago? I hardly put anything in the safe now. Digital security, ha!'

He picked up his mug and strode into the other room. Pumpernickel trotted after him. Leo took down the

Warhol, revealing an old-fashioned combination safe, also a bargain, cemented into the wall. He twisted the lock, muttering numbers to himself, and the door swung open. The space was crammed with papers; Leo took some out and blew the dust off them. He glanced at the names, shook his head, put them down on one of the visitors' chairs, and grabbed another handful. On the third attempt, he found what he was looking for.

'Dr Nancy Chen,' he read. 'A sealed envelope addressed to herself in Ealing. Hm.' He took the envelope and his coffee over to his chair, and threw himself into it. Pumpernickel made a flying leap into his basket and sat up expectantly.

'Now why,' Leo continued, brushing dust off the sleeve of his caramel-coloured cashmere jacket, 'would she want this kept safe? It's a cheap way of registering copyright in something – we had a whole sheaf of songs by that lyricist, very gifted she was, before your time, anyway she gave up and went into teaching Pilates. But Nancy Chen: she was a scientist of some sort, I seem to remember. Her family were very proud of her.'

He sipped his coffee, and made a face. 'Cold already,' he said. He tapped the envelope on his desk while thinking. Pumpernickel waited patiently. 'I suppose,' Leo said, 'I should give this to her family. Except they went back to Hong Kong when she died, and I've no idea where they are. And I doubt Mr Chi is in touch with them: when he took over the lease, there was a big argument over repairs that should have been made and weren't. I helped sort it out, remember? That's why I was allowed to stay when he chucked out all those boys who claimed to be inventing computer games, though I'm sure they were into porn. I could ask Mr Chi if he knew where the Chens went, but I bet he won't know. He's from Taiwan.'

Pumpernickel barked encouragingly. Leo got up. 'You're right,' he said, 'I need more coffee. I wonder if she made a will? I don't remember her doing so – she was only in her mid-twenties, after all, twenty-eight tops: at that age, you think you're going to live forever, don't you?' He wandered towards the other office. 'Marjorie made a list of all the wills we hold, of course she did. I've got a copy on my computer. But if Nancy's isn't among them, then what do we do? Apart from tidying up this mess . . .'

He refilled his mug, returned to his desk, and turned on his computer. He tapped a few keys, peered at the screen, scrolled down, then pushed the keyboard aside.

'Nothing,' he said, drinking some coffee. 'Nancy Chen never made a will, or if she did, she didn't lodge it with us. At least my memory's not entirely shot. The big question is, what was the woman who got in here looking for? She was obviously not a burglar, or she would have taken something of value, like the Warhol. I should get that insured, by the way, but the premiums are ridiculous.'

He looked at the dog accusingly. 'And why did you pick on the Nancy Chen file? Just because it smelt funny? That's meant to be a help?'

Pumpernickel barked and gave his owner a reproachful look. 'OK, OK,' Leo said. 'I'm not saying you did wrong. Let me guess. You smelt something distinctive on that one folder. Which I suppose could mean that our intruder spent longer examining it than the other files. Yes?'

The dog gave a throaty yap that Leo took for agreement. 'Right,' he said. 'Now I'm not as smart as you when it comes to smells – that's another thing that dulls with age, but let's not go there. For me, what's on that folder could be a trace of perfume, or a cream she was using, like a moisturiser, or maybe the woman's own body odour, who knows? We won't know – *I* certainly won't know – what it is or who it belongs to until we smell it again. Or you do. Which may never happen.'

Pumpernickel shook his head. 'I'm sorry,' Leo said, 'but it's the truth, and you know it. However...' The dog raised his head hopefully. 'The fact that you chose a file relating to a sealed envelope hidden in our safe may well have some significance. Did you have a proper sniff around everything in there?' The dog yapped. 'And the Chen folder is the only one with a distinctive odour?' Another yap.

'Well,' Leo continued, 'I trust your judgement on matters like this. Not to mention the fact that it's the only clue we've got. The question is, what do we do with it? It's no good taking it to the police: all they'll do is give me an incident number, which is not much use as I'm not going to make an insurance claim, am I?'

He drank more coffee and swung round in his chair to see if the yoga class would give him inspiration. All it did was make him shudder, and he swung back to face his dog. 'I think we should open it,' he said. 'If we can't find her family, and we don't know if she left any beneficiaries, it's all we've got to help us identify our intruder. Which will be our justification if anyone asks. But I'd better do it in front of a reliable witness.'

Pumpernickel stood up, wagging his tail. Leo shook his head sorrowfully. 'I'm sorry, my friend,' he said, 'but unfortunately your testimony would not be accepted in a court of law. Ridiculous, I know, as you're at least as intelligent as many of the people I've encountered there, and if the Solicitors' Regulation Authority accepted canines, you'd be a partner, you know you would. But for now, it'll have to be a human.'

He looked at his watch. 'Ten past ten,' he said. 'A couple of hours till we meet Dennis for our usual. We can make a start on tidying up next door. And you can have another sniff around. You never know what you might find.'

~ ~ ~

Dennis Arbuthnot, the world's most fearless crime reporter, according to his byline, occupied a settle built for three at the usual table in the usual pub where he met his old friend Leo, and Pumpernickel, for a lunchtime drink if none of them had anything more pressing to do.

He was a large man with a fleshy face that inspired confidence rather than acting as a warning against excess. His eyes were sharp, his nose was prominent and not, surprisingly, empurpled, he always wore a double-breasted dark suit with shirt and tie, and his voice was like apricots marinated in brandy.

'You're late,' he said, as Leo arrived with Pumpernickel, who slid under the table where there was a bowl of water awaiting him. 'You are also dusty and dishevelled, and it's your round, not that any of these things are unexpected or unprecedented.'

'We've been burgled,' Leo responded, slapping down Nancy Chen's envelope, 'and you're going to act as a witness. Are you up to the task? Is that your first or second carafe?'

He nodded towards a small jug of Beaujolais which was half-empty. 'I'm having a spritzer. And before you give me that bollocks about it being neither fish nor fowl nor good fresh herring, it contains fewer calories than a pint of beer, and I still care about being able to see my knees without using a periscope.'

Dennis waved a dismissive hand. 'Pure vanity,' he said. 'Your knees are nothing to boast of. In fact, as I have frequently remarked, I cannot think what the fair Marion sees in you. She must have a generosity of spirit to match the generosity of her build. Why would anyone bother to burgle you, when you possess nothing of value?' Pumpernickel growled from under the table. 'Except the mutt, of course,' Dennis amended. 'A creature of superior intelligence, if lacking in articulacy. Are you getting them in, or not? One miserly carafe merely lays the dust.'

'Marion could drink you under the table,' Leo said, 'without breaking sweat.'

'She is a woman of impeccable pedigree,' Dennis said, 'and she would not sweat, she would glow. As to a drinking competition, I would welcome the opportunity.'

'Susan might have something to say about that.'

'Susan?'

'The wife of your bosom and mother of your innumerable children?'

'Ah. She enjoys seeing me rise to a challenge. And if you were about to make a fatuous comment concerning my sexual prowess, desist!' He drained his glass, and emptied the wine jug into it.

Leo sighed, went to the bar, and returned with another carafe, a white wine spritzer, and a bag of unsalted peanuts which he opened and put on the floor for Pumpernickel. He clinked his glass against Dennis's, took a sip, smacked his lips in exaggerated enjoyment, put the glass down, and dusted off his hands.

'Now,' he said, picking up the envelope. 'Are you ready for this?' Pumpernickel looked up from his nuts. Leo paused. 'I suppose,' he said, 'I should take a picture. Before and after, you know what I mean?'

He got out his phone. Dennis regarded him gravely over his wine. 'You have always been a drama queen,' he said. 'I recall the night of one of those

15

innumerable parties you and Deirdre gave. Well, perhaps "gave" is not the *mot juste*; they "happened" in that basement flat you had in Notting Hill, when all sorts of undesirables would turn up claiming to be pioneers of bohemian excesses.'

'You were there often enough,' Leo remarked, taking pictures of the envelope from every angle to show it was properly sealed.

'Purely to add tone to an otherwise disreputable gathering. I needed some respite from the demanding task of reporting the foul crimes of my fellow citizens, with the eloquence for which I am renowned. Anyway, one of your guests, an aspiring architect as I recall, was talking to a not unattractive young woman, an actress, when his new wife appeared, grabbed the ukulele on which you erroneously claimed to be an expert performer, and smashed it on her husband's head, thus performing a great service to those of your friends with any musical discernment. You made a great fuss, not, to my surprise, over the destruction of your instrument, but because you were afraid a case of assault and battery would be brought, and you did not welcome the attention of the local constabulary in case they discovered you were growing weed on your windowsill. And while you were gibbering hysterically, it turned out that the cause of this altercation was your own wife Deirdre, who enjoyed making trouble when she was high. I wonder if all that cannabis hastened her dementia? Anyway, she had apparently told the young wife her husband was about to bed the actress, which was a complete fabrication. You, however—'

'George Ramirez,' Leo interrupted, absorbed in the papers he'd taken out of the envelope and reading them with growing excitement. 'Could that possibly be the same—'

'The chairman of Zarastro Oil,' Dennis snapped. 'What about him?'

'This is a report addressed to him when he was head of their research department,' Leo said. He turned the pages, rapidly scanning and exclaiming at their contents. He reached for his glass and took a big swig.

'It predicts what will happen if they go on drilling for oil and gas. All the things we've seen in recent years – floods, fires, global warming, loss of species, acidification of the oceans, destruction of the environment–'

'Old hat,' Dennis said dismissively. 'People are already suffering from disaster fatigue. Such news is now relegated to the inside pages, except in the *Guardian*, whose readers enjoy being bludgeoned into despair.'

'But this was written twenty years ago,' Leo said, 'and nobody talked about it then, did they? Obviously it was suppressed, which is scandalous! This could be a scoop for you, Dennis! A crime against the truth! I had no idea...'

'Heard it all before,' Dennis said, emptying his glass in one swallow.

'How?' Leo demanded. 'I've only just found this in my safe, and you are my witness! Maybe this is what the burglar was after, though I've no idea how she might have known of its existence.'

'Rumours of just such a report were brought to my attention,' Dennis said darkly. 'Such is my reputation–'

'Who approached you?' Leo asked.

'You know I never reveal my sources.'

'Do you want me to tell Susan about you competing with Frank Naylor to see who could eat a box of chocolate truffles quickest?'

'That was for a charitable cause.'

17

'Since when was the Society of Beaujolais Drinkers a charity?'

'Well,' Dennis huffed, 'as I never used the story, and nor could anyone else without corroborative evidence, it came from the office of the late Sidney Playfair MP. In the person of his special adviser, a quite personable young woman called Ginny Larue.'

Leo lowered his voice, and tapped Nancy Chen's envelope. 'Sidney Playfair, the champion of honesty and accountability, knew about this report?' he said.

'One of his constituents turned whistleblower. The report existed only in rumour. As I told Miss Larue—'

'But here it is!' Leo said excitedly. 'In black and white! The evidence you need!'

Dennis poured himself more wine, and sighed. 'Let us assume,' he said, 'that Mr Ramirez actually received it...'

Leo fiddled with his hearing aids, then took one out in frustration. 'Bloody things,' he said. 'I can't hear with them, I can't hear without them. Of course Ramirez suppressed it!'

'I said *received* it,' Dennis said more loudly. 'There is no proof—'

'*This* is the proof!' Leo said, flourishing the report. 'Why would she bother addressing a copy to herself and having me look after it if she didn't think evidence of its existence would be needed? Obviously Zarastro buried it, because nobody's heard of it!'

'Did she say anything to you about it when she deposited it?'

'No. Or if she did, I don't remember. She brought it in, postmarked as you can see, then went off skiing and got herself killed. It was supposed to be an accident, but maybe...'

Dennis held up a podgy hand. 'Maybe if you drank decent wine instead of that acidic juice, you would be less prone to conspiracy theory. Even if the rumours about that report's existence now turn out to be true, it means very little. Let us assume it landed on Mr Ramirez's desk, along with the hundreds of reports commissioned on a regular basis by the research department of a large oil company. Its conclusions would damage the company's profits: of course Mr Ramirez would prevent them from being made public. There is nothing illegal in that, as you should know. The report is their property, and they are entitled to do with it what they will. Big corporations, like government departments, bury reports all the time. No surprises there.'

'But...' Leo protested. Pumpernickel pushed his head into his lap. He knew, even if Leo didn't, when there was no point in arguing. Leo patted him, and put his hearing aid back in.

'Even if you could prove they suppressed it,' Dennis continued, 'no one would bat a jaded eyelid. People expect oil companies to behave badly: your trouble, my friend, is that you are an idealist in a world that runs on realism. You remain stuck in the 1970s – I am surprised you don't still appear in a flowered shirt and address me as "man" while puffing on a loosely stuffed joint.'

Pumpernickel gave a huge yawn. 'That flowered shirt came from Carnaby Street,' Leo said, 'and if I could button it across my *boyech* I'd be wearing it now. Why did Sidney Playfair's spad – what was her name? – Danny Larue...?'

'Now you are showing your age,' Dennis said. '*Ginny* Larue approached me on her employer's behalf because the whistleblower insisted, like you, that a damning report had been suppressed. Sidney, knowing of

19

my extensive contacts, wanted to know if I had heard anything about it. This was, of course, before the whistleblower met an untimely end.'

'Which didn't make you suspicious?'

'If a young gay man is foolish enough to go running late at night wearing expensive trainers, in a park notorious for harbouring homophobic addicts of various kinds, what do you expect?'

'Wait a minute. Was his name Larry Coombs?'

'It was. His death made a para on page twenty-nine. I did not write it myself.'

Leo emptied his glass and banged it down. 'His foster mother came to me. She'd been to see Sidney Playfair to get the police to investigate Larry's death properly. She was not happy with his response, and the next thing she knew, Sidney had died. You don't have to be paranoid to suspect these things might be connected! And it's your round.'

'Much as it pains me to have to pay for something that resembles the urine of a diabetic donkey, put it on my tab. Are you aware who is the main financial backer of Sidney Playfair's campaign for accountability?'

'No,' Leo said, getting up to go to the bar, 'but you're going to tell me.'

'I never cease to be astounded by the depths of your ignorance. The answer is George Ramirez. Why would a businessman who prides himself on playing his cards close to his impeccably tailored chest, finance a maverick's attempt to bring in a law to punish politicians who break their manifesto pledges? Which they do as regularly as they brush their teeth and cheat on their partners.'

'You're asking me?' Leo said. 'You're the one who's always saying I don't know how the world works.'

'Your expertise, if I can dignify it with that name, extends a little way into the law, and occasionally to domestic cookery. Susan praises your recipes, but then her palate has coarsened with age. I do not know why Mr Ramirez was behind Sidney Playfair's campaign, but the corrosive connections between finance and politics are so common, they scarcely raise a ripple of controversy. An idle mind like yours may seek distraction by investigating such matters, but my readers are more interested in a sanguinary murder.'

'Like that of Larry Coombs?'

Dennis waved him towards the bar. 'A drug-induced homophobic robbery?' he said. 'I need something worthy of my talents, that will make the front page!'

~ ~ ~

'The secret,' Leo informed Marion while cutting an aubergine into inch-wide chunks, 'is to marinate them for as long as possible. One thing I've learned, most stews are better the day after, when the flavours have been properly absorbed.'

'As long as that doesn't mean,' Marion said, 'that we have to wait until tomorrow to eat this delicious – what's it called?'

'A *caponata*.'

'I'm starving!' She was sitting with a glass of Greek red wine, a Xinomavro, at the kitchen table of the flat she had inherited from her father in a mansion block overlooking Hyde Park. She was a couple of years older than Leo, and a couple of inches taller, though as he was fond of pointing out, it made no difference when they were lying down. She was generously built, with a solidity that inspired respect, and she had the sort of face that combined the ruddiness of an outdoors person with fine features that radiated kindly concern. Her expression had

21

an openness about it that made you want to be her friend, and her head was topped by a helmet of short, fine hair dyed whatever colour took her fancy. Today it was a coppery bronze.

She watched Leo slice a red pepper to go with the chunks of aubergine and courgette already bathing in olive oil, along with quartered shallots and a couple of garlic cloves, kept whole to add flavour but not to be swallowed, as it was a school night and neither of them wanted to offend the clients they would see the following day.

'You're sure there's nothing I can do to help?' she said.

'I promise it won't take long,' he assured her. 'I've just got to add the sun-dried tomatoes, olives, capers and a tablespoon of maple syrup, and it'll be ready in half an hour, three-quarters tops. I could knock up some hummus if you're that desperate. Or should I distract you by chasing you naked around the sofa?'

Pumpernickel covered his ears. Marion stole an olive. 'I'm sure that would be very nice,' she said, 'but it would be such a fag having to get dressed again, wouldn't it? We can't do justice to one of your creations wearing pyjamas. What about your burglary? Shouldn't you report it? You just missed my last client, a detective chief inspector with a morbid fear of seagulls.'

'Did you find out why?' Leo said, using his hands to mix all the vegetables in the baking tin to ensure they were covered in oil and seasoning. He wiped his fingers on a paper towel and shoved the tin in the oven. Then he washed up the knives he'd been using and sat down opposite Marion with his glass.

'We traced it back,' she said, pouring him more wine, 'to when he was making love to a young woman on a secluded part of the Sussex downs.'

'*Is* there a secluded part of the downs?'

'Apparently so. Anyway, just as they were getting down to business, a passing seagull dropped a used condom on them. Which made him impotent for several months.'

'Did you sort him out?'

'I helped him to see it was a chance encounter, not that he was being picked on by a moralizing bird intent on exposing promiscuous policemen. Gulls pair for life, but I don't think we can credit them with teaching other species how to behave. Who might have attacked your office?'

Leo shrugged. 'I thought it might be an ex-con with a short fuse we couldn't help, but Pumpy found the only clue so far. He sniffed out a folder that led me to unearth a report that's been in my safe for twenty years. To me, it could lead to a huge scandal, but Dennis says I'm naive, nobody's shocked by anything anymore. I suppose he has a point.'

'That doesn't mean you shouldn't follow your instincts, does it?' Marion said encouragingly. 'Dennis is a journalist, it's his job to be cynical. You're not like that. One of the many things I love about you is your enthusiasm.'

'And I thought it was my body and my cooking,' Leo said, looking pleased. Pumpernickel rubbed himself against Marion's legs. He was a fiercely loyal creature, and though he could be critical, he totally approved of people he respected giving his owner praise. She scratched behind his ears.

'Those too,' she said, 'and that – *caponata?* – already smells delicious. But don't let Dennis put you off looking into something you think matters. I know he's one of your closest friends, and I like the old rogue, even if he

23

does believe he's a plus-sized Adonis and hides his sensitivities behind a facade of rhetorical flourishes. But if you're convinced there's something seriously wrong...'

'You're always telling me I'm not a detective!' Leo complained in that slightly wheedling tone men use when they want confirmation they're on the right track, as if they weren't convinced themselves. The tone that hints they want to venture slightly beyond their comfort zone, and are concerned about looking foolish, though they would never admit it.

Marion drank more wine. 'I only said it requires considerable training,' she said, 'and that it's dangerous to jump to conclusions without sufficient evidence. Also you tend to get emotionally involved, which is a good thing in many ways, but not when it comes to judging guilt or innocence.'

'What, you don't make those judgements?' Leo said. 'How can you avoid it when people tell you their most intimate secrets?'

'It's precisely then that I need to be impartial. I try and help people come to terms with their mistakes, whereas a detective's job is to ensure they get punished for them. But I'd never try and stop you investigating something you feel strongly about. What's in this report that Dennis dismisses?'

Leo got up to see how his dish was doing. 'She was a client of mine,' he said, stirring the vegetables around with a wooden spoon and putting them back in the oven. 'Five more minutes. A young Chinese scientist who worked for Zarastro Oil. Shall we eat in here? It's easier.'

Marion nodded, and pulled out a drawer in the table to get utensils. 'I know Zarastro. I was at finishing school with the daughter of the founder. She called herself

24

Persian – I dare say she still does. Mehrnaz Faruq. I wonder if she's still around?'

She laid knives and forks in their places. Leo automatically straightened them. Not that he was obsessive, he just believed that if you took trouble over the cooking, you should take trouble over how you presented and ate it.

'When I first met you,' he said, 'at the Rivoli Bar—'

'You put that ridiculous deerstalker on the stool next to yours.'

'I was reserving it for you! And it keeps my ears warm. Anyway, I didn't realize you knew everybody who was anybody. I only chose The Ritz because it was central. To be honest, I was surprised they let you in wearing Doc Martens. Not that anyone would have dared trying to stop you.'

'Confidence is all. That's what I tell my patients. You struck me immediately as a self-confident person.'

'I did?' Leo said, trying to look surprised. 'I wasn't, though. I didn't know what to expect. The dating column in *Private Eye* doesn't insist on accuracy. Shall I serve from here?'

'Why not? Is that flatbread going with it?'

'Shit. I forgot to warm it.'

'It'll be perfectly fine cold. Do you know why I knew you were confident? Because you asked me what I wanted, rather than telling me. Which, in my experience, is what most men do on a first date, in an attempt to assert their manliness. That's enough for me.'

'You call that a proper helping?' Leo asked rhetorically. He wiped a dribble of the sweet-and-sour sauce from her plate with the edge of his stained apron, and put it in front of her. Then he shoved the flatbread on another plate, helped himself to the *caponata*, took off his apron, and sat down. Marion had already started eating.

'Delicious!' she said, tearing off a piece of flatbread to mop up the gravy. Leo tasted his.

'Could have done with a splash more wine vinegar,' he said.

'Nonsense. You're just fishing for compliments.'

'Cooking is an art. The law is a profession. You can be confident about your professional skills, but with a work of art, you never know how it will turn out. Cheers!'

They clinked glasses, drank and ate in appreciative silence until Marion put her knife and fork together with a contented sigh.

'I really enjoyed that,' she said.

'I don't want to sound like a Jewish mother,' Leo said, 'but you had so little, if you don't have more, I'll worry there's something wrong with it.'

'Didn't you say it would be even better tomorrow?'

'Yes, but that might mean it wasn't quite good enough today.'

'Do you,' Marion asked with mock severity, 'want me to take back what I said about you being self-confident? Or will that cause you to question my view of your irresistible attraction, extraordinary sense of humour, penetrating intelligence and generosity of spirit?'

'I've shut up already,' Leo said, with his mouth full.

'Good,' Marion said, sitting back to drink her wine. 'Because I also hope you're going to follow up this case involving Zarastro. Don't let Dennis put you off. Not that I'm telling you what to do...'

'I love it when you do,' Leo said, chewing on the last of the flatbread.

'No you don't. Not really. You're an independent spirit, Leo Wengrowski. You care about what's happening in the world, when most men – most people your age, our age – have resigned themselves to grumbling about it. They'll say it's the young's turn to protest, then they'll criticize their tactics and strategy and ignorance of history. Like Dennis, they relish reporting on failure. You still believe in the possibility of success. Don't you?'

'You're getting me all stimulated,' Leo said, draining his glass. 'And it's only Tuesday.'

Pumpernickel shook himself all over, stalked across to his basket next to the stove, turned round three times and curled into a ball.

'He may be supple enough to lick his own penis,' Leo commented, 'but he's still a bit of a prude.'

Two

The following morning Leo's granddaughter Jazz arrived at his office only forty minutes late. A young man, Robin Pocklington, trailed at her side looking anxious. Pumpernickel was delighted to see them both and greeted them effusively. Leo, who believed in punctuality, though he invariably left himself less time than he needed, partly because he hated hanging around waiting, partly because he believed being in a rush got the adrenaline going as well as keeping his weight down, allowed Jazz to give him a big hug. She was his only grandchild and he adored her.

Jazz, short for Jasmine, was the daughter of Leo's and Deirdre's only child Tina, who Leo had wanted to call Janis, after Janis Joplin, but they settled on Tina, after Tina Turner with whom she had absolutely nothing in common. When Leo and Deirdre split up following ten years of hazy indulgence and mild recrimination, Tina stayed with her mother and Leo was convinced she had disapproved of him ever since. She was the ferociously well-organized head of geography at a comprehensive school, married to a biology teacher called Raymond who nobody took seriously, which suited him fine. Tina chose the care home which Deirdre contentedly agreed to enter when she developed dementia. Leo paid for most of it and didn't, in Tina's view, go to see Deirdre often enough. He felt guilty, but did little about it, though he was careful not to cancel visits he had promised to undertake. His ex-wife didn't always recognize him, which was both a disappointment and a relief.

Jazz had won a scholarship to Balliol College, Oxford, which Tina deprecated as an elitist institution, though she was secretly immensely proud of her daughter, who was now in her second year reading History. She also coxed the women's first rowing eight: she was on the short side, like her grandfather, and she had his grey-blue eyes and curly hair, though hers was still brown and she had a lot more of it. She also played real tennis, drank pints of beer without putting on weight, visited immigrants held in detention centres while their status was being decided, and had twice been beagling, much to her mother's disgust, though Jazz insisted it was just getting to know the enemy. She had no hang-ups whatever about sex, which Leo pretended to be shocked by but actually admired. His formative years were the 1970s, he had had many affairs, he had never forced himself on anyone against their will – for him and his friends, no meant no, and any other behaviour marked you out as a male chauvinist pig, a term now as outdated as flared trousers. The kind of sexual freedom Jazz enjoyed seemed to be the only lasting legacy of the revolution Leo's generation had fervently believed in. He was shocked that their failure to change the world was blamed for turning an alarmingly high number of today's youth towards right-wing populism, with its hatred of foreigners, homosexuals, people whose skin colour was anything but white and anyone who ate tofu – the very people whose company Leo enjoyed. Jazz, fortunately, was both tolerant and progressive, as well as being a vegetarian like her grandfather.

'We're worried about our friend Felix, Gramps,' she said, throwing herself into one of the visitors' chairs and crossing her legs. She was wearing a short black skirt over leggings with a hole in them, which Leo noticed but knew better than to comment on. The young man who'd accompanied her was dressed entirely in black except for a long rainbow-coloured scarf wrapped flamboyantly round his neck. He perched on the edge of a chair with his knees together. If he'd had a handbag, it would have been on his lap, secured by both his hands.

'This is a professional consultation?' Leo asked, hovering by his desk. 'I thought you were just popping in to say hello after one of those all-night orgies. You want coffee?'

'Coffee would be great,' Jazz said, uncrossing her legs, 'but I can get it.' She prepared to stand up, but Leo waved her down.

'There's a bit of a mess next door,' he said. 'We were burgled. Or, to be strictly accurate, as your mother would say, we were broken into and a lot of papers were thrown around. We're sorting them out, but you can't rush these things. I hope you both take it black. If not, you'll have to pop down and buy some milk, Jazz. I do those stairs six times a day, and it's enough already.'

'Black is fine, Mr Wengrowski,' Robin said, in a surprisingly deep voice for someone so pale and thin. He had a slight accent that Leo thought might be South African or Australian, and dark floppy hair which he tossed back frequently.

'Was anything stolen?' Jazz asked. 'I take it you weren't around when it happened. They didn't try and hurt my Pumpy, did they?' The dog obligingly bounded over to her and allowed himself to be petted.

'Fortunately,' Leo said, 'your Pumpy, not to mention your beloved grandfather, were a bit late getting in. He found the only clue we have, to give him credit. He has a good nose.'

'It's a lovely nose, isn't it, Pumps?' Jazz said, smoothing the hair on the dog's face. 'So do you know who broke in? Is my clever Pumpy going to make a citizen's arrest?'

She addressed this question to Pumpernickel, and gazed at him as if expecting a reply. She got a short bark.

'He's not saying,' Leo explained, 'at least until we've got more evidence. I'll get the coffee.'

He went into the next office, where some of the floor was now visible thanks to Leo piling up the papers in untidy heaps.

'I could murder one of your chocolate digestives, Gramps,' Jazz called. 'Unless you're going to take us out for lunch. I haven't had any breakfast.'

'I've got a two o'clock,' Leo said, appearing with a tray on which were three mugs of black coffee. He put it down on the edge of his desk, indicated that his visitors should help themselves, sat in his chair, and pulled open a drawer. He held up an open package.

'Two left,' he announced, pushing the pack towards them. 'Don't say I don't make sacrifices for my family. And their friends. So who's this Felix?'

Jazz grabbed one of the biscuits and bit into it. 'He's on suicide watch,' she said, through a mouthful of crumbs.

'In the Warneford,' Robin added, taking the remaining biscuit and nibbling at it fastidiously. Pumpernickel kept an eye on them both. He knew chocolate was bad for him, but he didn't entirely believe it. Like his owner, he was an optimist.

'That's in Oxford,' Robin helpfully explained. 'All they do is keep him drugged, so he's like a zombie. Half the time he doesn't know where he is or who we are. And it's all my fault!'

He gave a deep sob that so moved Pumpernickel he went straight over and put his head in Robin's lap. That he was still holding his biscuit was pure coincidence.

31

'It's not *all* your fault, Rob,' Jazz said firmly. 'You did some things which weren't helpful, but if you'd just kept them to yourself...'

'What "things" are we talking about?' Leo asked, sipping his coffee. Robin was trying to finish his biscuit so he could pat Pumpernickel's head. Jazz answered on his behalf.

'He's Felix's boyfriend,' she said, 'and he strayed. Happens all the time, right? Who knew it would push Felix over the edge? And who goes in for confession in this day and age? If Robin wasn't a fucking theological student...'

'People still study theology?' Leo said. 'With all the *tsurrus* religion causes, you can get a degree in it? No wonder your mother disapproves of Oxford!'

'I believe in honesty,' Robin said sadly.

'Only because it makes you feel better!' Jazz snapped. Robin looked as if he was about to cry. She backtracked. 'Sorry, I didn't mean that,' she said. 'It just you don't realize – maybe men in general don't realize – that honesty can be very hurtful.'

'If you've come here just to philosophize,' Leo said, finishing his coffee, 'you can do it next door, while helping me to put letters in the right files. A relationship counsellor I am not.'

He put his hands on the arms of his chair to push himself up when Jazz said, 'Actually, Gramps, it wasn't your help we came for. It was Marion's.'

Leo collapsed back into his seat. 'Marion's?' he echoed.

'Jasmine says she's the best in the business,' Robin said.

'So is Gramps,' Jazz said loyally, 'when it comes to defending drug addicts and sex workers and stuff. People who are screwed-up? Not so much.'

Pumpernickel gave a little bark of disagreement that made Robin's hands fly to his face. 'It's OK, Pumps,' Jazz said soothingly. She patted her lap for him to come over. He hesitated. 'I wasn't criticizing,' Jazz continued. 'Gramps knows I love him just as much as you do. It's just, you know, horses for courses.'

Somewhat mollified, the dog trotted over to her. She scratched behind his ears, whereupon he lay on his back with his legs in the air so she could rub his tummy.

'You are such a pushover, Pumpy,' Leo remarked. 'Luckily, I need more persuading. If your friend Felix is already under medical care...'

'They're not doing him any good,' Robin said.

'Quite the opposite, in fact,' Jazz said. 'They're making him worse. Marion was my idea. And who better than you, Gramps, to persuade her to take Felix on? You're the most persuasive man in the world!' She gave him a dazzling, wide-mouthed smile that was both artificial and coquettish. Leo held up his hands in surrender.

'Alright, already,' he said. 'You'd better give me some details.' He opened his notebook and clicked his ballpoint pen.

'His name's Felix Playfair,' Jazz said.

Leo wrote it down, then looked at her. 'Playfair?' he said. 'Is he by any chance—'

'Sidney Playfair's his grandfather.'

'Was,' Robin said. 'Felix found him dead. They were very close.'

'He'd just finished a constituents' surgery, and Felix was going to drive him to the final meeting before his Accountability Bill was debated in the House of Commons.'

'Felix thought he was having a catnap. He was a diabetic. Sidney, I mean. Felix isn't. At least not as far as I know.'

'You'd know,' Jazz said tartly.

Leo shook his head to clear it. Pumpernickel returned to his basket beside the desk.

'This is so weird,' Leo said. 'I was talking about Sidney Playfair with my friend Dennis only yesterday. In connection with our burglary, as a matter of fact. I thought his death sounded suspicious.'

'Funny you should say that,' Robin commented. 'Felix thought he'd caused it.'

~ ~ ~

Earlier that morning, DC Alan McNeill had got out of bed as quietly as possible so as not to wake his partner Katy, who knew him as William Flanagan. He had prepared the six a.m. feed for their son Midge, and picked him out of his cot before he started fussing. He fed and burped him, changed his nappy – a proper cloth one, not a disposable – and settled the boy down, where he cooed contentedly and became fascinated by his fingers. His father returned to bed and gently stroked Katy's arm. She smiled sleepily.

'No trouble?' she asked.

'No trouble.'

She turned towards him, her eyes still closed. 'You're a really good dad, William,' she said.

'I know,' he said. 'I'm an angel in human form. You wanna feel my wings?'

She snuggled closer to him and opened her eyes. 'Doesn't feel like a wing to me,' she said. 'And I thought angels didn't have cocks.'

'Hell's angels do.'

34

'Oh,' she said. 'Right. Just a quickie, then. You don't mind if my eyes close? We were up very late planning the new campaign.'

'You keep 'em closed. Just think of me as part of the dream team.'

Afterwards, he brought her a cup of Fairtrade tea. The baby was still waggling his fingers in amazement. Katy sat up and he helped make her comfortable against the pillows. She yawned and rubbed the sleepy dust from her eyes.

'I could get used to this,' she said. 'You mustn't spoil me.'

'Why not, if you deserve it?'

'You're the only one who thinks so. Lots of rows, last night.'

'Over what?' he asked, sipping his tea from a chipped mug saying 'Just Stop Oil'.

'Tactics, of course. Like always.' Katy Shaw had short dark hair framing a small, fine-featured face with large brown eyes that gazed unblinkingly at a troubled world. She worked as a part-time paralegal in a firm of solicitors who did a lot of pro bono work defending victims of a hostile bureaucracy, and she refused to feel guilty about owning a flat in Battersea thanks to the generosity of her maternal grandmother, who had a big win on the Lottery and went to live in Spain to escape the disapproval of her relatives at her taking up with a much younger man.

'Let me guess,' William said. 'They wanted to block traffic on Waterloo Bridge, you said it would piss people off.'

'Westminster Bridge, but otherwise correct.'

'They want to climb Nelson's Column and pour paint on his head.'

'Nice idea, William! Bit difficult, though. Could we organize a drone to drop paint from above?'

'They'd shoot it down.'

'But that would scare the pigeons. Any protest that causes harm to animals is doomed.'

'Even police horses?'

'Including police horses,' Katy said firmly. 'And especially dogs.'

He looked at his watch. 'I'd better get ready,' he said. 'I can walk Midge round the park before taking him to the baby-minder. Then I'm on duty till four.'

She put a small hand on his arm. 'You work so hard,' she said.

'Not as hard as you,' he said lightly. 'It's only organizing people in a recycling plant. Hardly rocket science. What have you got on today?'

Katy yawned. 'Sorry,' she said. 'Zarastro Oil. Not boring or anything, just that I never catch up on sleep. Even when you get up to feed him, I'm still aware of what needs doing.'

'What, you don't trust me?' he said jokingly.

'Of course I do. It's just, I don't know, instinct or hormones or whatever. I can't let go. Maybe I should try meditation or something.'

'Or drink more.'

'You know I'm a lightweight when it comes to booze.'

He cupped her chin in his hand and looked at her with troubled eyes. 'I love you, Katy Shaw,' he said, and kissed her delicately on the nose. Then he got up and stretched. Naked, he had a slim body with some scarring he claimed came from being beaten by his stepfather until he grew big enough to fight back. He was small, neatly bearded, with close-cropped brown hair that had a touch of red. His teeth were slightly chipped – another childhood legacy – but they added an allure to his smile, which he was sparing with. A serious young man, they all thought, who could be trusted to do whatever he promised.

The baby lost interest in his fingers and uttered a little cry to see what would happen. William went over and scooped him up. 'Here,' he said, taking him over to the bed, 'have a cuddle with your mum while I get dressed.' Katy took him and nuzzled the back of his fragile neck, inhaling the smell that vanishes so quickly but that parents always remember. William looked down at them and allowed himself a smile.

'Zarastro Oil?' he said casually, on his way to the bathroom. 'Is that the one run by George Ramirez, everyone's favourite polluter?'

'That's the one,' Katy said, her voice slightly muffled by Midge's neck. 'We're building a case against them. They're claiming to be one hundred percent behind the government's clean air policy, while lobbying to water it down. If we make the case stick, it could be more effective than anything our campaign committee is planning. But of course I can't tell them that.'

'What can you tell them?' he asked.

'Not a lot, at the moment,' Katy replied, blowing raspberries on her son's bare back which made him giggle and squeal. 'That whistleblower who was stabbed – he came to lots of meetings – he said there were rumours of a damning report into the firm's activities that was made twenty years ago. The practice I work for is trying to find out what happened to it. Obviously Zarastro suppressed it.'

'But that's not against the law, is it?'

'Maybe not, but misrepresenting the truth is. Think how it would look if a huge oil company that claims it never knew the damage its products caused, turns out to have known all along, and kept quiet about it! That's going to sink their share price, isn't it, baby?' She turned her son over and blew raspberries on his belly button. He giggled so much he could hardly breathe.

~ ~ ~

Leo gave Ginny Larue lunch at the Groucho, of which he was a member for three reasons: it was round the corner from his office, it welcomed Pumpernickel, and its members had blackballed his friend Dennis when he applied for membership. They sat at a corner table at the back of the restaurant and Ginny insisted on facing the room so she could network.

'I need a job, you see,' she said, sipping a Campari and soda while her eyes darted around, looking for likely possibilities. She had glossy brown hair which grazed her shoulders and a long lively face with flared nostrils that reminded Leo of an intelligent horse. She was tall and not ashamed or awkward about it: her posture suggested purposeful elegance.

'What kind of job?' Leo asked, helping himself from the bottle of Soave the waiter had left in an ice bucket. He didn't bother diluting it with soda water: that would spoil the mushroom risotto he'd ordered. Pumpernickel lay quietly under the table. He'd had his lunch at the office, and was busy digesting it.

'I don't know,' Ginny said frankly. 'I'm tempted to say anything that'll pay the mortgage, apart from pole dancing, but I've not been besieged with offers. Special advisers are two a penny, aren't they? In the food chain they come just above interns, and who wants a spad whose boss made a lot of enemies and then died just before bringing his life's work to fruition? Is that Alastair Campbell over there?'

'Probably,' Leo said, without looking. 'Do you want to stay in politics? See Sidney's Accountability Bill through Parliament and all that?'

'Oh, it won't pass now he's gone,' Ginny said airily, 'not unless someone with real charisma – someone like Mayor Mike McDonald, say – took it up, but he's far too busy, and he's not even an MP anymore. And the MPs who said they'd support it? They'll all be very relieved the Second Reading's been cancelled. Turkeys voting for Christmas, isn't it? Why would you vote for a bill that makes you accountable for promises you only made to get elected? Oh, thank you,' she said sweetly to the waiter who brought her a bowl of minestrone. 'Yes, pepper and parmesan, please. Thank you *so* much.'

Leo, who wasn't having a starter – he had *some* willpower – played with a breadstick while the waiter showed off his peppermill. 'How did you get the job in the first place?' he asked.

'My mum is a teacher at the school Sidney's wife Beth is head of,' Ginny said cheerfully. 'I mean, I went to Oxford, I've got a two one in PPE, but it's who you know, isn't it? I thought about being a dancer, but I'm a bit tall; I flirted with being a journo – I was deputy editor of *Cherwell*, doing all the boring stuff – but let's face it, the old media don't have much of a future, do they? You'd be far better off being an influencer on TikTok or whatever. There's always the City, I suppose, but that'd be like being back at Oxford, with a bigger expense account. So when Mum suggested I have a chat with Sidney, and he offered me a job, I jumped at it. I'd been a member of the Labour Club, mainly because my boyfriend at the time was president, but Sidney had just got the funding to galvanize his campaign, and he wanted someone to help organize it. I may be hopeless at organizing myself, but I'm quite good at organizing other people.'

Her face suddenly widened in a radiant smile, she put down her soup spoon and gave a little wave to someone Leo didn't recognize. The smile vanished as quickly as it came, and she pushed her soup aside. 'Arsehole,' she said. 'He was always looking for stories to discredit our campaign. I'm surprised he didn't come over to gloat. Or perhaps that's against the club rules.'

She drained her Campari noisily. Leo filled her wine glass. 'The funding,' he said. 'Was that from George Ramirez?'

'Gluttonous George? Though that's not fair; I should really call him Generous George, as he paid my salary. Do you know him? Yes, thank you, it was delicious,' she said to the waiter who removed the remains of her soup.

'Only by reputation,' Leo said.

'Oh, ketchup *and* mayonnaise, that would be lovely,' Ginny said in answer to the waiter's question as he put down her burger and chips. Leo slipped a chip to Pumpernickel and spread his napkin over his lap as his risotto arrived.

'You would think,' he said casually, 'that Sidney and George would be unlikely bedfellows. A left-wing MP who resigned from the front bench because his leader reneged on all his promises, and the head of a global oil company who fiercely defends his industry while insisting they're investing heavily in renewables?'

'If you'd met George, you'd know it makes sense,' Ginny said, biting into her burger unconcerned about the sauces dribbling down her chin. Leo approved of anyone who enjoyed their food. He had a forkful of risotto and waited for her to chew and explain.

'He hedges his causes the way other people hedge their funds,' she said, wiping her mouth. 'He'll support anything that looks as if it has a real chance of success, because he prides himself on always being on the winning side. Of course, if the cause fails, he'll deny he ever had anything to do with you – he's a bit of a shit that way.' She picked up a chip and dunked it in mayo. 'He talks to the royals about the environment and puts money into the republican movement. And he turned down a knighthood.'

''Cos he was waiting for a peerage?' Leo asked.

'Correct,' Ginny said, preparing for another bite of her burger. 'And he gives great parties, though he's ruthless about dropping people who don't come up to his expectations.'

'My!' Leo said. 'He sounds like a total *shmegegge* to me. I still don't see why he'd back Sidney. What have they got in common?'

Ginny swallowed more wine. 'If I'm being charitable, I'd say that George believes that a world where people say what they mean and do what they've promised is a good place to do business. Sidney's bill would have done away with the bullshit and seen people penalized for breaking their pledges. What businessman could resist?' She attacked the remains of her burger with gusto.

'OK,' Leo said toying with his risotto. He would have been more generous with the mushrooms and added a bit more stock. And possibly a dash of vermouth. 'I won't ask what you'd say if you were being uncharitable. So I have two questions. Why, if the Accountability Bill was so popular, won't another MP take it up? And how did Sidney and George come together in the first place?' He

41

stole another chip, this time for himself, not his dog. Who stirred beneath the table but didn't complain.

'I don't know the answer to the second question,' Ginny said, clattering her knife and fork together and throwing herself back against the cushions with her glass in hand. 'That was before my time. All I know is the campaign office was financed by Zarastro, and whatever we asked for, we got. Which brought results, let me point out, that proved the investment was worthwhile. As for the first question – I don't think I could, thank you,' she said in response to the waiter asking if she wanted to see the dessert menu. Leo shook his head and asked for a decaffeinated double macchiato. Ginny indicated she was happy with her wine.

'As for the first question,' she resumed, 'it was a matter of personality. Sidney had... they call it charisma, but I'd call it integrity. You could believe what he said, and people did. Can you think of many other MPs that's true of? Even the ones who said they'd support him didn't really mean it. They were just jumping on the bandwagon. Sidney gave you hope, and that's electoral gold.'

'Are you saying you don't think it would have got enough votes to pass?'

'A First Reading is a formality. But a Second Reading for a bill that sets up citizens' juries to decide whether a politician was justified in breaking their manifesto promises? Come on! They would have cut off its balls in committee. It's lucky, in a way, Sidney didn't live to see that happen. It would have broken his heart.'

'OK,' Leo said, as the waiter brought his coffee, 'another question. How did he die?'

Ginny peered into her glass and swirled her wine around it. 'No one's quite sure,' she said eventually. 'The inquest, as I'm sure you know, brought in an open verdict.

Something stopped his heart beating. It could have been stress over whether or not the bill would pass the next day—'

'Convenient for his opponents that he should die just before introducing it,' Leo said.

'You could say that,' Ginny said with a grim smile. 'His constituency secretary said they had a pretty lively surgery before he was supposed to attend a big rally that evening; maybe somebody said something to upset him.'

'I was told he was a diabetic.'

'I kept him off cake and sweeties.'

'I was also told Sidney knew about a damning report Zarastro kept suppressed for twenty years.'

'How did you know about that?' Ginny demanded. 'Did that whistleblower approach you too?'

'Can't tell you. How did Sidney react?'

'He got me to check it out. Which I did by going to one of the best reporters in the business.'

'My friend Dennis.'

'If he's your source, I imagine he would have said the same thing to you as he did to me. That he wouldn't write a story based on rumour and gossip. Not without proof.'

'As a matter of fact, I showed him proof,' Leo said. 'But guess what? Dennis said it wasn't news anymore. People are no longer surprised by what those bastards get up to. What about Sidney's grandson Felix? He found him, right? After they'd had some sort of row?'

'Felix!' Ginny snorted. 'What a drama queen he is!'

'Seriously? You know he's had a nervous breakdown?'

'And I'm sorry, but not surprised. Maybe he gets it from his mother Sally. She's your original wild child. I wouldn't call her a disappointment to Sidney and Beth, not really; they're very good to her, considering.'

'Considering?' Leo said, emptying his macchiato in one swallow.

'They didn't speak for years. I'm not sure why, but Sidney's not one for holding grudges; he'll have a blow-up, then forget about it, and wonder why people act sulky around him. But Beth is someone who takes her responsibilities seriously. Anyway, Sally turned up at their place one day, out of the blue, with baby Felix. The father had a hotel on a Greek island, with a wife and several children of his own. You know the kind of thing. Sidney and Beth brought Felix up, and he's quite bright – he got into Oxford, and came up the year I went down, though we never bumped into one another, not until I started working for Sidney. Felix helped with the campaign from time to time, but he was a bit useless. He gets quite stroppy if you ask him to do something he thinks is beneath him.'

'Such as?'

'Stuffing envelopes. Cold-calling to sign up supporters. Getting people to donate money or raffle prizes. All the little things a successful campaign relies on.'

'So what did he do?'

'Drove Sidney around, mostly. Especially to the big rallies; he liked those, the whole rock star thing. Sidney used to bring him onstage and say stuff like, "This is why I'm doing this, to be accountable to my grandson, because we all want to be able to look our grandchildren in the eye and say, we did what we promised!" Which is why he was so upset when Felix attacked him. Though he is a little – what do they call it? On the spectrum? Felix, I mean. I had to have words.'

'What kind of words?'

'I said he had no business upsetting his grandfather just before his big rally. He tried to tell me I didn't understand; I told him *he* didn't understand, and if he had any idea of how important this was for the country, for the whole world, really – how much it mattered to Sidney, the man who had acted like a father to him and loved him and encouraged him – I said Felix should really go in and make it right.'

'And?'

'He left it too late, didn't he? When he went in to collect him after his last appointment, he found Sidney dead. And of course Felix went all to pieces.'

'You know,' Leo said, signalling for the bill, which brought Pumpernickel out into the open for a stretch and a yawn, 'that young Felix is in hospital – the Warneford, is it called? – on suicide watch?'

'So I'd heard,' Ginny said, 'but that's not down to me. I was just doing my job, protecting Sidney, to get him over the line. Oh look, there's Andrew Neil.'

Leo twisted round, just as the bill came. 'Would you want to work for him?'

'God, no! Anyway, he's just another doomed dinosaur, isn't he?'

'Careful,' Leo said genially. 'We dinosaurs can still bite, even if we're vegetarians.'

~ ~ ~

'Underdressed?' Marion boomed, with a laugh that made the glasses tinkle on the waitresses' trays. 'Don't be ridiculous. Compared to me, you're Beau Brummell!'

They were at a gallery in St James's for the opening of an exhibition of children's book illustrations by one of Marion's clients, whom she had rescued from depression and creative block. The women wore little black cocktail dresses, the men were in dark suits with white shirts and striped ties. Leo was in his caramel-coloured cashmere jacket, which he wore over a slightly wrinkled blue shirt, open-necked because he couldn't bear anything tight around his throat. His blue corduroy trousers, which had an expandable waist, ended in brown brogues, highly polished as always, another legacy from his father, a man with romantic ideas about revolution who made a decent living selling shoes. Marion's long and shapeless black cardigan covered a faded check shirt tucked inside baggy jeans. She wore trainers.

'So why are they all so poshly got up?' Leo asked. 'Are they expecting royalty?'

'I'm sure Camilla's been asked,' Marion said airily. 'She's always been a friend of Jeremy's, who trades on it shamelessly, the little shit. He does decent canapés, though, and offers proper fizz. And the pictures are good, aren't they?'

'Scary is the word I'd use.'

'Kids love being scared, provided it all comes right in the end. Just like us, really.'

'You scare me sometimes,' Leo said, sipping champagne and fiddling with his hearing aids. 'I'm sure they told me there was a setting on these things specifically designed for parties.'

'Why bother?' Marion said heartily. 'They won't be talking about anything interesting. They're mostly here to be seen with the Queen, if she turns up, not admire the pictures.'

'That's what's scary about you. Your honesty.'

'I thought you liked my honesty.'

'I love it. To be honest, what frightens me is that you'll see me for what I really am, and go off me.'

46

'Perfection is boring. That's why the greatest masterpieces are either fashioned out of unpromising material, like Michelangelo's *David*, or left unfinished, like Milan cathedral. Which would you rather be, unpromising or unfinished?'

'Being called promising is usually the kiss of death to a career. Can I be a work in progress?'

'Of course you can,' Marion said. She kissed him on the top of his head, which he found both a pleasure and an embarrassment. 'Where shall we go for dinner?'

'Why do we spend all our idle moments thinking or talking about food? Is that healthy?'

'Because it's more interesting than sex,' Marion said loudly, causing a few well-coiffed heads to turn. 'What is there new to say about sex, at our age? But we still tear out recipes that promise a little wrinkle on something familiar, even if we never get round to trying it. Good cooking, such as yours, doesn't just provide filling, it stimulates the imagination, it tickles all the senses, it is soothing and satisfying, and it requires patience and skill whose rewards are long-lasting. People may, when young, have similar expectations about sex, but they are invariably disappointed. And I speak from experience, as many bring their disappointments to me.'

'God help me if I cock up a recipe, then,' Leo said. 'I have a favour to ask you.'

'You can always ask,' Marion said, grabbing a canapé from a proffered dish and allowing her glass to be refilled. Leo accepted the refill but declined the canapé.

'Jazz came to see me this morning.'

'How is she?'

'She's fine. But she has a friend—'

'Who is in need of therapy?'

47

'How did you guess?' Leo said in mock wonder. 'You have the wisdom of the oracle.'

Marion sighed and drank more champagne. 'What's their problem?' she asked.

'All I can tell you is that he's on suicide watch because he thinks he's responsible for the death of his grandfather.'

'OK,' Marion said seriously, 'if he's already under medical supervision, there's not much I can—'

'His grandfather is, or was, Sidney Playfair. The MP who—'

'Was about to introduce a bill to make politicians accountable *between* elections. Which is one of the most sensible proposals I've ever heard, short of turning Westminster over to pasture, which is what William Morris suggested in *News from Nowhere*. What's the boy's name?'

'Felix. Jazz, and Felix's boyfriend Robin, think the Warneford is not doing him any good. In fact, they're convinced it's making him worse. Jazz thinks you're the best in the business, according to this Robin. She's obviously got my genes and knows how to appreciate excellence.'

'Don't go overboard,' Marion said, with a wry smile that indicated to Leo she was thinking about the possibilities and complications. Her willingness to get involved made his heart soar with gratitude and admiration. 'It would have to be Felix's decision,' she continued, snaffling another canapé, 'and he'd have to convince the doctors he's capable of rational thought. Is he?'

'I've no idea,' Leo said happily, 'but I can ask Jazz. And we could talk about it at Wiltons. I will even watch you eat oysters, despite my grandmother describing them as tasting like cold snot.'

'It's a deal,' Marion said. 'I should warn you, however, that medical science has poured cold water – see what I did there? – on the oyster's aphrodisiacal qualities.'

'I would never use an innocent shellfish as a weapon for seduction,' Leo observed, 'though a psychologist might find it interesting that the conversation has moved from food to sex. I will book us a table.'

He got out his phone. As he was talking, a waitress came round and offered to refill his glass. He accepted, as did Marion. They toasted one another. There was a flurry around the door as Queen Camilla arrived. Leo groaned.

'Does this mean we can't leave until she does?' he asked plaintively. 'They've had a cancellation and will hold the table till half past. Nothing against her personally, though if she makes us miss our reservation, it will make me even more of a republican.'

Marion put her head close to his ear. 'There's a way out at the back,' she said. 'Follow me.'

Leo hastily finished his champagne. 'When have I ever done anything else?' he said.

Three

Leo considered he had made good progress on clearing up the mess left by the intruder of two days before. He had shredded enough redundant correspondence to fill three black bin bags, and was feeling quite pleased with himself, despite backache from all that bending and a pain in his right knee he was sure was arthritis. One of the dubious delights of getting older was discovering that there were some aches and pains you learned to put up with even though they were as annoying and hard to get rid of as mice in the roof. You could go to the trouble and expense of having them checked out and dealt with, but you didn't bother until they did something you could no longer tolerate, like the mice chewing up your wiring. In the organ recital of ailments old people go through, you either exaggerate your problems or make light of them, depending on whether you want sympathy or admiration. Marion was always sympathetic; Leo's daughter Tina would briskly tell him to go to a doctor as well as reforming his lifestyle. Which reminded him he should call her and arrange to go and see Deirdre with her. Or maybe Jazz would come with him. Dealing with a daughter who disapproved of him and an ex-wife who didn't always recognize him was like walking two spirited dogs: exhausting, but the hope was they would keep each other too busy to turn on him.

He heard the door to the main office next door open with a bang, and Pumpernickel began barking furiously. Leo got up painfully and went to see what was happening. He found a small, round, angry black woman in nurse's uniform shouting at Pumpernickel to be quiet.

'Mrs Macouba!' he exclaimed. 'Did we have an appointment? Thank you, Pumpy, that will do!' The dog gave a final bark to show he wasn't intimidated, then stopped.

'No, we did not have an appointment, Mr Wengrowski,' Mrs Macouba said. 'I came here to tell you I no longer want your services. I could have texted you but I wanted to do it in person, because I don't run away from things!'

Pumpernickel growled. Leo said, 'OK, Mrs Macouba. You want to tell me why? Take a seat. Can I offer you coffee?'

'No coffee,' Mrs Macouba said, plonking herself defiantly in one of the visitor's chairs. 'My shift starts in one hour. I tell you why, then I go. What have you done about Larry? Nothing!'

Leo eased himself behind his desk. What she was saying was not accurate. He had found the actual report Larry had only heard rumours of, and he had discussed it with Dennis, who was not prepared to do anything about it. Disappointing though that was, Leo was ready to share all this with Mrs Macouba, when she was in a calmer state of mind. Nobody likes being fired, especially if they have done nothing wrong. And at his time of life, when he didn't need hassle, it was a blow to his pride to be dropped by a client, rather than do the dropping himself.

The dog sniffed Mrs Macouba, then started barking again. She tried to shoo him away, but he ignored her.

'Pumpy!' Leo said reproachfully. 'I apologize, Mrs Macouba. He doesn't usually behave like this. He's a bit discombobulated, you see. We both. We were burgled—'

Pumpernickel's bark turned into a growl. He looked from Mrs Macouba to Leo. 'What?' Leo said. The dog made a warning noise, deep in his throat. Leo raised his eyebrows interrogatively. He got a series of short yaps in response. This conversation, if we can call it that, made Leo sit up and turn to his visitor.

'Mrs Macouba,' he said formally, 'forgive me for asking, but did you by any chance call here two days ago, saying you wanted to leave me a surprise birthday present?'

Mrs Macouba rose from her chair in fury, but when Pumpernickel growled at her, baring his teeth, she hastily sat down again. She clutched her handbag protectively.

'Yes, it was me,' she said, 'and I'm not sorry. Just keep him away from me, alright?'

'Pumpernickel,' Leo said quietly, 'let's just listen to what the lady has to say, shall we?' The dog snorted, then stalked over to his bed by the desk, and sat in it, staring at her intently.

'OK, Mrs Macouba,' Leo said. 'Let's hear it, and then we'll decide what to do. Burglary is a serious crime—'

'I did not steal anything!' Mrs Macouba exclaimed.

'But you came here to find something, right? Technically—'

'The Chinese gentleman very kindly let me in!' Pumpernickel growled impatiently. 'Why does he keep doing that?' she demanded.

'My canine colleague has highly developed detective skills,' Leo said proudly. 'Those nostrils of his can sniff out scents we are scarcely aware of. He knew you were looking for Nancy Chen's report: he could smell you'd been handling her file. Why did you think I would have it?'

'I told you when I first came to see you. You don't listen.'

'Maybe I don't hear. Tell me again.'

'Larry had heard about it. He knew you were her lawyer. But what did you do? Nothing! You and that Member of Parliament: my Larry gets stabbed, and nobody cares!'

'And you thought wrecking my office would help?'

'I didn't mean to do that,' Mrs Macouba said sullenly. 'My Joshua, rest his soul, he always said I got carried away. You don't know what it's like, when you suddenly become invisible. They want you to do something, they all smiles; you want them to do something, it's like you don't exist. You make a fuss, you done for. But when it really matters, I make a fuss, what else can I do? What happens? Nothing! You understand why I get carried away?'

'I understand, Mrs Macouba, and I imagine you thought making it look like a burglary would mean no one would suspect you. Though you reckoned without Pumpernickel.'

The dog bared his teeth in what could have been a smile or a threat. Mrs Macouba sniffed. 'I never cared for dogs,' she said. 'Nor cats neither. We had a parrot for company, Joshua and me. That and twenty-nine children.'

'How many?' Leo said, startled into adjusting his hearing aids. 'Did you say—?'

'Twenty-nine,' Mrs Macouba confirmed. 'We were champion foster parents for Leyton. There was a piece in the paper!'

'Right,' Leo said. 'And Larry was...?'

'The last. My favourite, though you not supposed to have them. Came back to live with me when my Joshua passed, even though he had a nice place of his own. Earning good money, he was, at Zarastro, which made it harder for him to blow that whistle. But he knew his duty, and he did it, even though he got himself killed!'

53

She got a tissue out of her bag and blew her nose. Leo fiddled with the mouse on his computer, then pushed it away. 'What made you think the report would be here?' he asked.

'I found his little notebooks!' Mrs Macouba said triumphantly. 'The police didn't bother doing a proper search, did they? They came across some gay porn, and that was enough for them. Case closed, like their minds.'

'OK,' Leo said patiently, 'but how did Larry know I was Nancy's lawyer? Didn't you tell me one of your nursing colleagues recommended me because I'd sorted out a problem with her landlord?'

'Yes, yes. And she said you did it in no time at all. You a regular Speedy Gonzalez, she said. So how come you all speedy for her and not for me?'

'You haven't exactly given me much time, Mrs Macouba. And I still don't know how Larry connected me and Nancy Chen.'

'Same way he heard of that report being locked away where no one could read it. A woman by the name of Patsy Finch. Worked with Nancy way back when. Retired long since.'

'Patsy Finch?' Leo said, waking up his computer and tapping keys. 'Doesn't ring a bell.' He scrolled rapidly down his screen, then pushed it away. 'Plenty of Patsy Finches, but none of them connected to Zarastro Oil.'

''Course there isn't!' Mrs Macouba said scornfully. 'She signed one of those whatdoyoucallems, where you go to jail if you breathe a word. Larry met her on one of his climate marches. He charmed her, of course he did – he could charm anybody and anything. And he was prepared to go to jail to do what's right: that's what I taught him!'

54

'I'd like to see these notebooks, Mrs Macouba. They could help provide the evidence—'

'You're not seeing them. You off the case!'

'Fine,' Leo said resignedly, 'but what do you propose to do with them? You don't have a very high opinion of police or politicians or lawyers; who does that leave in the fight for justice for your foster son? Journalists? Let me assure you, I've already tried them!'

'You say you got the report, so what are *you* going to do with it? You tell me that!'

'I could do a lot with it, Mrs Macouba, if I had something that cast light on what happened to it in the twenty years since it was written!' Pumpernickel growled in support. Mrs Macouba regarded them both suspiciously.

'You do something first,' she said, 'then I see.'

Leo's first instinct was to tell her to get lost. A distinguished lawyer and fighter for justice for more than half a century does not relish being set stupid tests by a wilful client. Yet there was something about this case that was beginning to grab him. What he had learned so far was more than enough to tempt him to go further. And he had Marion's encouragement. He sighed.

'What would you like me to do, Mrs Macouba?' he asked.

'How about you find this Patsy Finch?' she suggested.

Leo and Pumpernickel exchanged looks. In this age of universal surveillance, how hard could it be to find a retired scientist who, despite signing a non-disclosure agreement, had started Larry on the path that led to his death?

~ ~ ~

DC McNeill met his minder in a greasy spoon off the Edgware Road. DI Susan Pringle looked like an upmarket estate agent in her crisp white blouse and black trouser suit, with her fair hair tied back in a business-like ponytail. A half-eaten blueberry muffin was beside her cup of black coffee; Alan, in overalls bearing a company logo, and nursing a thick mug of strong tea, could have been a building foreman discussing the repairs needed to the various slum properties in his employer's portfolio. In fact they were talking about his seven-year-old daughter Yvonne, who had been suspended from her primary school for giving a black eye and a bloody nose to a boy called Darren who had accused her of trying to steal his trainers.

'I'll kill him,' Alan said.

'He's eight, and in care,' Susan said. 'I spoke to your wife Linda: she said he was trying to snog Yvonne, who dealt with him forcefully. The trainers were his cover story. Evie will be back at school on Monday, the boy won't go near her again, I promise you. Your daughter can look after herself. Maybe she gets that from you.'

'How can she, when she never sees me?' Alan said gloomily. 'She'll be a teenager by the time I've finished this operation. She'll be lost to me altogether. A girl who had to spend her formative years without a male role model...'

Susan cleared her throat and rolled some muffin crumbs around to give her fingers something to do. 'There's Clive, of course,' she said. 'He pops in every so often to keep an eye on things. Linda says he and Evie get on really well.'

'Really well?' Alan echoed mockingly. 'What does that even mean? Helps her with her homework, takes her to football practice, reads her a bedtime story? *I'm* the one should be doing all that!'

'You've got Midge to look after,' Susan said firmly, 'and that must be your focus right now. You're well embedded, doing a grand job, and the mission's at a crucial stage. That report they're sniffing around, that could scupper the clean energy summit the PM's chairing. Any scandal involving Ramirez is going to make us all look stupid, the PM relies on him so heavily. You dealt brilliantly with that whistleblower...'

'He was a pushover. Katy's a lot tougher. Once she gets hold of something, she doesn't let go easily, I can tell you!'

'Then you'll have to stop her getting hold of anything, won't you, DC McNeill? You volunteered for this job, no one forced you. You've done very well so far; complete it properly, and there'll be a promotion for you, I promise you that.'

'And Linda and Evie still think I'm in Washington?'

Susan nodded. 'We route your messages to them via our American colleagues' server, not that they would notice. Those little gifts you buy are delivered by FedEx. They miss seeing you, of course – we'll have to give you some home leave soon, but not till after the summit. Which isn't that far away.'

'It may not seem far to you, ma'am, but it sometimes feels like an eternity to me!'

'Of course it does, Alan,' Susan said, softening. 'But think how important it is to prevent those campaigners from dictating the agenda.'

'They think they're helping!' Alan said, taking a sip of his cold tea and shaking his head. 'I can never get my head around the fact that such intelligent people can be so deluded.'

'It's all a question of perspective,' Susan said, taking one more bite of the muffin. 'They insist they're the only ones with answers, but they don't understand, they refuse to accept, what the consequences would be if their policies were put into practice. People wouldn't stand for it! There would be constant battles over land and water and fuel and fur to keep you warm. But that's never the future your campaigners talk about, is it? They just attack the government for trying to keep a decent standard of living for everyone and still save the planet. Never forget, Alan, that you're working for the good guys, regardless of what your new friends tell you. And the good guys want you to find the source of this report before everything goes tits up. Understood?'

'Understood, ma'am,' Alan said, trying to sound as if he meant it.

~ ~ ~

Leo was being driven to his ex-wife Deirdre's care home by his granddaughter Jazz, who had borrowed her mother's car. Leo had given up driving when he moved in with Marion, partly because he didn't enjoy it anymore, especially at night, and partly because his old Mercedes was clapped-out and Marion had a comfortable Toyota hybrid, even if she was, in Leo's affectionate view, a lousy driver. Jazz's driving style was exuberant, but at least Leo didn't feel he had to keep his legs rigidly braced whenever she exceeded the speed limit. Not that he let that stop him *kibbitzing*.

'There's no rush,' he said. 'Your grandmother's not going anywhere. She probably won't recognize us anyway. Last time she thought I was a plumber and complained about the heating.'

'She recognizes *me*,' Jazz said proudly, braking suddenly as the lights changed. 'She knows I'm at Oxford and warned me about LSD. I didn't know you were into hallucinogenics, Gramps!'

'Me? Never!' Leo spluttered, being thrust against the back of his seat as Jazz roared off to beat a white van to her left whose driver was making lewd signs at her. 'We smoked a fair amount of dope, your grandmother and me – that's what we called it then – but when it came to tripping, alcohol was our drug of choice. Everyone knew people who tried LSD and walked off balconies convinced they could fly. Luckily, we lived in a basement.'

'You know Mum thinks your lifestyle is what gave Nana dementia?'

'I know your mother thinks I'm to blame for most things, whether it's war in the Middle East or the rise of populism. I wouldn't be surprised if she didn't hold me responsible for potholes like that one,' he added, as they bounced over a puddle that almost cracked the car's axle. 'It'll be my fault if her car's out of action.'

'That's OK,' Jazz said cheerfully, 'I'll blame you anyway. You can afford it, whereas all I've got is my student loan, which is maxed out. But you did get Marion to take on Felix, so you get loads of brownie points.'

'Has the place in Oxford let him go? Won't he need a secure place to stay?'

'He's staying with us,' Jazz said. 'Whatever you think of Mum, she's very good with waifs and strays.'

'She gets that from me! I understand why she resented me moving out all those years ago, but Deirdre and I got on much better after I did. All those stupid rows we used to have...'

'Like when Nana threw a knife at you and you caught it in the breadboard?'

'Yeah, but that didn't happen *all* the time. It just wasn't the best atmosphere for someone like your mother, who likes stability. Nothing wrong with stability, though it can get a tad boring, but maybe boredom was better than all the *broyges* that used to go on. I just wish she didn't disapprove of me all the time, you know what I'm saying? Parents need their children's approval just as much as the other way round.'

'I approve of you, Gramps,' Jazz said, slowing down on passing a police car, 'and Mum approves of Marion, so you're halfway there. Mum's probably worried I'm going to turn into a version of you.'

'That's a bad thing?'

'She thinks you're an optimist who wanders off into fantasy land. She's a realist, like you have to be if you're head of geography in a comprehensive, and she wants me to keep a grip on the world.'

'She doesn't think I have a grip?'

Jazz reached out and patted his hand before changing gear to go up a steep hill. 'You are a bit of an idealist,' she said, 'which is why I love you, and so does Marion, obvs. It's just that there aren't many idealists around, not ones who look forward like you do. Most people at Oxford specialize in looking back.'

'You sound like my friend Dennis,' Leo said, a bit mollified. 'Talking of looking back, what really pisses me off is that all the -isms I thought we'd defeated forever – racism, sexism, fascism, to name but three – seem to be making such a triumphant comeback. They're breeding and morphing like viruses, growing stronger and smarter all the time!'

'Do you think the bill Felix's grandad was going to introduce would have made any difference?' Jazz asked, pulling into a petrol station. 'The one that would have made politicians accountable between elections? And you don't mind paying to fill up, do you? Mum's disapproval

60

would be off the scale if I left the car empty. She wants an electric one, but she says she can't afford it on her salary.'

'Of course I'll pay,' Leo said, getting out his cards. 'What are parents and grandparents for? As for Sidney Playfair's bill, I was talking to his spad, and she thinks it would have been neutered in committee.'

'But it got such popular support!' Jazz said, stopping behind a Range Rover that took as long to fill up as a truck. 'Surely someone else will take it forward in Sidney's place? That would help Felix over his depression.'

'The spad – her name's Ginny Larue – didn't think so.'

'Ginny Larue? She was president of the Union when I came up. She's a hero of mine!'

'Well, she's looking for a new job. And she doesn't think anyone is going to fill Sidney's boots. The optimist in me doesn't believe her. The realist – and I do have a bit of realism in me, or I'd be a useless lawyer – sees her point. Why would politicians want to limit their promises to what they can deliver? It would be the end of politics as we know it! We'll have to find another way of helping Felix.'

'Ginny Larue,' Jazz said, getting out of the car. Leo wound down his window so he could continue talking to her while she was operating the pump. 'She should stand for Parliament. She was one of the best speakers I ever heard.'

'Maybe working in the Commons put her off,' Leo said. 'Even to someone as warm-hearted and generous-spirited as me, she came across as a bit of a cynic. Like a client of mine this morning. I know this will astonish you, but she has a low opinion of lawyers in general and me in particular. She was about to fire me, can you believe it?'

'Maybe you're better off without her, Gramps,' Jazz said absent-mindedly, watching the petrol bill mount. 'I'm glad I'm not paying for this. I thought prices had dropped.'

'They have, but the oil companies are never in a hurry to lower prices for the consumer, are they? Call me an old cynic—'

'You're an old cynic who's going to be poorer by fifty-some quid,' Jazz said, replacing the petrol cap. 'Do you want me to take your card to the till?'

'I'll do it,' Leo said, unclipping his seatbelt and grunting his way out of the car. 'Maybe they'll have a box of those chocolates Deirdre likes. Though then she'll probably accuse me of trying to poison her. While I'm gone, here's a question for you. How would I find out the contact details of a woman who doesn't appear to exist on the internet? Google couldn't trace her when I tried.'

'What's her name?' Jazz asked, as she got back into the car.

'Patsy Finch. Worked at Zarastro Oil around twenty years ago. You find her, you can have a chocolate too.'

'Better make it a box,' Jazz called, getting out her phone as Leo walked stiffly towards the tills. Her thumbs flew around the little screen with a speed her grandfather would never master, not that he'd want to.

~ ~ ~

'How would you like,' Marion asked, scrubbing a saucepan in the sink while Leo waited with a drying-up cloth, 'to come to a party in the House of Lords? Would it offend your socialist and republican principles? Which I share, though I was quite fond of the old queen.'

'I'm always up for a party,' Leo said. 'Who's giving it, and would I have to wear a tie?'

'Jimmy Northolt, and no tie will be necessary. You have to go through security, but they don't make you take off your shoes, so there's no need to worry about the state of your socks.'

'What's wrong with my socks? I can still put them on without sitting down, though I sometimes have to lean against the wall. My balance isn't what it was either, though part of my exercise routine is standing on one leg for a count of thirty, then a count of ten with my eyes closed. Which is a lot more difficult than you would think. It's supposed to help my brain keep me upright, though I still puff a bit tying shoelaces.'

'That's why I wear shoes I can slip in and out of,' Marion said, handing him the dish, 'and I did wonder what took you so long in the bathroom. Anything else to wash up?'

'Just the silver. The dishwasher tarnishes them. Who's Jimmy Northolt?' He handed her a bunch of silverware which she plunged into the washing-up bowl. Leo was going to say how well her rubber gloves complemented her hair, which was the green of new-mown grass, but he thought better of it. He had never been to the House of Lords, and as an old radical he despised the corrupt way in which its members were chosen to reward either their failures in office or the size of their donations. But he was fascinated by its rituals and the mystique of the hereditary peers whose families still owned vast estates from which the general public was excluded.

'He's the Earl of Brixton, which is not his fault, and I helped him to get over a crippling shyness that prevented him from speaking out on things he cares about, like supporting the English walnut industry. I was at school with his sister Laetitia, who is the bossiest woman I know. Fortunately she is kept busy running a stud farm.'

'I bet she still finds time to tell her brother what to do,' Leo said, drying the spoons carefully. 'My sister Becky tells me how to behave, and she's three years younger than me!'

'That's perfectly normal with siblings. I love Becky.'

'Everyone does,' Leo said with mock gloom. 'Actors fight to work with her, even though she pays them *bupkes* and breaks them down before building them up again. Talking of which, how are you getting on with Felix Playfair?'

'Starting next week,' Marion said, peeling off her gloves. 'How's the clearing-up after your burglary? I meant to ask before, but your zabaglione put everything else out of my mind.'

'We found out who was responsible, thanks to Pumpy's olfactory skills,' Leo said, carefully draping the dish towel over the handle of the oven. The dog got up to receive compliments in person, and also to clear up any remnants of cheese or cream that had escaped attention. Marion sat at the table to finish her wine and tickled the fur under his jaw, which made his eyes close in pleasure.

'Yes,' Leo said, joining her at the table, 'Pumpy even got a confession out of her. Boy, does she need lessons in anger management!'

'A woman burglar?' Marion asked. 'Not that common.'

'It wasn't actually a burglary,' Leo said. 'She didn't, as she pointed out, steal anything. She was looking for something, and when she couldn't find it her frustration boiled over. I wouldn't like to be the doctor who got the wrong side of her, though I'm sure she's great with her patients. And she did have twenty-nine children.'

'You'd've thought she'd know about birth control. Maybe that's the source of her anger.'

'They were foster children,' Leo said, dividing the last of the wine equally between their glasses. 'The last of them was that whistleblower who got stabbed, and she wanted me to ginger up the police investigation. But I didn't move quickly enough for her, so she decided to fire me. To give her credit, she came in to do it personally. But I persuaded her to give me another chance.'

'Because you were intrigued by what happened to the whistleblower.'

'Whose case you encouraged me to pursue,' Leo said, sipping his wine.

'If it's the one we talked about yesterday,' Marion said, 'I could see that's what you were going to do anyway. You're responsible for your own decisions.'

'When have I ever tried to blame you for anything?' Leo exclaimed rhetorically. 'You inspire and encourage me! I'm not complaining!'

'Good to hear,' Marion said, and drained her glass. 'I'm off to bed.'

Leo hastily followed suit. 'I'll join you,' he said, 'as soon as I've taken Pumpy out for a pee. Then maybe.... He stood up, looking hopeful. Marion smiled.

'I won't say it would be hard to follow the perfection of your pudding,' she said lightly, 'but after expending all that energy and all those skills on another wonderful meal, I worry that anything too energetic would drain you for tomorrow. You know how much I admire your ardour, but you're already looking a little tired, which is hardly surprising, considering all that you've had to deal with.'

'I have had a lot on my plate,' Leo admitted. Like most men, he was very suggestible, and if the woman he loved told him he appeared to be under strain, he would immediately allow himself to crumble a little and feel in need of rest. Marion's sympathetic attention was a sign of her concern for him, and why risk that by pushing for something that might only be a crude coda to the delights he had already served up? He had nothing to prove, after all.

He was, he told himself, as he stood shivering at the entrance to the park waiting for Pumpernickel to relieve himself, a very lucky man.

Four

People who knew his mother said he looked like her, and Felix wished they wouldn't. But then he'd never met anyone who knew his father, and couldn't remember what he'd looked like – dark-haired with blue eyes and white teeth in a tanned face, presumably, like the Greeks he saw in movies. His mother had no pictures of him – she said, and according to his grandfather she meant it kindly, that Felix was all the reminder she needed – and she was considered pretty, which Felix didn't think he was, though he didn't obsess about it. It was one of those things, like having a second toe longer than the rest, that you could do nothing about.

There were things you could do something about. Figures, you could keep in order. Food, you could control. Exercise, you could regulate. Running in particular: the only sport where you could get away from everybody else and receive praise for it. Felix was never sure what people meant when they praised him, and had never praised anyone in his life; if you happened to be good at something, or cared enough about it to make yourself better at it, the results were obvious, weren't they, so why point them out? Wasn't it more use pointing out what you got wrong? Though people didn't like that as much. They preferred a warm shower to a cold one, and Felix recognized that. He liked a bit of heat: that might have been the Greek in him. He had once had vague thoughts about seeking out his father in Naxos or wherever it was he'd been taken away from as a baby, but as the man had made no effort to get in touch with him, though he must have known where he was, it was low on Felix's list of priorities.

That list was small, because things happened to him more often than he made them happen, which was something he had to cope with. He found himself reading mathematics at Oxford because numbers made sense to him. He was asked to join the university cross-country team and saw no reason not to, as it was an activity he enjoyed. He rarely went to dinners in hall because he liked to limit the amount he ate and cook it the way he wanted. He had friends on his staircase who looked after him whether he wanted them to or not. Especially Robin, who he enjoyed sleeping with, and Jasmine, who made him laugh. They had burst into his room the day after he'd found his grandfather dead, when he hadn't felt like getting up or doing anything. They'd hustled him to see a doctor, who sent him to a hospital, who put him in a room not that different from the one he had at college, including the bars on the windows to stop people getting in, and nurses kept waking him up when he would rather have stayed asleep. Then Jasmine had told him he was going to stay with her, and he could sleep for as long as he liked providing he went to see this friend of hers.

Which is how Felix found himself in Marion's consulting room overlooking the park, running his fingers along the sinuous lines of an ebony carving of a runner whose legs were way longer than his body, which wasn't natural but was pleasing to the touch. Marion was the same height he was, but a lot broader. She had a nice face, kind, considerate, like a nurse except that she had green hair and did more listening than telling you what to do. She was a doctor, though not, she told him, of the useful kind that could help him if he pulled a hamstring. She asked about his running. What was there to say?

'I've got a Blue,' he said eventually. That seemed to impress most people.

'I'm guessing,' she said, 'that's not the reason you do it. I played hockey at school because it came before elocution lessons which I hated, though I liked the teacher and she was very understanding if I'd managed to get myself injured. As you can see, I do not have the body of a natural athlete. I enjoy riding, though, and I'm not a bad dancer. I don't suppose you like dancing if it involves touching people, but have you tried getting on a horse?'

Felix looked at her in astonishment. How did she know he didn't like touching people, except for Robin? Why would you bother touching people unless you're enjoying sex with them? He shivered, and said, 'I don't like horses. They run away with you.'

'That's true, if you let them,' Marion said. 'You can control them, though, provided you know what you want them to do and communicate that to them. How are your communication skills?'

He thought about this and said, cautiously, 'I'm not sure. I don't pay them that much attention.'

'Because you don't need to, or because you can't be bothered?'

'I've got friends,' Felix said defensively. 'We talk, we laugh, we...do things.'

'Like what? Sporting things? Discussing philosophical matters? Or are we talking about sex, which is what students spend a lot of time doing, as well as drinking and drugs and getting their essays in late?'

She'd pretty well covered the ground, Felix thought. Though she hadn't included finding his grandfather dead, which was all because of him. He shivered again, and put the ebony carving back on her table. He didn't want to break it: strong and hard though it was, everything has a breaking point.

'Sex is part of it,' he admitted.

69

'Do you want to talk about it?'

'Not particularly.'

'Then let's not. Why did you choose running as your sport?'

'Because I was good at it?'

'Not because it was a good way of getting away from people, fast?'

Felix had never thought of it like that, and said so.

'What's obvious to one person may not occur to someone else,' Marion said cheerfully. 'It's a bit like humour: one person's giggle is another one's groan, my grin could be your grimace. When did you start running?'

'In primary school.'

'Were you bullied?'

That was a question that required careful consideration. Was being called names like Paki and thicko bullying? Was being knuckle-punched on the shoulder so hard your arm went numb? Was being called a mummy's boy and jeered at because you put your hand up ahead of everyone else when Miss Arkwright wanted the answer to a sum? Things like that happened to other people, didn't they, so that made them normal, didn't it?

'I don't think so, no,' Felix said, eventually. 'But I suppose I did like getting away from people. And they liked me for doing it, so it was win-win. And I do quite like winning. Giles says it doesn't always make you friends, but that shouldn't stop you from doing it.'

'Who's Giles?' Marion asked.

'He lives with us. With my mother and me. In Henley. He's a carpenter. Well, a joiner, actually. He makes very good cupboards where the drawers always close easily.'

'Tell me about your mother.'

'What is there to tell? She's my mother. She's got long black hair and wears long dresses and she's a dancer with a group of people who play flutes and tambours and she designs things with intricate patterns though she often gets her measurements wrong.'

'Does she ask you to check them?'

'She asks Giles. Or she doesn't ask but he does it anyway. I could do it but she doesn't think I'd be interested.'

'And are you interested?'

'Not really. I like big problems.'

'How big? Are we talking about the meaning of life, or something a bit easier to solve, like what happens in a black hole?'

Felix looked at her with respect. 'Black holes are interesting,' he said, 'but most people get depressed when you talk about them. Or bored.'

'Why do you think that is?'

'Robin says it's because they make you doubt the point of existence. Jasmine says it's because trying to explain them leaves no room for jokes. My grandfather—'

He stopped suddenly. Marion waited. She was good at it, it's what had made her reputation, when other therapists watched the clock and made suggestions that would lead to a speedy box-ticking conclusion.

'I just remembered,' Felix said, staring at his hands, 'my grandfather comparing politics to a black hole. He said it sucked up all your energy and all your ambition, so that even the brightest star disappeared without fulfilling their promises. He said he was going to change all that with his accountability campaign. I asked what the point was, if the campaign was going to be swallowed by a black hole. He said he was merely making a comparison, and I shouldn't take things too literally. I tried to follow his advice, but it's difficult when people say one thing and mean another. How do you know which to believe?'

He retreated behind the wings of the chair Marion's clients were offered if they didn't want to lie on the sofa, and made a snuffling noise.

'Did your grandfather come and watch you run?' Marion asked gently.

Felix leaned forward to pluck a tissue from the box on a table beside his chair. He blew his nose, examined the tissue as if it contained something exotic, and stuffed it into his pocket. 'Whenever he could,' he said.

'And what did he say when you didn't win? Which I assume must have happened occasionally.'

Felix gave a wintry smile. 'A few times,' he said. 'To him, the most important thing was to get off to a good start. People were always trying to push you aside, elbow you out of the way, trip you or make you stumble. He said you had to do whatever was necessary to make sure you got the start you deserved. Once you were clear of the field, it was a matter of staying-power. But if you let people get in your way, you'd never make up the distance you'd lost.'

'Did you follow his advice?'

He looked down, and mumbled, 'I tried. But I couldn't always make it work.'

~ ~ ~

Leo found himself ripping open boxes of baby food with a Stanley knife he'd been handed, and stacking the contents on rickety steel shelving in a depot that had once been a sorting office for mail and was now a drop-in food distribution centre. Pumpernickel stood by, allowing himself to be patted and petted by toddlers with cold hands.

'When you've filled that bay,' said the woman he'd come to meet, 'you can have a coffee. Though personally I'd advise the tea. The coffee's from jars that are so out of date it comes out in lumps. Some donors are more charitable than others.'

Patsy Finch was a well-rounded woman about the same age and height as Leo, with neatly coiffed grey hair, warm brown eyes, a carefully made-up face whose powder flaked a little when her jowls wobbled, and bright red lipstick. She moved with energy and purpose, spoke with authority leavened with laughter, and was persuasive rather than demanding. Leo liked her immediately. So did Pumpernickel.

The place was like a supermarket, with people filling their baskets quicker than the handful of volunteers could stock the shelves. There were checkout points, but vouchers were offered instead of money. Some of the customers had the shuffle of the homeless, some the scuttle of the desperate, a few had the defiance of those determined to make shopping an event.

'It's my first time as a shelf-stacker,' Leo said, a little defensively, as Patsy straightened the bottles and jars he'd laid out. 'My granddaughter's done it in vacations, to pay off a piddling part of her student loan. I never realized how demanding it is, and I'm mildly obsessive about having things in order.'

'I suspect this would drive you mad, then,' Patsy said. 'You get it looking nice and tidy, then people come along and spoil it. Sisyphus had it easy by comparison.'

'How often do you volunteer?' Leo asked. 'I mean, it's wonderful and disgraceful all at the same time, isn't it? That in a country as rich as ours, people are forced to rely on charitable handouts in order to feed their families. Though,' he said, glancing around, 'some of them look exactly like the people you see in Waitrose, squeezing the mangoes for ripeness.'

'That's why we have the vouchers,' Patsy said. 'At the start it was open to anyone in need, but when the Range Rover set took to dropping in to see what they could pick up, we limited it to people on benefits. To each according to their needs is another example of Marx misunderstanding human nature, but then he was hopelessly middle-class himself, wasn't he?'

'I never got beyond the first chapter of *Das Kapital*,' Leo admitted. 'And the paper of those translations smelled funny, didn't it? As if the bleach hadn't been properly washed out.'

'You're absolutely right,' Patsy said, 'but I ploughed through all three volumes nevertheless. I didn't want to be one of those scientists who couldn't handle philosophy. I think you've earned a break now, you and your dog. A reward for the dignity of labour.'

Pumpernickel yawned, as he often did when he heard people talking about him, then shook himself as yet another small child pulled his tail. He didn't complain, but trotted gratefully after Leo as they walked towards the back of the depot, where a kitchen had been set up in a draughty corner by the loading bays. Patsy made tea, insisting she didn't need any help. She offered Garibaldi biscuits, warning they might be a bit stale. Leo took one to be sociable. Pumpernickel, who had more willpower, lapped at some water.

'So,' Patsy said, sitting on a rickety wooden chair and crossing sturdy legs beneath a sensible skirt, 'you want to know about Nancy Chen's report, even though I'm forbidden from talking about it under the terms of the NDA they made me sign. My golden goodbye paid off the mortgage on my flat by Primrose Hill, which I am not about to jeopardize.'

'Quite right,' Leo said. 'The last thing I want to do is add to the ranks of the homeless. But we're talking about a murder here. You knew Larry Coombs?'

'Two murders, actually,' Patsy said calmly. 'Larry is one and yes, I met him campaigning on the climate crisis, another of the things I do to avoid watching daytime television. But you know Nancy's death was never satisfactorily explained? At least not to me.' She sipped her tea and regarded Leo gravely.

'You worked with her at Zarastro Oil, right? When George Ramirez was head of research?'

Patsy snorted so derisively Pumpernickel was startled. 'He was no scientist!' she said. 'He had an A level in physics, but his degree was in business studies! Still, he did recruit me and Nancy, though she was a much better scientist than I was.'

'She was also quite well organized,' Leo said, 'which, if it's not sexist to say so, you are too. How did the two of you get on?'

'Nancy was more serious than I was, as well as being more determined and more attractive.' Leo started to make a chivalrous interruption, but Patsy held up a hand. 'I was known as Party-girl Patsy,' she said, 'which is only slightly better than Pushover Patsy, owing to my inability to say no to unsuitable men. Nancy was much braver in standing up for herself and ending relationships she regarded as going beyond their sell-by date. With Nathan Flowers, for example: they were together for months, years even, but that didn't stop her giving him his marching orders.'

Pumpernickel raised his head as Leo nodded excitedly. 'Nathan Flowers! He wanted me to hand over her letters!'

'A man who doesn't take kindly to rejection,' Patsy observed, 'and look where it's got him.'

'Where has it got him?' Leo asked.

'Why, jail!' Patsy said, as if Leo should have known all along.

'Forgive me,' Leo said. 'All I know about him is that he found out I was Nancy's solicitor and thought I might have her letters and papers, as her family went back to Hong Kong after she died. What's he in jail for?'

'In my opinion, it should be for getting Nancy killed,' Patsy said. 'He followed her to Zermatt, even though she'd dumped him – she was a keen skier, which was another big difference between us. This was long before Zermatt became the most expensive resort in Switzerland, when it was a very lively place, especially for the after-ski parties, which is all I went for.'

'I knew she died in a skiing accident,' Leo said, 'but there was no suspicion of foul play. Are you saying this Nathan...?'

'I'm saying that I thought it odd that her binding should come loose when she went off-piste. She was meticulous in everything, whether it was the report she delivered shortly before going on holiday, or getting the right gear for whatever route she was planning. And Nathan had good grounds for getting rid of her.'

'Revenge? Jealousy?'

'Those too,' Patsy said, 'but mainly because he was working for Zarastro as well. And I knew they weren't going to like Nancy's report, which is why I resigned soon after she died. I didn't want that happening to me!'

'Wait a minute,' Leo said, helping himself to another stale Garibaldi. 'You think Zarastro used Nathan to kill Nancy? Why didn't you say anything at the time?'

'Shock. Fear. Lack of proof. Scepticism that it would make any difference. The Swiss decided it was an accident, and they're known for their thoroughness. Then Nathan got promoted. I didn't know him well, but I wouldn't have said he was capable of running a company. They put him in charge of some subsidiary, and then blamed him when it all went wrong. You must have read about it.'

'Remind me.'

'That particular company made its profits from exploiting foreign workers, especially from places like Myanmar and Korea. One of their lorries was packed full of illegal immigrants when it broke down. The driver abandoned them. Two days later the police broke it open to find twenty-three dead people. The driver was arrested, and said his boss had told him he would sort it out. His boss was Nathan, who Zarastro promptly blamed. He was given a thirty-year sentence for manslaughter with no possibility of parole.'

Leo dunked his stale biscuit in his cold tea while he absorbed all this. 'So Nathan is still in jail,' he said, 'and you were paid for your silence.'

'I couldn't *prove* anything,' Patsy said, 'and of course they buried the report. I wasn't as brave, or as foolhardy, as Nancy, or Larry Coombs. Poor Larry. They said he was killed for his trainers, but I don't believe that anymore than I believe Nancy's ski fell off. But of course I might just be paranoid. Would that surprise you?'

'I try not to be surprised by what goes on,' Leo said, 'and though I've been trying for a very long time, I don't always succeed. You, however, strike me as perfectly normal. Who isn't paranoid about things we're afraid of or can't explain? My partner's a therapist; I've picked up a bit here and there. But how can someone as committed as

77

you obviously are keep quiet about the deaths of two people you knew quite well?'

'I told you,' Patsy said, picking up his mug and hers and washing them in a plastic bowl, 'I am not someone who sticks their neck out.'

'You've told me your suspicions.'

'Because, without evidence, that's all they are,' Patsy said briskly. 'I'm like most people, I seethe, but I don't act. I watch the news in disbelief, I read *The Sunday Times* and turn to the reviews in despair. I do a tiny bit to make life better for people a lot worse off than me, but I wouldn't jeopardize the comforts I enjoy. I leave that to other people. People like you.'

Pumpernickel moved towards Leo. People were always dumping their problems on him. Luckily he was there to help.

~ ~ ~

'Flowers!' the officer said. 'You know the rules. You've been here long enough!'

'Just comforting him, sir,' Nathan Flowers said, withdrawing his arm from his visitor Malcolm Beamish. 'He's been through a hard time.' He held up both his hands. 'Nothing exchanged, other than a little warmth and friendliness.'

'Yes, well,' the officer snorted. He was looking forward to retirement and didn't want any trouble. 'Keep your distance, that's all.' He went to lean against a wall and stare at a young visitor in a short skirt and knee-high boots and a blonde mane of hair he was sure was a wig. In fact he was positive the visitor was a man in drag, but as he couldn't recall any regulations forbidding such a thing, he contented himself with keeping a close eye on them.

'Thanks, Nathan,' Malcolm said dolefully. 'You must have seen my dad a few times, on visits. He stayed

78

with my crazy mum even after she was struck off, he agreed the move to High Wycombe, which led to all my troubles, then to die in his sleep when he seemed perfectly fit – he didn't even make a fuss about that!'

'You shouldn't joke about death, Malcolm,' the older man advised. 'We both know it's a serious matter, don't we? Are you going to stay with your mother?'

'Are you kidding? We'd kill each other! And where would Gilda go? She's an illegal, remember!' He was in his late twenties, large and muscular from taking up bodybuilding at Nathan's suggestion, though he never went in for steroids. His size and strength had not filled him with self-confidence, however, and he remained a fidgety young man with troubled hazel eyes.

'Better than this place, though, right?' Nathan said. He was not notably tall, but he held himself with a certainty that made people respect him. His head and face were shaved and bony, with eyes that could outstare anyone, even the governor, and though his skin was beginning to sag and wrinkle, it still encased a body of sinewy strength.

'You know, I miss it, sometimes?' Malcolm said. 'I didn't have to think all the time what I should be doing, or how I should do whatever it is. And now Dad's gone...'

'I'm still here,' Nathan pointed out. 'And I'm not going anywhere. You've got a job to do. We've talked about it often enough.'

'I'm doing it, aren't I?' There was a slight whine in his voice, like a dog hoping for a treat.

'Yes, you are, Malcolm, and you're managing it well. But you're not finished, not by any means. There'll be more to do—'

'What if I don't want to?' Malcolm broke out.

79

Nathan sighed. 'We can't always do what we want, Malcolm. Surely you've learned that by now?'

'It's easy for you! All you have to do is sit in here! I'm the one facing the problems!'

'And you don't think there are problems in here?' Nathan said quietly. 'I solved several for you, don't forget. I know you're upset about your dad, but don't let that wipe out all memory of what you owe me.'

'I don't. It hasn't,' Malcolm said earnestly. 'But you know, in here, nothing changes. Out there, it changes all the time. You never know what you're up against, especially when you're living with someone like Gilda. What worries me is, what if I'm asked to do something I can't? Or if I get it all wrong?'

Nathan spread his hands in an expansive and reassuring gesture. 'Worst case scenario,' he said, 'you end up back in here. Would that be so terrible?'

~ ~ ~

Katy Shaw worked as a paralegal in a set of chambers in Gray's Inn that could charitably be described as Dickensian, meaning they were small, cramped, malodorous, with few conveniences as they were in a listed building. Katy had use of a desk on the top floor, where the pro bono work was done. She was part of a team that offered what help they could to illegal immigrants, asylum seekers, evicted tenants, victims of slavery and people trafficking, and protesters arrested for peacefully demanding that the largest despoilers of the planet cease their climate-destroying activities forthwith. Dickens would have recognized the situation immediately. Katy hadn't got round to reading Dickens, and would have been critical of his attitude to women, in his own life as well as that of his fiction, but she knew he took the side of the oppressed against the oppressor, and felt he was a kindred spirit. She loved her job, even though much of it was infuriatingly frustrating.

'That Zarastro report,' her starchy boss Helen Wilson said, 'do we know how the unfortunate, or foolhardy, Larry Coombs heard about it?'

'He wasn't foolhardy,' Katy protested. 'He came to lots of meetings of the climate campaign group I'm a member of, and was very passionate.'

'Passion is all very well,' Helen said severely, 'but not always practical. Especially if it gets you killed. What did he tell you?'

'That he'd heard about this report being buried when it was presented twenty years ago. From someone who worked with the author, a scientist called Nancy Chen. Larry never mentioned his source, but he may have told his MP, Sidney Playfair, who he went to with his suspicions, hoping Sidney, being big on accountability, would do something about it.'

'And Sidney inconveniently died. Is that all we know?'

'Larry mentioned a solicitor who acted for the late Dr Chen. Larry was going to see them, but then he got stabbed. Larry, I mean, not the solicitor. Which is more than a little suspicious, don't you think?'

'Did he name this solicitor?'

'Leo somebody,' Katy said, leafing through her notebook. 'Surname sounded Polish?'

'Leo Wengrowski?' Helen said, surprising her colleagues with a sudden smile. 'Is he still practising?'

Katy finally found the page she'd been looking for. 'Apparently so,' she said. 'Somewhere in Soho. You know him?'

'An old schmoozer with a sharp mind,' Helen said. 'Go and see him. And give him my love, though he may not remember me. Mention Heythrop.'

Katy was going to ask more, but Helen had moved swiftly on to other business.

~ ~ ~

At the House of Lords Leo found himself talking to a blonde peeress who overflowed from her dress like a soufflé escaping its baking dish. She was constantly pushing back a lock of hair with the hand that didn't hold a glass, and had a laugh that never reached her eyes. Leo told himself he gravitated towards her purely because no one else was talking to her, which seemed a shame. Marion was busy with her friend Jimmy Northolt, who she'd rescued from crippling shyness, and Leo didn't want to interfere. It seemed only chivalrous to strike up a conversation with a solo stranger, just to show he wasn't intimidated by his surroundings, which were shabbily grand in a way that was peculiarly British: gilded on the outside, gimcrack within.

'I'm sure I should know who you are,' he said boldly, 'but you won't know me from a hole in the head, so I'm Leo Wengrowski, I'm a solicitor who's still working because boredom is what kills you, and the only reason I was allowed in here is standing over there with purple hair, talking to an earl.'

'Well, Leo Wengrowski,' said the peeress with a carefully controlled giggle, 'I'm Maxine Ensor, I'm here because everyone thought I'd had an affair with the previous prime minister but three, whereas in fact my lover is a major party donor who would prefer to have me here than be bored by attending himself. And I was an MP who was on *Question Time* a lot until that cow Fiona Bruce decided I was drawing attention away from her, so maybe

82

that's why I look familiar. Do you need a refill, or are you one of those tedious people who don't drink because it's January or your driver's on holiday?'

Leo's resolve to do everything in moderation was no proof against a challenge. He quickly drained his glass and looked round. An elderly man with sparse hair severely parted and plastered to his head, dressed to look like a funeral director in breeches, snapped his fingers and a young woman appeared with bottles of wine and refilled both their glasses. 'My lady,' she said, bowing her head. Leo got a polite nod.

'If I just call you Maxine, will I never get another drink?' he asked. 'I mean, they can probably tell I'm a revolutionary by the fact I've undone my tie, but my shoes are properly polished, which my father maintained was enough to pass as a gentleman. It worked for me in the old days when you wrote a cheque if you didn't have enough money on you. The man in Fortnum & Mason, whose tailcoats are more colourful than your guys' here, just glanced at my patent leather boots and said that would be fine. My dad despised patent leather, but the rot was already setting in. Who's your lover, or should I not ask?'

'You can ask,' Maxine said with another giggle. 'It's not exactly a secret. George Ramirez. He runs a company called Zarastro Oil. If you're a revolutionary, you'll despise him too. I think he's rather good news.'

Leo's mind snapped to attention. Be discreet, he told himself. Don't blab why you're interested. Make chit-chat like in the gossip columns. Don't get heavy.

'So how good is he under the duvet?' he heard himself asking. Maxine's eyes, which were a cloudy grey when her hair wasn't covering them, opened a little wider. Then she leaned closer to him.

'I thought gentlemen didn't ask questions like that, Leo. Or do you like to shock people before you seduce them?'

Great, Leo thought, with relief. She thinks I'm flirting. 'My days as a seducer ceased,' he said, 'when I met Marion, the purple-haired Amazon over there. But before then, I assure you, I would have besieged you with my subtlest charm and sparkling witticisms, not to mention plying you with strong drink and offers of romantic assignations in restaurants where you have to know not only the maître d's first name, but those of his wife and children. Now I am grown old and faithful, but unfortunately neither wiser nor more discreet. And the first thing a man, or a man of my age, is interested in, when it comes to fulfilling the desires of beautiful women, is performance. You'll understand that when you get older.'

Maxine looked at him seriously, then blinked rather than winked, and drank some wine. 'As a matter of fact,' she said, 'things haven't been great in that department. The trouble with George is, if things don't go exactly the way he wants, he gets very impatient. You know what I mean?'

'I think so,' Leo said carefully. 'Maybe my partner Marion could help. She's a psychotherapist with quite a reputation. And I'm not on commission, I promise you.'

Maxine gave a wintry smile. 'It hasn't got to that stage yet,' she said. 'When you're expecting great things from someone, and they let you down, it's not just disappointing, is it? It can affect your entire outlook, as well as your performance.'

'Who are we talking about? I'm a lawyer, you know your secrets will be safe with me. Though maybe that's like a stranger coming up to you and saying, "I'm a doctor, take off your clothes"?'

This made Maxine giggle again. She took another swig of her wine. 'It could be me,' she said, avoiding his question. 'I can be...enthusiastic in the bedroom, when maybe a cooler approach is required. I thought George would want to join me in celebrating the death of someone I was sure he despised as much as I did, but in fact he was rather upset.'

'About you?' Leo asked. 'Or about the dead person?'

'Whose name was Sidney Playfair,' Maxine said. 'Sanctimonious little shit! I led the opposition in the Commons to that ridiculous Accountability Bill, you know, but most MPs are too stupid to avoid a bandwagon that's going to crush them beneath its wheels.'

'But the campaign was wildly popular, wasn't it? Holding politicians to their promises, and punishing them for not doing so unless they have convincing reasons? What's not to like?'

'You obviously read the *Guardian*,' Maxine snorted.

'I do,' Leo said proudly, 'and I'm not ashamed to admit I occasionally eat tofu, though only if it's been marinated and is then fried so it tastes of something more than blotting paper. And who remembers blotting paper these days?'

'The accountability campaign,' Maxine said, 'would have crippled not just politics, but business, finance, industry and democracy itself. Who would want to stand as an MP, or for any elective office, if every promise they make has to be performed to the letter?'

'This may not be the best place to argue that with you,' Leo said, 'but mightn't it have helped politicians to offer promises they *could* keep?'

'The real world doesn't work like that! You wouldn't have any business at all if people just kept to their word!'

'True,' Leo admitted cheerfully, 'but as you've already discovered, I'm an idealist. And I do think that when a politician acts surprised that no one believes them, they're deliberately forgetting the fact that they've gone back on every pledge they've made. Why would anyone have faith in a proven liar, unless they were selling something that makes you thin?'

'Because you want to!' Maxine said defiantly. 'Politics is a shitty business, like most businesses, and the human beings who take responsibility for it – a responsibility most people are happy to hand over to them – grab at whatever offers happiness. It's like an affair: you want it to end well, you know it won't, but you promise you'll do your damndest to make it happen. And people believe you, however many lies you may have told in the past, because they'd prefer a happy ending to the miserable truth. We're in the dream business, Mr Wengrowski, and voters will go for fantasies over nightmares every time!'

Having made her point, she looked around, as people do at parties, for someone else to talk to, but Leo snagged her attention by asking, 'Do you believe Sidney Playfair died of natural causes?'

'Why?' she said, squinting at him roguishly through her hair. 'It's still being investigated, isn't it? Are you going to accuse me of murder on our first meeting? That would be a little forward!'

'You've got the killer instinct,' Leo said disarmingly, 'and you've made me realize how many people must have hated him for running a campaign that was hugely popular. I thought, naively and obviously wrongly, he had enough supporters inside and outside

Parliament to give his bill a genuine chance of becoming law. His death prevented that from happening. I'm a lawyer, I'm naturally suspicious. What can I tell you?'

Maxine gave a mirthless laugh. 'I'm not sorry he's dead, but I still paid him tribute at the memorial,' she said. 'Someone told me he was diabetic, but in that case he shouldn't have stuffed himself with cakes and pastries, should he? Or is that what you do to balance the blood sugar? He never could resist a box of chocolates, our Sidney, but much as I might have wanted to send him one laced with poison, I didn't.'

'What about your lover, George?'

'Now you're being ridiculous.'

'Marion often tells me I shouldn't try and play the detective, but what if Sidney had something over him? Maybe George wanted rid of him for that?'

'All I know,' Maxine said, draining her glass, 'is that Sidney's death has not brought the bedroom bonus I was hoping for. And as we have got onto personal matters, your partner over there is taller, broader and quite possibly older than you are, and obviously knows everybody. Are you her toyboy, and if so, why did she choose you?'

'The answer to the first question is yes,' Leo said happily, 'and as for the second, I can be surprising when I try. Even if I do sometimes need a little assistance.'

~ ~ ~

In bed that night, Leo and Marion's usual routine was that he would turn his light off and slide down under the duvet while Marion caught up with the latest publications on her laptop. Leo would try and stay awake until she had finished, in the hope of a cuddle, but he was mostly fast asleep by the time she turned her device off. Tonight was an exception: Marion, being multi-talented, could easily hold a conversation at the same time as flicking through abstruse scientific articles, and was able to express intelligent views on both.

'I promise you this has nothing to do with me,' Leo began, 'but I was talking to Lady Ensor and I rather suspect her lover, who happens to be George Ramirez, has erectile dysfunction.'

'He should go to one of the specialist clinics,' Marion said, her eyes on her screen.

'She – my new friend Maxine – said she was hoping he would be rejuvenated by the death of Sidney Playfair, but on the contrary, he sagged. Maybe there was something going on between those two guys. Felix hasn't mentioned anything about that, has he?'

Marion sighed. 'You know I can't say anything about–'

'Just a yes or no.'

'No.'

'No he hasn't, or no you're not going to say anything?'

'Both.'

'OK. Understood. But in general terms, you would agree that disappointment in bed can be caused by psychological as well as physiological concerns? Remember, this is not me we're talking about.'

'Yes, the willy can wilt if the mind is elsewhere. If you're asking for reassurance–'

'No, no,' Leo assured her. 'I'm just trying to understand what kind of relationship Sidney and George had. If Sidney's death led to George's impotence...'

'The two may not be connected at all,' Marion said. 'Impotence can be caused by performance anxiety or – and this frequently happens with older people, though George is only, what, in his late fifties? – by the sudden realization of how absurd sex is.'

88

Leo sat up. 'Wait a minute,' he said. 'What? You're saying sex is ridiculous?'

Marion looked at him fondly over the top of her reading glasses. 'It can be,' she said, 'and when it is, we laugh about it, don't we? A laugh is as good as an orgasm any day!'

'I'm not sure I'd go that far,' Leo said. 'I mean, I like a laugh as much as the next man, but an orgasm, well, for a start, it's—'

'Rarer?' Marion suggested.

'Maybe now,' Leo said, 'but you should have known me when I was younger!'

'I thought,' Marion said, returning to her screen, 'this wasn't all about you.'

Five

In the head of security's office overlooking the Zarastro Oil refinery, delivery trucks were coming and going despite the protesters who gathered daily in front of the gates. Malcolm Beamish leaned against the door while his boss, P J Rotherwick, known as PJ, demolished an almond croissant, covering his overalls in icing sugar.

'The thing is, Malcolm,' PJ said, through a mouthful of crumbs, 'we didn't take you on because of your brains.'

Malcolm said nothing. He was used to being insulted, everyone did it except Gilda, who thought he was wonderful, and he'd learned to accept it without retaliating. He tried to act like a gutter and let it all flow by him so that his anger was contained, but occasionally something would catch and stick and he could no longer control himself. He knew that some people, aware of his record, not to mention his impressive physical presence, thought it was OK to push him to see how far he would go, but he mostly avoided them, preferring to drink vodka with Gilda in the basement bedsit he rented in Camden Town. He couldn't avoid PJ, though, and just hoped his summons wouldn't involve anything too challenging. Nathan's attempts to build up his self-confidence had not been entirely successful, but given his background, and a mother who rubbished him at every opportunity, especially now she no longer had a husband to use for target practice, Malcolm thought he was doing alright.

'Nor,' PJ said, washing down the croissant with noisy slurps of milky coffee, 'was it your beauty. All that bodybuilding you do hasn't exactly made you a babe magnet, has it?'

You haven't seen Gilda, Malcolm thought. Dark-haired, dark-skinned, dark-eyed, sleek as a seal, she'd been cleaning the toilets in a coffee shop he used and had asked him for a cigarette. As he didn't smoke, he offered her a drink instead, and she told him her story, walking across Europe from Beirut or somewhere to find a cousin in Battersea who tried to abuse her. It made Malcolm's story seem quite ordinary, and he just wanted to protect her, to show her that there were men who weren't only interested in screwing her one way or another. She accepted his protection and never questioned him about anything except whether he liked her bean soup. Even PJ would like her soup, and he was supposed to be on a strict diet.

'Was it your extraordinary talents that led to your employment by one of the world's largest oil companies?' PJ asked rhetorically, brushing flakes off everywhere except his chin, screwing up the paper bag that contained the croissant, throwing it at his empty wastepaper basket, and missing. 'Oh, wait a minute, remind me what those talents are. IT skills? Non-existent. Technical expertise? Zero. Knowledge of the hydrocarbon industry? Zilch. You don't even have a fucking HGV licence!'

Feeling that some response was required, Malcolm bent down to pick up the paper bag and put it in the basket.

'Litter-picking!' PJ said. 'That must have been it. That, and the fact that we get a government grant for taking on useless ex-cons like you because it's cheaper than keeping you in jails that are already full, sewing mailbags for a postal service that doesn't exist, feeding, housing and supposedly training you at taxpayers' expense to rejoin a world you don't recognize. Am I right?'

'Yes, PJ,' Malcolm said dully.

'Well, I'm glad we've got that cleared up. Have you anything to do that might conceivably be considered useful, other than cluttering up my office?'

'You summoned me, PJ. And told me to bring you a croissant without anyone knowing. Other than that, I was checking out the alarm system in the loading bay.'

'Important work that could be done better by a robot. I want you to go and see someone.'

Malcolm's heart sank. It wasn't likely to be his social worker or anyone like that. It was probably someone PJ wanted to settle a score with. A driver who'd got out of line, a union official who'd demanded too much, a petrol station manager who'd made one complaint too many. PJ never did anything so crude as send in the killer dogs, not at first. Men armed with wrenches weren't immediately despatched to terrify the target's wife or children. Instead massive Malcolm trudged round with a warning: stop doing whatever you're doing, or worse will follow. A lot worse. You might think it's bad to get a visit from someone who's done a stretch for a murder he didn't commit, someone you wouldn't want haunting your house, upsetting your gran or your neighbours because he was convicted of stabbing a kid, an innocent kid, twenty-seven times, including once in the eye. And if you don't take notice of what he's got to say, the next person to turn up won't be nearly as nice.

That was why PJ was not just head of security, he was a senior manager who was reputed to be the fixer for the top brass in Zarastro's London office in Blackfriars, overlooking the River Thames. Which also explained why PJ's wife didn't drive a Ford Fiesta, but a convertible Mercedes with heated leather seats.

'OK,' Malcolm said reluctantly, because he had no alternative. 'Who am I seeing?'

'A nice lady – or she used to be, until she started getting loose-lipped – called Patsy Finch,' PJ said. 'She lives in Primrose Hill, so you won't have much in the way of travel expenses. She used to work for us, and retired around twenty years ago, but instead of being gratefully discreet, she's been talking to people, despite signing a non-disclosure agreement. One of the people she talked to was another employee with little regard for company loyalty. Can you guess who that was? Unfortunately I don't have the time to waste while you work it out, so I'll tell you. His name was Larry Coombs.'

Malcolm, who was pale to begin with, went the colour of a vegan alternative to milk. Of course he knew the name Larry Coombs. He'd been instrumental in killing him.

~ ~ ~

'I was told,' Katy said, 'that I should mention Heythrop?'

Leo looked puzzled for a minute, then threw himself back in his chair with a laugh so loud it made Pumpernickel bark.

'God!' Leo said when he'd recovered, 'I had a hangover that lasted a week!'

Katy couldn't imagine her boss Helen having a hangover. Even a good time seemed beyond her. 'What happened?' she asked. 'What is Heythrop, anyway?'

'It's a village in Oxfordshire that was the centre of a hunt.'

Katy looked puzzled. 'A hunt?' she said. 'For what? Spies? Terrorists? Treasure?'

Leo laughed again. 'Foxes,' he said. 'People used to dress up in jodhpurs and jackets to get onto horses and chase poor little foxes into corners so they could be torn apart by a pack of hounds.'

93

'That's disgusting,' Katy said.

'I agree. Another reason I'm a vegetarian.'

'But what were you and Helen...?'

'Oh, we didn't go *hunting!*' Leo said. 'Can you imagine me on a horse? Besides, I don't think they accept Jews, or not vegetarian ones. But once a year they hold a party, a point-to-point, they call it, which is basically a piss-up by a racecourse, and it so happens that Helly and I were each invited to attend by clients of ours.'

Katy had never heard her boss called Helly. 'And?' she said.

'It was cold – there may even have been snow on the ground. Watching horses run round a track isn't the most exciting thing in the world, unless you're a gambler, which I'm not, or you know something about form, which I don't. The clients were talking to other clients about the things clients talk about, which is usually how their lawyers overcharge them for doing fuck all. But there was a free bar. And Helly and I found ourselves on adjoining barstools drinking martinis until we fell off.'

'You fell off your stools?'

Leo nodded. 'I'm afraid so,' he said. 'Being a gentleman, I suggested we should book a room in a nearby hotel, in order to assist our recovery. My suggestion was gravely accepted, and my next memory was of waking up in a strange bed, fully dressed, with my shoes neatly placed on my chest. Naturally I cannot and would not reveal what actually happened, but I believe I behaved with perfect decorum. And as my friend Dennis might say, I was not at that period in my life someone whose behaviour would normally be described as decorous.'

Katy tried to look shocked, but found it hard not to giggle. 'Have the two of you met since?' she asked.

'I don't believe we have,' Leo said, 'but not because we've been avoiding one another. At least, not on my part. Naturally I sent Helly a note offering an apology, if one was merited, and she replied saying there was nothing to apologize for, which was a source of relief as well as regret. What more can I tell you?'

Katy pulled herself together. 'We think it's possible,' she said in a business-like tone, 'that you might be able to help us over a report commissioned by Zarastro from a former client of yours, Dr Nancy Chen? This would be about twenty years ago?'

Pumpernickel sat up in his basket. Leo fiddled with his pen. 'And who made the connection between me and Nancy Chen?' he asked. 'Was it Larry Coombs?'

Katy tried not to look surprised. Helen had said Leo had a sharp mind.

'You're wondering,' Leo continued, 'how I knew. Larry's mother, or to be accurate, his foster mother, came to me about his murder. Has she now hired you to look into it?'

'Oh no,' Katy said earnestly. 'Our specialty is corporate crime. We don't do—'

'Common or garden murder? I'm not saying it's far more interesting, but you do meet a nicer class of person. Which is the main reason I gave up corporate law about twenty-five years ago. Helly, obviously, is still writhing in its tentacles.'

Katy felt she had to defend her boss. 'Actually,' she said, 'she does a lot of pro bono work, with a small team I'm part of. We're building a case against Zarastro's far-reaching involvement in the forthcoming climate summit.'

'On whose behalf?'

'Actually, for the families who lost members fleeing Myanmar, a few years ago. You probably remember the case: twenty-three of them were found dead in a container lorry belonging to one of Zarastro's subsidiary companies. Zarastro blamed the company's chief exec, who was given a thirty-year sentence, but we reckon that was just cover for their trafficking activities. Which was one of the things poor Larry wanted to expose.'

'Poor Larry? You knew him, then?'

Katy blushed. She wasn't sure why. Larry had attended meetings of the campaign committee she was on, and as she'd always been, in the words of one of her colleagues, 'a bit of a fag-hag,' she and Larry had grown close enough for him to ask her opinion of his new jogging bottoms, and whether she would doubt his commitment if he had a go with another member of the committee he fancied, the somewhat manic Robin Pocklington. Katy had pointed out that she'd had a child with one of their most dedicated campaigners, William Flanagan, and she trusted no one doubted her commitment. She'd wished Larry luck, and the next thing she knew, he'd been killed. Maybe her blush was guilt that she hadn't done more to find out what happened, though she had a brand-new baby and had hardly taken any time off work. Maybe it was just grief that someone as brave as Larry, who was prepared to take on a multinational corporation and at the same time sigh that he wished he had shoulders like her William, should be set upon by a gang of kids, none of whom had been caught.

'We campaigned together,' she told Leo. 'Larry was going to come to the office in Gray's Inn and meet Helen, but she was delayed, he had to rush off somewhere else, and before we could reschedule, he was dead. But he did tell us he'd heard about this report...'

'From Patsy Finch? I've already talked to her.'

'You have?' Katy said, surprised. 'You move quicker than we do.'

'The advantage of being a one-man band,' Leo said. Pumpernickel gave a huge yawn to draw their attention. 'One man and a dog,' Leo amended. 'Just suppose I could lay my hands on a copy of Nancy's report. What would you do with it?'

'Well,' Katy said, 'I'd confront Zarastro with it. But I'm only a paralegal.'

'They would of course deny receiving it,' Leo said. 'I've talked to my journo friend Dennis Arbuthnot, and he says rumours of this report had reached him, but people are so used to the dirty tricks of multinational companies, it would hardly make a splash.'

'I don't believe everyone's stopped caring altogether!' Katy protested.

'Nor do I,' Leo said firmly. Pumpernickel sat up. 'The thing is, you have to make it personal, don't you? A scandal affecting a company's balance sheet would only matter to the shareholders; one where an innocent young woman, as well as a young man, got themselves killed by trying to expose the truth, that's a *story*!'

His vehemence made Pumpernickel bark in encouragement. Katy's face lit up, then equally suddenly darkened.

'What?' Leo asked.

'It's just...our practice couldn't, wouldn't handle anything like that. It's not...the way we do things. Helen would never—'

'She sent you to check out Nancy's report, didn't she? What if you tell her I've got a copy, which I'm willing to let her see?'

'I don't know,' Katy said dubiously. 'She's very...focussed. She wouldn't like anyone criticizing her approach, or even worse, trying to get her to shift it. I mean, I'd like to help, of course I would, though I do have a baby to look after as well as the day job and all my campaigning...'

'OK,' Leo said decisively. 'I'll talk to Helly. But here's what I think might have happened. Patsy Finch was a colleague of Nancy's, and believes her death was suspicious. She mentions her suspicions to Larry when he turned whistleblower—'

'Because,' Katy interrupted, 'he saw from the inside what Zarastro were doing, and was disgusted that they were pretending to support climate action while influencing government policy against it.'

'Exactly,' Leo said. 'And then Larry gets himself killed. Patsy is convinced that's suspicious. I'm convinced it's suspicious. You're convinced it's suspicious, right?' Katy nodded. Pumpernickel gave a short yap. 'Even the dog's convinced. So what we should be concentrating on is not whether they suppressed the report, but whether they had Nancy and Larry killed to keep it under wraps!'

Katy shivered, more with excitement than dread. Pumpernickel came over and put his head on her thigh to give her courage. 'How do we find out?' she asked, almost in a whisper.

'I could talk to Nathan Flowers, for a start,' Leo said.

'Nathan Flowers? He's the one Zarastro blamed for the death of those asylum seekers!'

'He was also Nancy's boyfriend, till she gave him the push. He should have something useful to say. As for Larry, his mother Sadie found his notebooks, which the police managed to miss.'

'They're not really interested in what happened, are they? Another gay protester: that's one less to worry about!'

'What if I persuade Sadie to let me see the notebooks? They might help you and Helly to build your case too. A two-pronged approach: would Helly be up for that?'

'I don't know, Mr Wengrowski,' Katy said doubtfully. 'She likes doing things her way.'

'It's Leo. And of course she does. I could try schmoozing her – that's something I'm good at – or we could work together without her knowing.'

'Well, Leo,' Katy said, blushing with pleasure, 'that would be—'

'That's settled, then,' Leo said. Pumpernickel snickered, and pawed Katy's arm. She automatically tickled him behind the ears. Leo got up and went over to his safe.

'I'll show you the report,' he said. 'It sure makes interesting reading. I can't give you a copy, of course, but just so you know, my printer is also a photocopier, and if I make us fresh coffee, I'd have to leave you alone for a few minutes.' Pumpernickel stretched each of his legs, then shook himself alert.

'If you need any help,' Leo continued, 'Pumpy's as good as I am with technology. Which isn't saying much.'

~ ~ ~

Malcolm kept watch on Patsy's flat from the cramped driver's seat of his battered Fiat Uno. The inside was clean – Gilda had seen to that – but the heater wasn't working properly, and he was aware that the car stood out among the Jaguars and Range Rovers of the Primrose Hill set. But skulking around the park in the cold while maintaining eyes on her front door would only make him

99

look like a drug dealer, and though he was confident he could see off a stray kid asking for a wrap, he didn't fancy getting involved with the gang whose pitch this was.

Patsy had gone in with a man who was carrying lots of shopping bags. He'd been wearing a hoody but he didn't look like much of a challenge. Malcolm hoped the man was just helping with Patsy's shopping, but he'd been in there for nearly half an hour and it was getting dark, on one of those grey January days when the only difference between day and night was that night was colder. Maybe they were having tea. Malcolm could just do with a cup of tea. Or maybe they were having sex: Patsy might look like an old turkey, but the way she dressed and used powder and lipstick showed she was a turkey who was still up for it. As Malcolm's dad used to say, 'Just because there's snow on the roof doesn't mean the fire's gone out.' Then he and Malcolm would look at his mum and snigger.

The Idea of anyone wanting to have sex with his mum was weird enough; Malcolm decided his dad only stayed around to keep an eye on him, though that hadn't stopped him getting in with the wrong set when he was trying to find kids of his own age to hang out with. A gang who set him a challenge, stabbing the brother of the leader of a rival gang, and when he bottled it, made sure he got the blame anyway. His dad came to see him in jail every week; his mum came once, and spent most of her time complaining he wasn't getting the rehabilitation that was his due. The screws had laughed about that. Luckily Nathan took him under his wing. And there was nothing funny about their relationship, whatever the whispers said. Nathan had taught him how to look after himself, and take care of business. Stuff his father would have taught him, if Malcolm had not been banged up, and if his dad had lived.

Malcolm shivered. Should he wait five more minutes? Or should he go in regardless? Lesson one, Nathan always said, was use surprise. Lesson two was don't get caught. Which was also lesson three: when the music stops, make sure someone else is holding the weapon. Which he'd managed neatly enough with Larry Coombs. Waited till the group got high, worked them up a bit, pointed out Larry as he went for his usual night run, same time, same place he always did. Take the trainers so it would look like a robbery: job done.

Somebody had stepped out from behind a tree when he was coming away. Malcolm nearly had a heart attack, especially as the man looked like a cop. You can tell by the way they hold themselves, by the way they move, as if they were in charge. Malcolm had stuffed the trainers inside his hoody, and of course he didn't have a weapon, but he kept his head, resisted the temptation to run, and said, strolling on, 'Alright, mate?' And the man had echoed him, 'Alright, mate,' and vanished. Weird, but Malcolm was used to weird.

He got out of the car, stretched his cramped muscles, and decided to go in. He was just a messenger boy, really; whatever Patsy was doing, if he interrupted her to deliver his warning, it would be even more of a surprise, wouldn't it? It would carry more weight, she'd be even more likely to remember it. And, he reasoned, if there was someone with her, they could take care of her after he left. It wasn't as if he enjoyed frightening old ladies, though if she keeled over Malcolm imagined PJ would be quite happy. He'd virtually said as much, for the record.

He pulled on his balaclava, even though it was already too dark for him to be recognized outside. He thought about putting on gloves to cover the tattoos on his hands and fingers, but decided that the daggers and tear-shaped drops of blood would make his appearance even more menacing. He flexed his fingers and rang Patsy's bell. Hers was the ground-floor flat, which should make it quick and easy to crash into.

'Delivery for Patsy Finch,' he mumbled into the intercom. The buzzer opened the front door. There were two internal doors, one to his left, one to his right. The one to his right started to open. He ran at it with his shoulder, because they wouldn't expect violence. The light spilled over him from a small sitting room crammed with furniture. Patsy was stretched out on the sofa, chintz-covered like his mother's, drinking what must have been gin, judging by the bottle on the coffee table in front of her. The man who'd been with her was nowhere to be seen.

Maybe, Malcolm thought, he's in the bedroom down the hall. He knew what he had to say. He'd sort of rehearsed it while sitting in the car, though he was relying on adrenaline to make it sound more threatening. He opened his mouth – and suddenly felt a sharp pain at the back of his knees, which made him stumble. He put out a hand to save himself, and had it savagely twisted behind his back. Before he knew it he was lying on the ground with his bum in the air. His balaclava was ripped off and a booted foot crushed his cheek painfully into the Axminster carpet. His shoulder felt like it was going to dislocate and his tattooed fingers were being crushed to the point of breaking.

'Hello, Malcolm,' a male voice said. 'And what are you doing here?' He put his face closer to Malcolm's. He looked familiar. It was difficult trying to remember something when he was in such pain, but something clicked in Malcolm's mind as well as his shoulder. It was the guy he'd seen after they'd stabbed Larry Coombs. The guy Malcom was sure was a cop.

~ ~ ~

'Honestly,' Felix said, 'I don't remember Grandad ever getting angry. Granny shouts occasionally, but only when she's had a hard time at school. Not from the kids, from the teachers. Grandad said it was on account of her high principles.'

It was his second session with Marion and he'd been looking forward to it. Staying at Jasmine's house was OK, and for sure it was better than that hospital in Oxford, but they wouldn't leave him alone. They wouldn't let him go running – Jazz said she'd never be able to keep up with him – and even if he announced he was going to do some reading, they kept checking up on him.

Robin came round a couple of times but he and Felix were never allowed to go to bed together. Jasmine's mum, who insisted on being called Tina, said she was broad-minded but would rather there were no 'goings-on' under her roof. Her husband, Jazz's dad, never seemed to say anything or do much apart from stroking his beard. A bit like Giles, really, who let Felix's mum do all the talking. He could have stayed with her and Giles in Sussex but according to Jazz the doctors advised against it. They wouldn't look after him properly and he wouldn't get the treatment he needed.

Granny had offered to have him at the cottage in Yorkshire they'd bought years ago to get away from everybody, but he couldn't face her. Not after what had happened. But being with Marion, curled up in her wing-backed chair with the carving of the runner to keep his fingers busy, Felix felt safe. Unhassled. Talking was easier when people didn't *make* you talk.

103

'My mother stopped speaking to anyone when I was about your age, or a bit younger,' Marion said casually. 'It was fun to begin with - it meant me and my brother could do what we liked when we were home for the school holidays - but after a bit it became scary. If you're not told how far you can go, most people become less daring, not more. I thought it was my fault.'

'Why?' Felix asked, intrigued.

'I thought she was punishing me.'

'What had you done?'

'That was the problem. I didn't know. Was it because I was a great galumphing girl, not the delicate and dainty person she'd always been? Was it because I couldn't cook or sew or clean in corners or keep everything tidy the way females of my generation were supposed to do? Was it because I kept butting into other people's conversations at the parties my father insisted we gave at Christmas - parties where no one noticed my mother wasn't saying anything as they were too busy talking about themselves? Was it because I looked like my father and had a laugh like a horse? It was impossible to find out, so I felt guilty about everything.'

'Did she ever tell you the reason?'

Marion shook her mane of hair, which was green. 'Never. When me and my brother Harold left home - me to get married, which didn't last very long, Harold to work in a theatre in Brighton where he could grow a beard and wear skirts - my mother entered an order of silent nuns. So I had to work it out for myself. With the help of a therapist, of course.'

Felix leaned forward in his chair, fascinated. 'And?' he said.

'We decided - *I* decided - she was punishing my father for abandoning her every week to live with his mistress. In this very flat, as a matter of fact. Of course,' she continued cheerfully, 'I'll never know whether or not I was right. But it enabled me to get over a failed marriage and gain enough confidence to train as a therapist myself. Which is the point. You don't have to feel guilty about things you didn't do.'

'But I *did* do something,' Felix said before he could stop himself. 'I killed Grandad.'

'How did you manage that?' Marion asked conversationally. 'Killing someone isn't easy. Unless you're handy with a gun or a knife or can mix up a mean poison. Did you do any of those things?'

'I killed him,' Felix said doggedly, 'because I told him he was a hypocrite. First he turned bright red, then he went as pale as your wall. It was like watching the tide go out: all that was left was sand.'

'And seaweed,' Marion said. 'And crabs and prawns and limpets and all sorts of living things. Why did you call him a hypocrite?'

Felix heaved a great sigh. He struggled to speak, swallowed, retreated to the back of the chair, then said with a rush, 'He was blackmailing someone.'

'Oh yes?' Marion said calmly. 'Who?'

'Only George fucking Ramirez,' Felix muttered, his face hidden. 'Who then financed Grandad's whole accountability campaign.'

'That's public knowledge. Why do you think George was being blackmailed?'

Felix came out of hiding. His face was angry, his voice trembled. 'Robin told me,' he said thickly.

'And how did Robin know?'

'He...' Felix stopped. Normally he didn't talk about things he found difficult. They sat somewhere in his head until their edges had grown smooth and they could

105

slip out easily. But the thing about Robin, his going with someone else, that was still jagged. He didn't want to hurt himself on it but maybe, just maybe, spitting it out might reveal it to be something smaller, slighter, smoother than he feared. Something he could handle. If he chose his words carefully, he could step over and around them and see them from a safe distance.

'He – he slept with someone who worked for Zarastro,' he said slowly. The admission didn't burn his mouth as he had half-expected it to. He went on, more confidently. 'He insisted on telling me about it. He said he needed to be honest. He's studying theology, you see.'

'Honesty can be hurtful, can't it?' Marion said sympathetically. 'Sometimes it can feel as if you've been handed a heavy suitcase the other person can't carry anymore. You're landed with it and you don't know what you're supposed to do with it. Is that how it feels?'

'A bit,' Felix said.

'Well, now you can put it down and have a breather. How did this person who worked for Zarastro know your grandfather was blackmailing the boss?'

'It's complicated,' Felix said, though this was easier than talking about being hurt by something that reason told him shouldn't hurt at all. 'Robin said the man – his name was Larry – heard from someone who used to work at the company about a report that laid out all the damaging things that would happen if the world continued to rely on oil. This was twenty years ago.'

'And what happened to the report?'

'Nothing. It was never published. Robin said Larry was convinced Zarastro had suppressed it. He already had evidence of how they were persuading the government not to act too quickly on climate change, and he took it to Grandad, who was his MP. And what did Grandad do? He went to George Ramirez and said he'd say nothing about it all, provided Zarastro financed his accountability campaign.'

'Which they did,' Marion said, 'and very successfully. The bill was on the point of becoming law, wasn't it?'

'But how,' Felix said heatedly, 'can you preach accountability if you're blackmailing the source of your funding? How can someone who's always talking about principles – who resigned from the front bench because the leader had gone back on his promises – live with suppressing information that is a matter of vital public importance?'

'How reliable is the information? I'm sure you've asked yourself that.'

Felix put the carving back on her table. He'd been clutching it so hard his fingers were white. 'I trust Robin,' he said slowly. 'I have to.'

'Even though he's not one-hundred-percent faithful?'

'He said it was like an itch that he had to scratch. I've been trying to understand that. But,' he added, brightening up, 'the man he slept with, this Larry, he was stabbed soon afterwards. That must be a sign of how important his information is, mustn't it?'

'It certainly could be. Anyway, you went to your grandfather, and confronted him with this story.'

'I had to! All my life he, and Granny, have urged me to be honest. Mum's always making things up to get herself out of a situation, but I'm not like that. I couldn't live with myself, keeping something like that secret, and I never thought Grandad could either. The first opportunity I had to talk to him was on the day of the final rally, the big one before the vote. I'd arranged to drive him there, and though I really didn't want to spoil it for him, I couldn't say nothing. So I came out with it, and he changed colour like I said, then I left him to recover. He had more people to see, and I thought he'll have an explanation, I'm sure he will, and it'll all be alright. But the next time I saw him, he was dead. And that was all my fault!'

Marion poured him a glass of water and pushed it towards him. 'You know they haven't established the cause of death yet,' she said quietly. 'You may think you gave him a heart attack, but there's no evidence that's what killed him.'

'What else could it be?' Felix demanded tearfully. 'He wasn't stabbed or strangled, was he? He ate more chocolates than he should have, being a diabetic, but he'd done that a million times before and lived to joke about it!'

'If you'd had the chance to talk to him about your accusation, what do you think he might have said?'

'I'll never know, will I?'

'You knew him well enough. How might he have defended himself?'

Felix reached out for a banana-shaped sculpture in bronze, and stroked it to calm himself down. 'I suppose,' he said eventually, 'he might have said that politics is all about compromise. That the accountability campaign was what mattered most to him, because it would have ushered in a different form of politics, where people have to answer for breaking their promises. And he'd probably have said he'd be the first in line to answer accusations of dishonesty, once the bill had passed. Which it didn't, and isn't likely to, now he's gone. That's down to me too!'

'That's not true, Felix,' Marion said firmly. 'Let's just talk about why you're being so hard on yourself, shall we? Why do you think that is?'

'I don't know,' Felix said sullenly. 'I was just trying to be honest, and now he's dead.'

'When Robin was honest with you, did you feel so crushed by it that you gave up the will to live?'

'Almost!'

'Yet you forgave him. Which shows that you are not only stronger than you think, you're also more charitable. Your grandfather had great strength of character, it's what made him and his ideas about accountability so popular. Let me ask you this: why couldn't you forgive him, as you forgave Robin?'

Felix looked dazed, as if this had never occurred to him before. 'It's – it's different,' he managed.

'Because Robin is your lover as well as your friend?'

'Well, yes, partly, I suppose. But Robin's...he's young, like me. Grandad was old.'

'And the old should know better?'

'Yes,' Felix said decisively. 'Yes, they should. If they don't, what's the point of growing up?'

'Good point,' Marion said cheerfully. 'But what if I told you we may know better, we may have learned a lot as we shoulder our way through life, but we don't always act on what we've learned? We're imperfect, I'm sorry to say, and I regard that as cause for celebration, not condemnation.'

'OK,' Felix said cautiously. 'I get that people don't behave the way numbers do. They're not that predictable. But when your lover tells you, not only that's he's been...with someone else, but that someone else was let down by your own grandfather, you have to do something, don't you?'

'To make the world a better place, or to make yourself feel better?'

'Fuck!' Felix said suddenly. 'Why can't you do both?'

'How did you feel after you forgave Robin?' Marion asked.

Felix considered this carefully. 'Better, I suppose,' he said grudgingly. 'But that doesn't mean I can forgive Grandad so easily.'

'Baby steps,' Marion said. 'Why don't you start by forgiving yourself?'

'How do I do that?'

'You're a mathematician. Consider the probabilities. How many heart attacks are brought on by shock statements?'

'I've no idea.'

'Look it up. It will be a very low number. Most are caused by a build-up of bad cholesterol in the arteries. Did your grandfather suffer from high cholesterol?'

'No, but he had diabetes.'

'Did you force-feed him éclairs to put him into a glycaemic coma?'

'Of course not!'

'You accused him of something which upset him, yet he went on to deal with the problems of his constituents, correct?'

'Yes, but—'

'The important "but", Felix, is that when you left him he was alive, if pale. You are trying to take responsibility for something that had nothing to do with you, to make yourself feel better.'

'I didn't feel better!'

'I suggest that's a combination of guilt and grief. Guilt that you so readily forgave your lover for burdening you with his confession, grief because you want to explain the death of your grandfather, who you loved in an entirely different way, and no other explanation has yet been advanced. Leaving a big pool of doubt which you're enjoying wallowing in!'

Felix stared at her. Tears formed in his eyes and ran down his cheeks. He did nothing to stop them.

'I'm sorry,' Marion said gently. 'Do you want to stop?'

Felix gulped. A tear splashed onto the back of his hand, and he stared at it in astonishment. Then he wiped his eyes with his fingers.

'I'm sorry,' he said gruffly. 'I don't think I've ever cried in public before.'

'How does it feel?' Marion asked.

Felix licked a tear from his upper lip. 'Good,' he said. 'It feels good.'

~ ~ ~

Malcolm trudged dolefully down the stairs to the basement flat he shared with Gilda. His shoulder hurt, he could hardly flex his fingers, he was sure there was a bruise on his cheek where the man who Patsy called William had ground his face into the carpet. He was ashamed that he had let himself be so easily ambushed, let alone facing Gilda with flaws on the body he spent so much time cultivating. He hoped she loved him for more than his formidable physique, yet that was the one thing he was most proud of, the one thing he could control – and it had let him down.

The room smelt of soup and sausages, as well as damp and mould, undercut by the sharp note of the cheap perfume Gilda used. She was lying on the bed reading an old magazine he had brought her from work to improve her English, and she jumped up the moment she saw him and said, 'What happened?' She was little and lithe and she had to stand on tiptoe to touch his cheek.

'An accident,' he said. 'Nothing to worry about.' He sat heavily on the bed, and she twined herself around him like a cat, rubbing herself gently against him.

'I worry,' she purred. 'Tell me.'

He tried to straighten his shoulders, and winced. He wouldn't be able to lift the weights he normally did, not for a while anyway. Maybe he'd skip the gym for a few days, but what would they say? What would PJ say, apart from mocking him mercilessly for letting himself be bettered by an old lady? He wished he could give up the Zarastro job and take up one of the offers he regularly received from other boys at the gym. There were always jobs for bouncers, and he'd never get the hassle he got from PJ. He might even be picked up for one of those game shows, which would make Gilda proud. Maybe it would even give his mother something to boast about. Except he couldn't give up Zarastro, because of Nathan. He hated letting Nathan down. Nathan could make him feel even worse than PJ did.

Gilda put the tips of her fingers on his bruise. They were cool and dry and it felt good. She knelt beside and just behind him, and gently started to massage his neck and shoulders. She had small hands but her fingers were strong and as she kneaded his muscles he felt the tightness going out of him and relaxed enough to roll his head to release the tension in his back. She unbuttoned his shirt to get at the front of his shoulders and ran her hands down his pecs. He closed his eyes.

'Tell me,' she said again.

'There's not much to tell,' he said as her fingers brushed his nipples. 'I just have to find some missing notebooks, is all. Piece of cake.'

'Who wants cake?' she said. Her fingers were working their way downwards, over his abs.

'This man I met called William,' he said. 'I'm sure he's a cop. He was there when – when something happened to the guy who was going to blow the whistle on Zarastro.'

'Blow the whistle? What this means?'

'Tell people things about the company they didn't want everyone to know. We could all have lost our jobs. That's why he had to be stopped.'

'The cops stop him?'

'No,' Malcolm said. 'That was my job.'

He wondered how the cops would have known what was going to happen to Larry. If they knew, why didn't they stop it? Did they want him out of the way too?

All this thinking made Malcolm's brain hurt nearly as much as his shoulder. It was much easier to let Gilda's fingers work their way down his body. Soon he didn't have to think anymore.

Six

Leo was never sure what to take when visiting people in prison, especially if they were in for life, but he settled on a pack of ten cigarettes, which cost more than the train fare, but could at least be used as currency.

'I am intrigued,' Nathan Flowers said. 'Why would a distinguished lawyer who should have retired years ago come to see a complete stranger? Unless you have decided to make an appeal on behalf of the victim of an egregious injustice?'

'But you're not a complete stranger,' Leo said, sitting at the table, ignoring the comment about his age and the mention of an appeal. He held up the still sealed packet of cigarettes so the guard could see it. 'You came to see me some twenty years ago, when the ground floor and basement of my Soho office were occupied by a pornographic cinema and strip club. They've since been replaced by a Chinese grocery, which is an improvement if you've reached the point when food matters more than sex. You wanted some love letters you thought an ex-girlfriend of yours might have left with me. Nancy Chen?'

'Nancy Chen!' Nathan said, taking the cigarettes and stuffing them into his pocket. 'I haven't thought about her for years. Some people have the ability to remember the pleasant things and block out the unpleasant ones. For me, unfortunately, it's the other way round. That's what prison does to you.'

'You wanted the letters – which I didn't have, by the way: she probably destroyed them – because you were getting married and didn't want your wife to know about your passion for someone else. How did that work out?'

'Rachida?' Nathan said. 'Not well. She ignored the bit about "for richer or poorer, for better or worse", and

114

took off with a fitness instructor while my trial was still going on. She was a bear of very little brain, sadly, as well as being of a jealous disposition. Not like Nancy, who was, I readily admit, far smarter than I was.'

'So what went wrong between you and Nancy?'

Nathan sat back in his chair and gave Leo one of his intense stares. 'Why are you so interested?' he demanded.

'She was my client,' Leo said. 'She left me a copy of the report she was commissioned to write on the future effect of oil exploitation on the climate. A very prescient woman: virtually all her forecasts have turned out to be true.'

'Of course!' Nathan said with pride. 'She was one of their best scientists!'

'You were working in the same department. Along with Patsy Finch.'

'Is she still alive?'

'Very much so,' Leo said. 'Or was last week, anyhow. How did you get on with her?'

Nathan's expression became crafty. 'She might have been a little jealous. Of my relationship with Nancy, I mean. Which was very close, very intense.'

'Is that why she ended it? Too intense for comfort?'

'I never pushed her too hard! I worshipped her, as a matter of fact: I would have done anything she asked. I could never quite believe that someone as beautiful and talented could fall for someone like me.'

'Maybe that was a turn-off. I'm not saying anything as sexist as women don't like a pushover—'

'I was no pushover!' Nathan said indignantly. 'I started out senior to her, as a matter of fact, and I encouraged her potential. It was thanks to me she was asked to take the lead on that report, even though I knew her findings wouldn't be welcome.'

'Did you ever see the final version?'

'She wouldn't show it to me. We'd split up by then.'

'You wanna tell me why?'

Nathan composed himself, and shrugged. 'She said she no longer loved me. Simple as that. She could be – she was – very direct. It was what I loved about her, even though it's sometimes hard to take.'

'Most of the time, in my experience,' Leo said with feeling. 'Honesty can be brutal. Yet you chased her to Switzerland. What were you hoping for? Reconciliation over a raclette? Forgiveness with a fondue?'

'First of all, we'd booked the holiday together,' Nathan said with dignity. 'It cost a lot, even then, and we weren't being paid enough to write it off. Second, we were both good skiers, good enough to spend most of our time off-piste, and I thought maybe that would somehow bring us back together.'

'Skiing's a mystery to me,' Leo admitted. 'In fact, I've never seen the attraction of snow and ice, unless you're a polar bear. I tried skating once, and nearly broke an ankle. Give me roller skates any time.'

'There are those who say a good ski run is more orgasmic than sex,' Nathan said. 'That's something I think about occasionally, in my solitary cell. But it was also an opportunity to check up on her, see who else she was seeing, maybe talk to her friends like Patsy in a relaxed atmosphere, and find out if there any way back. There's nothing like a skiing holiday to burnish your optimism, and give you the courage to say and do things you wouldn't dream of doing at home.'

'Such as?'

'Such as daring someone to go for a run – a ski run – that everyone said was too dangerous, in the hope that if anything happened, you'd be on hand to help.'

'A knight in shining ski boots coming to rescue a fair damsel from an avalanche or whatever?'

'I can tell you have a romantic streak, Mr Wengrowski. Which is uncommon in people of your profession.'

'I'm glad you recognize it. So how did you lure her onto this dangerous slope?'

'I did not need to lure Nancy. She was always up for a challenge.'

'You set off first, confident she'd follow?'

'For someone who cares nothing for skiing, your guesses are pretty accurate.'

'That comes from years of studying human nature, often at its most depraved. How did you ensure she had an accident?'

'I beg your pardon?'

'You wanted her to fall, break a leg, whatever, so you could come swooshing to her aid, right? What did you do, saw through her skis? Tamper with her binding? Loosen her clips? Put itching powder in her bobble hat?'

Nathan stared at him, then laughed. 'What kind of person do you think I am, Mr Wengrowski? I loved Nancy! Why would I want her dead?'

'Call me fanciful, but you're in here for manslaughter. She'd broken off your relationship, a relationship that meant a lot to you. You were hurt, devastated, jealous, vengeful; why wouldn't you be out to get her? Maybe you didn't intend to kill her, any more than you set out to kill those unfortunate asylum seekers, but that's how the cookie crumbled. Only the Swiss authorities couldn't find anything wrong. So you got away with that one. And as a result, you got a big promotion at Zarastro. What did you do, quietly take the credit for ridding the company of someone whose report was only going to cause them trouble?'

Nathan stood up. 'Take me back, boss,' he said to the guard. 'I have nothing more to say to this gentleman, and I never want to see him again.'

Which, Leo reckoned, was as much of a confession as he was likely to get.

~ ~ ~

Sadie Macouba slapped down a tattered Sainsbury's shopping bag on Leo's desk. Pumpernickel watched her warily.

'Open it!' she commanded. Leo peered inside the bag, and pulled out a large, old hardback book with a stained cover.

'*The World's Best Book of Curries*,' he read. 'I wouldn't mind a copy of this! I never make them hot enough for Marion. She must have a gullet of steel!'

'You haven't opened it yet,' Sadie pointed out. Leo did as instructed. The inside of the book had been hollowed out. Nestling in the space was a notebook. Leo looked at Sadie, who folded her arms across her chest and nodded.

'I said I'd bring them, and I always carry out a promise,' she affirmed. 'You found that Patsy woman, you got that report, now you got Larry's notebook. What're you going to do with it all? Put a bomb under them and get that investigation going double quick!'

Leo held up a warning hand. Pumpernickel shrank into his basket. 'It's not going to happen instantly,' Leo said. 'To make sure we get justice for Larry, we have to identify the people who killed him, and those who were behind them. That's going to take time. You and I both know it isn't a simple case of a robbery that went wrong, which is what the police currently think. I'll start work on it immediately – in fact, I've already started – but it's not something I can do all on my own.' Pumpernickel growled softly. 'Even with Pumpy's assistance,' Leo went on, 'we need help with the bigger picture. There's a practice I'm working with, a reputable firm in Gray's Inn—'

Sadie reached out and snatched the notebook from his hands. 'You don't show this to no one!' she said.

Leo scratched his scalp in frustration, then leaned back in his chair. 'If you want my professional services—' he began.

'I'm not sure I do!' Sadie flashed back.

'I thought we agreed—'

'We agreed I let you see one notebook. Not share it with the whole world!'

'Mrs Macouba – Sadie – either you trust me or you don't. I've been in this business a long time.'

'And what you got to show for it? A dusty office up two flights of stairs, and a smelly old dog!'

Pumpernickel registered his objection to this description by sitting up and barking. 'Pumpy and I are the same age,' Leo said firmly, 'and our record speaks for itself. If you want a swish office where they start charging you hundreds of pounds per hour the moment you step out of the lift, where your case will be handled by an overworked twelve-year-old who knows less than Pumpy and is still putting lotion on his spots, then by all means take your custom to them. I wish you luck, because you'll need it!'

Sadie looked at him. Then she giggled. 'You still got a spark, old man, eh? I like that.'

'I'm glad you do,' Leo said stiffly. 'So are you going to stop playing games now? Because if not, I'm going to charge you for wasting my time!'

'I wouldn't pay.'

'I'll take you to court.'

'Old white lawyer against widowed black nurse grieving for her dead boy? How's that going to look?'

'OK, you got me. Now, you going to give me the book, or are you going to give me the book?'

Sadie held it out to him. 'I'm giving you the book,' she said, 'but—'

'No buts,' Leo said firmly. 'You want me to sing "I'll Do It My Way"? Pumpy can do a mean howl, if required.' He took the notebook and opened it.

'Interesting,' he said, leafing through the pages. 'Private briefings for government ministers; this will be just what my colleagues in Gray's Inn are looking for to build their case against Zarastro.'

'How's that going to help Larry?' Sadie demanded, though her tone had changed from aggressive to plaintive. Leo hated bullying of any kind, but he felt his strong stance was vindicated by the alteration in her mood. He wouldn't forget her jibe about his and Pumpernickel's age, and the state of their offices – where, he reminded himself, Sadie had made such a mess – but he might forgive it. Her impatience, and mistrust of the slowly grinding cogs of justice, was something he understood and shared. Solving Larry's case would not only bring some comfort to Sadie, it would also be proof that Leo still had what it takes. At his age, he frequently allowed his mind to be assaulted by niggles of doubt about his own competence, his knowledge – was he up-to-date? Was that worth worrying about? – his energy, sometimes even his judgement. Finding Larry's killer, and all the ramifications of his case, would silence those doubts. At least for a while.

~ ~ ~

'My sources,' Dennis said, swirling Beaujolais around his glass and peering critically at Leo through it, 'tell me that scientists are investigating the possibility that Sidney Playfair was killed by a deadly toxin that could be the Korean equivalent of Novichok. Zarastro own a subsidiary in Korea. Even someone as dull of mind as you might find that coincidence interesting.'

'Fascinating,' Leo agreed, wishing he'd bought something more warming than a white wine and soda. Mulled wine had too many calories. So, sadly, had Guinness, of which Marion was fond. He'd already had enough coffee, even though he drank decaffeinated, and if he'd ordered a bowl of soup Dennis would have mocked him unmercifully. For Dennis, drinking and eating were two pursuits that should be kept separate, except at proper mealtimes.

'Is that all you are going to say?' Dennis rumbled. 'I've had better conversations with your hound. I thought you were concerned about Mr Playfair's fate.'

'I am, I am,' Leo assured him. 'Especially as Marion is treating his grandson. But disentangling Zarastro's inky tentacles is hard. And I don't mind telling you, Dennis, I sometimes feel I'm losing a bit of that zip I've always relied on.'

'Tchah!' Dennis snorted. 'You could never keep your zip done up, never mind harnessing it to some useful purpose! What brought this on?'

'Don't you ever feel you're banging your head against a brick wall?'

'If I do, I take care to winkle out the mortar, so the wall falls without resistance.'

121

'Do you never think, I've paid my dues, I've done my bit, it's time to step aside and let the young ones have a go?'

'I have yet to meet a young person who knows enough about a subject to expatiate about it with any confidence. I have never encountered a young person who even approaches my mellifluities of style. I have never seen a young person at a press conference, of which I have attended far too many, pose a question that caused the slightest ruffle to cross a politician's brow. So no, I do not contemplate giving up when there is so much for people with wisdom and experience to challenge. I do not consider my capacities, which were always much larger than yours, to be in any way diminished. Of course your experience is far more limited than mine, and if you have ever possessed wisdom, I have seen little of evidence of it, so I understand your doubts, even if I do not share them. But before you go and throw yourself in front of a bus, if the streets are not completely gridlocked, I would have you know that while I am prepared to champion Marion, should the position fall vacant, my generosity does not, regrettably, extend to your dog. And it's also your round. If it's to be the last, make it a generous one.'

Pumpernickel emerged from under the table to show solidarity with Leo. Who laughed and got to his feet. 'Shall we have a Calvados to keep the cold out?' he said. 'Then you can tell me more about this Korean poison. Has it got a name, and why would one of Zarastro's companies be manufacturing it? More importantly, why would they use it on Sidney, whose campaign they were backing?'

Dennis shrugged his massive shoulders. 'Those are all questions to occupy what passes for your mind,' he said, 'and they might prove more fruitful than the self-obsessed melancholy to which you seem increasingly prone. If you give up, you will just die of boredom, as you are too incompetent to kill yourself efficiently. God knows you can be boring on occasion, but I have put up with it for so long we might as well continue for a little longer. The name of the poison was something like ginseng. Minseng, possibly? Meanwhile, a Calvados would be most welcome. Especially if it was a double.'

~ ~ ~

Leo returned to the office in cheerful mood, though Pumpernickel gave an excited couple of yaps when, on the second-floor landing, a large man, not fat like Dennis but broad and muscular, pushed past them in an obvious hurry to get down the stairs. They could not see his face, which was hidden by the shadows, but Leo thought there was something familiar about him, and Pumpernickel obviously agreed with him, as he stopped, looked down the stairs, and give a disappointed whine as the man disappeared. Then he bounded after Leo and arrived at the office just as his owner was catching his breath in front of their door, which they both realized had been forced open.

Pumpernickel went ahead to check for possible dangers. Leo, seeing that the Warhol covering the safe was still on the wall, walked rapidly to his desk. All the drawers had been pulled out. Leo sat heavily in his chair.

'We seem,' he said, 'to have become a soft touch for burglars. Larry's notebook is missing.' Pumpernickel gave an angry bark. 'I know,' Leo continued, 'I should have put it in the safe. It must have been taken by the man we passed on the stairs, no? You recognized him, didn't you?'

The dog growled and wagged his tail enthusiastically. 'Me too,' Leo said. 'But where from? Was he a client?' Pumpernickel sighed and put his head between his paws. 'Listen,' Leo continued, 'you're the one

123

with the great memory. Me, I can't even go shopping without a list these days. But never mind that, how did he – how did anyone – know I had the notebook? Apart from Sadie, of course, and Katy. I was going to give it to her, wasn't I? Maybe she talked about it to her colleagues at the practice. Or members of her campaign committee. But why would they want to steal it, Pumpy, if they knew I was going to let them see it anyway?'

The dog didn't have an answer. Leo pulled out his phone. 'Let's ask her,' he said, tapping at the screen. 'After all, she seemed keen enough to work with us. This could be her first criminal investigation!'

~ ~ ~

Felix, Jazz, and Robin were having a coffee in the British Library. Felix was absorbed at stirring sugar into his cup, first one way, then the other. Which seemed to irritate Robin, who snapped, 'Can you please stop doing that? You don't even take sugar normally!'

'It gives you energy,' Felix said mildly. 'And I'm going to need it if I'm to persuade this guy Grandad admired – he's called Mike McDonald – to take up the accountability campaign!' He tapped his spoon against the rim of the cup, put it in the saucer, took a sip, made a face, and pushed the cup away. 'A muffin would give me more energy, though,' he added.

'I'll get you one,' Robin said, jumping up. 'Maybe eating something will stop you fidgeting like a puppy!' He stomped over to the counter. Felix looked puzzled, then hurt. Jazz patted his arm reassuringly.

'He's been worried about you,' she said. 'We all have. Who is this Mike McDonald?'

'He was an MP, but now he's mayor somewhere. Mayor Mike McDonald: sounds good, doesn't it? He and Grandad shared the same ideas, so I thought I should talk to him. But you don't need to worry about me anymore. It's all straight in my head. Thanks to Marion, and you and your grandfather, who Marion says is also interested in what's happening.'

'He is,' Jazz said earnestly, 'but from a different angle. Gramps is a lawyer, and I don't understand the way he works, but it seems to produce results. The *really* good thing, Felix, is that between them they've made you feel better. But shouldn't you take it easy for a bit? I mean, it's great that you no longer feel it was your fault Sidney died, but what Gramps told Marion about that poison – we can't yet be sure that's what killed him.'

'The poison exists,' Felix said. 'There's some literature about it. I came across it while pretending to be researching the Korean war.'

'You're doing a maths degree!'

Felix flapped his hand in the air. 'They don't know that here in the library, do they? What do they care? Anyway, Minseng got a mention. Of course I didn't understand it – it was in some chemical journal – but just seeing the word, and knowing it has an organic structure, is enough. Granny will insist it's looked into. Grandad always said she was the real terrier in their house.'

'Who are you talking about now?' Robin demanded as he returned with a muffin on a plate. 'I brought a knife, in case you want to share. Not that I want any, but Jazz is always hungry, isn't she?'

He sat down, and wrapped his hands around his coffee cup. Jazz reached out, broke off a piece of the muffin, and popped it into her mouth. 'You can't let Felix eat that on his own!' she explained, through a mouthful of crumbs. 'What are friends for?'

Felix cut the muffin in half, then started cutting the half into smaller sections. Robin was about to protest, but Jazz stopped him. 'We were talking about Felix's granny,' she said. 'Apparently she's a terrier.'

'You met her, Rob,' Felix mumbled, absorbed in cutting up the muffin. 'She came to support Grandad when he spoke at the Union. You thought she was terrifying.'

'The kind of woman,' Robin agreed, 'who can turn you to a pillar of salt with one glance. The very model of a modern headmistress.' He shivered.

Felix looked up and smiled. 'She liked you,' he said, 'because you were nice to me.'

'I'm always nice to you!'

'Not always,' Felix said, 'but—'

'Let's not go there!' Jazz interrupted hastily. 'What will your grandmother think if you try to persuade this guy, Mayor Mike McDonald, to pick up the accountability campaign?'

'She probably won't like it,' Felix said, chewing on a tiny portion of muffin. 'She might say it killed Grandad, and it could kill me. But that's why I have to do it, isn't it? For Grandad's sake!'

'I think,' Robin said, 'it's too soon. You're still...vulnerable.'

'I don't *feel* vulnerable!' Felix insisted. 'I feel strong, strong enough, anyway, to talk to Mayor Mike McDonald. He'll understand my reasons, even if you don't!'

'We get that, Felix,' Jazz said gently. 'Of course we do. But I agree with Robin: you're still recovering. You don't want to rush into things.'

'Marion said I didn't have to go back for more sessions if I didn't want to!'

'I *think* what she said, according to Gramps, was that she'd like to go on seeing you for a while, if you're willing. If you start rushing off in different directions—'

'I'm only going in one direction! The direction Grandad would want me to take!'

'What if you're wrong, Felix?' Robin said roughly. 'What if this mayor doesn't want to know? You'll be crushed, you'll have another breakdown, we'll have to start all over again. Is that fair on us, the people who love you?'

Felix looked at him through lowered lashes. 'If you loved me, *truly* loved me,' he said, 'you'd support me. Despite the risks – and of course I know there are risks, I'm not stupid! – it matters to me more than anything. It's the one way I can show that I'm better, don't you see that? I want your help to keep the campaign going – I need it, now more than ever – but if I have to, I'll do it alone. I don't want to upset you, either of you, because I do love you, both of you, in different ways. But I can't *not* do this, not after all I've learned, about myself as well as Grandad. We could do it, the three of us, I know we could. But if you won't, I'll do it myself. I don't have a choice: you do.'

Jazz and Robin looked at each other. Robin threw up his hands in a gesture of surrender. 'OK, Felix,' Jazz said, snatching another bit of muffin. 'Can I make a suggestion?'

'Are you going to try and stop me?' Felix asked suspiciously.

'Not at all,' Jazz said. 'On the contrary, I think it'll help persuade this mayor of yours, more, anyway, than you bursting in waving your arms around and saying, "You've got to avenge my grandfather!".' She did a wildly exaggerated impression of a crazed Felix rolling his eyes and waggling his fingers.

127

Felix giggled, then started to object. But Robin forestalled him. 'Let's hear what she's got to say, Felix,' he said reasonably. 'You must admit she's been pretty good so far. Everything she's suggested has turned out for the best, hasn't it?'

Felix managed a grudging shrug of agreement. 'OK,' he said to Jazz. 'So what's your idea?'

'Ginny Larue,' Jazz said. 'I know you and she had your disagreements when she was your grandad's special adviser, but she could persuade anybody of anything. You never went to any debates at the Union, but she was president when we first came up, and she was brilliant. I think if we could get her to talk to Mike McDonald, he'd listen. Especially as she more or less ran the accountability campaign, and knows what works and what doesn't.'

'But...' Felix started, then stopped. Robin looked at him enquiringly. 'It's just,' Felix continued reluctantly, 'she treats me like I was nothing more than a spoiled brat. She doesn't take me *seriously*.'

'We do. Don't we, Robin?' Jazz said, nudging Robin into nodding. 'And if we're there to put your case, I think she will too. At least it's worth a try, isn't it? You're doing this for emotional reasons, which is totally understandable; Ginny knows the nuts and bolts, and anyone who takes the campaign on is going to need those nuts and bolts, aren't they? As Gramps would say, am I right, or am I right?'

Felix looked at Robin, who gave him a wry but encouraging smile. Felix sighed. 'You could be right, I suppose,' he said slowly. 'If I let you finish my muffin, will you call her straightaway?'

~ ~ ~

128

When William returned to the flat he shared with Katy he found her frazzled, and not just because their son Midge was teething.

'What?' William said, in that defensive, slightly grumpy voice men put on when they think they're about to be criticized for not doing something. Even with a single syllable, the tone implies that their partner may think they've just had a hard day, but they should hear what a *really* hard day feels like.

'He's been grizzling for the last hour,' Katy said. 'I've tried the dummy, I've tried rusks, I've tried Bonjela, nothing works. And I'm in trouble at the practice.'

'Why?' William said, taking Midge and bouncing him on his knee. The child stopped grizzling, tried a giggle, then burst into tears. William got up and walked him around, hushing him. When that didn't work he stuck his little finger in the boy's mouth, which shut him up.

'That's not very hygienic,' Katy objected.

'It's done the trick, hasn't it? Because my hands are cold. When we had our –' he nearly said 'daughter', then rapidly changed it – 'puppy. When she was teething we kept a plastic bone in the fridge and let her chew on it. Worked like a charm. Why are you in trouble at work?'

Katy poured herself a glass of red wine. She waggled the bottle enquiringly at William, but he shook his head and continued to walk around with Midge. Katy sank onto the sofa with an exhausted sigh.

'I went to see the solicitor who acted for the author of the report we believe Zarastro suppressed,' she said. 'I think he and my boss Helen might have had a fling in the dim and distant, which is weird enough. She amazed me by agreeing to share stuff with him, with me as the go-between. He has a copy of Nancy Chen's report—'

'He does?' William said, his voice lifting in surprise. That was something he was really going to have to get hold of. Something he'd probably have to do himself, not leave to an Incredible Hulk like Malcolm. Katy didn't seem to notice his concern.

'He let me photocopy it,' she said. 'But the big surprise was him saying he had access to poor Larry's secret notebooks. Apparently Larry's foster mother found them and allowed him to see one. Leo said he would share it with us, which got Helen – Leo calls her Helly, which is *so* not her – anyway she got very excited about that. But Leo rang just as I was about to leave the office, to say it had been stolen. And now Helen thinks she's being played for a sucker, and she blames me.'

William paced up and down with the baby while thinking how to react. He had the notebook: he'd forced Malcolm to steal it. He had a hold over Malcolm anyway: he knew he was behind the killing of the whistleblower his police superiors had wanted to control just as much as Zarastro did. Zarastro were the main backers of the forthcoming clean air summit, and the Home Secretary wanted to make sure nothing would jeopardize it. Which meant neutralizing anyone who could cause trouble, whether it was a whistleblower or a campaign group like Katy's. That was the reason he had infiltrated it.

He put the baby back in the battered cot they'd got third- or fourth-hand from a member of the campaign committee. Midge whimpered, then went to sleep. William poured himself a glass of wine and sat next to Katy, close enough to share her body warmth, distant enough to talk seriously.

'Maybe I can help you with that notebook,' he said slowly.

Katy gave him a look that was half-hopeful, half-amused. 'How?' she said quietly, so as not to wake the baby. 'If this is a way of getting me into bed, don't bother; I'm honestly not in the mood. And Leo thinks it was nicked by someone who looked like a bodybuilder. Are you going to track him down and then wrestle him for the book? We could sell tickets for that, and raise some funds!'

William gave her a wintry smile. 'You know Patsy?' he said. 'Of course you do. She's one of the campaign's most loyal supporters. And she was a friend of Larry's.'

'Everybody was a friend of Larry's,' Katy said. 'Except you. You didn't trust him, did you?'

'I don't trust anyone who works for Zarastro.'

'Patsy did.'

'Years ago. Anyway, she's proved which side she's on. Larry Coombs was a recent convert, and I've never trusted converts. But Patsy trusted him, so maybe I got him wrong.'

'And you're admitting it! That's a first!' Katy said with a grin. 'But what's this got to do with Larry's missing notebook?'

'I bumped into her when she was shopping. She was struggling with her bags, so I offered to help and see her home.'

'That was very nice of you.'

'I can be very nice when I try,' William said. 'Anyway, she told me some interesting things she'd shared with Larry. Not just about that old report, about briefings Zarastro gave to government ministers to ensure they didn't get too radical about phasing out fossil fuels. They've been lobbying for years, which we all suspected, of course, but Patsy had some proof that their lobbying got results. And though she didn't want to come forward with it, she was only too happy to let Larry have it when he

131

turned whistleblower. She told him all she knew, and he must have made a note of it all. But his notebooks weren't found—'

'Because the cops didn't bother looking properly!' Katy said. The baby stirred. She lowered her voice. 'Larry's mother – foster mother – found them, and gave them, or one of them, to Leo. He's trying to get a proper investigation into Larry's death, though he hasn't made much progress. We were going to look at the notes too, but then they mysteriously vanished.'

'I've got them,' William said.

Katy looked at him in astonishment, then laughed, before shushing herself. 'Oh yes?' she said softly. 'They just happened to fall into your lap?'

'You could say that,' William replied seriously. 'I was having a drink with Patsy – she insisted, though I only had tea – when this guy burst in. The bodybuilder you were talking about. I knew I'd seen him before somewhere, and then I remembered. It was with Larry Coombs. I thought maybe they were lovers, and I was a bit suspicious...'

'You're always suspicious!'

'It keeps me alive. Sadly, it didn't work for Larry. Anyway, this guy, Malcolm his name is, burst into Patsy's flat and I was able to trip him up before he did anything. He admitted he was sent by Zarastro to warn Patsy to stop talking about the past. She swallowed another gin and said all the non-disclosure agreements in the world wouldn't stop the truth coming out. She was sure Larry's notes would turn up, and maybe the solicitor – that's your friend Leo – would know something about them. Which is when I had my idea.'

Katy listened to all this while gravely sipping her wine. 'And your idea was?' she asked.

'To get hold of the notebooks so the committee could use them.'

She frowned. 'But if Leo was going to let us have them anyway...?'

'I didn't know that, did I?' William said self-righteously. 'I thought, if we, the campaign committee, get our hands on them, we can ensure they're put to proper use. Lawyers are all very well, and I know you work for them, but you can't really trust them, can you? They're part of the system we're trying to smash!'

'Ye-e-e-s,' Katy said slowly, 'but still...'

'Maybe it was crazy, but I had this big guy on the ground, saying I was breaking his arm, and I thought, I could kill two birds with one stone. I said I'd let him go, and say nothing about him coming to threaten Patsy, if he stole the notebooks and handed them over. I would have done it myself, but that could link the burglary to the committee, couldn't it? I thought I was being clever, but maybe I wasn't. You never told me you were seeing Nancy Chen's solicitor: if you had, I wouldn't have bothered. I thought it would really help the cause, but if you think I've done wrong, just say so. I've got it, anyway. It's only one notebook, but it's dynamite.'

'What, here?' Katy said, putting out her hand to show she appreciated his efforts, even if they were a bit crazy. It was his passion, his willingness to take risks, his impatience with the caution of some of her colleagues, that had attracted her. If he sometimes went a bit mad, that wasn't always a bad thing, was it? You didn't get to smash the system by being cautious. You didn't get anywhere at all.

He took her hand and kissed it. 'Not here,' he said. 'But I can get it tomorrow. It's somewhere safe.' It was with his minders. They'd use the notebook to discredit

133

what the campaign was about, probably by cooking something up to show that Larry had got his facts all wrong. But that wasn't William's concern. He had to convince Katy he was on her side. And he seemed to have succeeded.

Seven

'You seriously think he was poisoned?' Ginny Larue asked incredulously. People at the next table in the big, crowded pub opposite Madame Tussaud's where they'd agreed to meet looked up and hesitated over their menus. Jazz leaned forward and bent her head so it seemed like she, Ginny, Felix and Robin were having one of those group hugs footballers get into on the pitch.

'It's a possibility,' Jazz said. 'Think Novichok, only a Korean version. It just needs a smear, and wham!'

'But who would do such a thing to Sidney? And on the eve of his great triumph?'

'We don't know, do we?' Jazz said. 'You were with him the day he...'

'Died,' Felix put in flatly. 'I saw him in his constituency office.'

'Yes, and you had a row that upset him greatly!' Ginny said. 'It was all I could do to calm him down to finish his surgery and get ready for the rally!'

'Felix was the one who found him,' Robin said protectively. 'He went all to pieces, thinking it was his fault. But now we know it wasn't a heart attack brought on by stress.'

'They're working on the poison,' Jazz said. 'Felix looked it up. It exists, and it could have been produced by a company Zarastro's invested in, in North Korea. Once they've identified it, the cops'll start investigating who might have administered it, won't they? You know who Sidney met that day, right? Who do you think could have done it?'

Ginny laced her fingers around her glass of white wine. 'It could have been anybody!' she said. 'There was an APPG reception on climate control, which Sidney

135

made time for, as George was supposed to be going, along with that awful Maxine Ensor—'

'What's an APPG?' Robin asked.

'An All-Party Parliamentary Group. They gather their supporters for a piss-up with the great and good. I told Sidney he had more important things to think about, but he insisted. He and Maxine had a stand-up row, but that was par for the course. I got Sidney away before they came to blows.'

'Sidney and George Ramirez?' Felix asked. He took a small sip of Diet Coke. 'They had an argument before I confronted Grandad with the blackmail thing?'

'No, Felix,' Ginny said impatiently. 'Sidney and George got on famously. I don't know where you got this stupid blackmail idea—'

'Felix isn't stupid,' Robin said hotly. 'I was the one who told him about the blackmail. I wish I hadn't, now, seeing what it did to him, but it came from a source I trusted, and I believe in telling the truth!'

'I worked closely with Sidney for over a year,' Ginny said, 'and I don't believe he is, or was, capable of blackmailing anybody!'

'You don't find it odd,' Robin said waspishly, 'that a whistleblower called Larry Coombs discovers Zarastro suppressed a damaging report twenty years ago, and tells Sidney about it so that he'll bring it to light? Only Sidney does no such thing: he goes to George Ramirez and tells him he knows about the report.'

'Which he asked me to check out,' Ginny retorted, 'and the people I spoke to, including the world's most fearless crime reporter, said that without hard evidence it had been suppressed, there was no story!'

'The story is,' Robin continued unabashed, 'that George Ramirez announces his support for Sidney's accountability campaign, which then takes off. And Larry gets stabbed to death!'

'I'm sorry,' Ginny said, banging down her glass, 'but I think you guys are deluded. People get stabbed all the time, just as people inexplicably drop dead when you least expect it. Yet you insist on linking it all to some paranoid conspiracy! I know Oxford is supposed to teach you to question everything, but you're taking it to ridiculous lengths.'

'I told you she'd be no help, didn't I?' Felix said bitterly. 'I'll do it on my—'

'When you were president of the Union, Ginny,' Jazz interrupted, 'you organized a debate on the motion "This House no longer believes I think, therefore I am". You attacked the idea that has been fundamental to philosophy for five hundred years, and thanks to your passion, and the way you talked about Artificial Intelligence, the motion was passed overwhelmingly. That was only a couple of years ago. Has becoming part of the system turned you into a robot? Don't you even believe in the accountability Felix's granddad gave his life for?'

'Of course I believe in it!' Ginny said furiously. 'I organized one of the most successful campaigns in recent parliamentary history, didn't I? But without Sidney, it's not going to happen! And all your fantasies about the reasons behind it are only going to get it rubbished and consigned to oblivion!' She emptied her glass, and made a big thing about gathering her coat, ready to go.

'Not,' Jazz said, 'if there is someone to step into Sidney's shoes. Someone you think is up for the job, or so you told my grandfather. Someone who needs your expertise and enthusiasm if he is to take the campaign on from where Sidney left off, rather than start from scratch. A bunch of students like us might not be able to persuade

137

him, but you could. You may not believe what we're saying, but I believe in you. He would too. I'm talking about Mayor Mike McDonald.'

'Mike McDonald,' Ginny muttered. Her whole body softened. She had been poised to leave, but settled back into her seat with a sigh. She looked at their faces, Felix's angry, Jazz's alight and eager, Robin's furrowed with concern. She sighed again. 'Alright,' she said. 'Who do I have to fuck to get a drink round here?'

~ ~ ~

Marion, Leo, and Pumpernickel took a pre-lunch stroll around Hyde Park as Marion had a cancellation and Leo's usual midday companion, Dennis, was at one of those awards ceremony he always complained about, unless he won something.

Pumpernickel took a polite interest in an elderly Jack Russell who was keener on investigating a discarded bag containing the remains of a doner kebab. Pumpernickel was put off by the pickles surrounding it. He would have had the fragments of halloumi left in the bag, but the Jack Russell got there first. Pumpernickel pulled Leo away.

'What?' Leo said. 'You don't like her table manners? Blame the owner!'

'It won't be anywhere near as good as what we get at home, Pumpy,' Marion said. 'When he gets bored with the law, he should set up a business called Leo's Leftovers.'

'My grandmother used to call them *shlorums*,' Leo said. 'All the best bits left on a chicken, minced and turned into fried rissoles, or of course soup. The Jewish penicillin.'

'Don't you miss meat? I would.'

'Not at all. I am sometimes tempted by a bit of pork crackling, but believe it or not I'm turned off by a bacon sarnie. All that water, all those preservatives; my vegetarian diet makes me feel fit as well as virtuous!'

'Virtue is alright in moderation,' Marion said. 'I was schooled by nuns, remember; any preaching makes me itch to do the opposite.'

'I never preach. Do I?' Pumpernickel made a snickering noise. 'When?' Leo demanded. 'When have I ever preached at anybody, never mind dumb animals?'

'You don't preach, sweetie,' Marion said, lengthening her stride so Leo had to almost trot to keep up. 'You just go on and on about something until I give in for the sake of peace and quiet. Isn't that right, Pumpy?' The dog barked, then stopped suddenly to sniff the bark of a tree. Leo gave him a few seconds, then pulled at his lead.

'It's too cold to hang around, Pumps,' he said, 'not that I'm nagging, or anything.' This was said loudly enough for Marion to hear. She ignored it, so Leo changed the subject.

'How's Felix getting on?' he said. 'I'm not asking for clinical details, I just want to know if you've signed him off, because Jazz says he considers himself cured.'

'He's functioning,' Marion said, returning the wave of somebody on a horse cantering along Rotten Row, 'and it's good that he's got something to occupy his energies. He will have dips and mood swings, of course – who doesn't? – but he's got good friends in his lover Robin, and of course Jazz. I just hope he won't be plunged into despair if his grandfather's accountability campaign doesn't immediately take off again. I don't think I'm revealing any secrets by saying he tends to see things as either black or white.'

'Is that such a bad thing?' Leo said, stopping so that Pumpernickel could have a poo. Leo, being the kind

139

of person who could never poo if the bathroom door was open, looked away. 'I mean,' he continued, 'isn't that what the accountability campaign is all about? Holding people to their promises, no ifs or buts?'

'Great in theory,' Marion said, 'very difficult in practice. Good parents try not to break the promises they make to their children, but once you're out of childhood, it becomes a lot more complicated, especially in the political arena.' She paused while Leo slipped a poo bag over his hand, bent down to pick up Pumpernickel's leavings, and stood up, a little pink in the face, to knot the bag and slip it into the pocket of the tweed coat he'd had for so long it had come back into fashion. Marion was indifferent to fashion; Leo still had enough vanity to care.

'But politics is where it matters most,' Leo said, as all three of them resumed walking. 'The reason no one trusts politicians is because they'll say anything to get elected and then just forget or ignore their promises without being held to account. If they were mis-selling goods, they'd be prosecuted under the Trades Description Act. Sidney Playfair wanted to set up an Office for Accountability that would act like one of those regulators who keep an eye on industry. You shouldn't be allowed to promise to invest in a cleaner environment and then say you can't do it unless you get loads more in government subsidies, or are allowed to raise prices. You shouldn't have made the promise in the first place!'

He had taken hold of Marion's hand and swung it in frustration. She patted his wrist fondly. 'Have you noticed,' she asked, 'that it's the right-wing politicians who come nearest to carrying out their pledges? Those on the left tack to the centre, whereas the right seem unafraid of at least trying to put their extreme policies into practice. Why do you think that is?'

'Because the left have run out of ideas, and courage? Or because people have lost faith in the system, and they think, let's elect someone who's promising to bulldoze the whole shebang, because how much worse can that be?'

'And how,' Marion said, plucking the poo bag out of his pocket and depositing it in a dog waste bin, 'is an Office for Accountability going to change that?'

'If people had their say on the things that matter to them,' Leo said, slowing to allow a small child to pat Pumpernickel, who patiently allowed his ears to be pulled, 'the political atmosphere might be less poisonous. Look at the Swiss. It only takes a certain percentage of the population to demand a referendum on a question, and their legislature has to take account of the result. OK, everyone has to compromise, and grey might become the predominant colour, but wouldn't people trust the process more if they were part of it?'

'Would that work?' Marion asked, swinging his hand as they resumed walking. 'I'm all for accountability – it's one of the key tenets of my therapy, persuading people to take responsibility for their actions – but how do you put it into practice?'

'Sidney's idea was to use a citizens' assembly to work out what penalties should be imposed on politicians whose explanations or excuses for breaking their promises failed to persuade a citizens' jury chosen at random. They'd be like coroners' juries, deciding on the facts, not guilt or innocence. I reckon that could work, but the only way we'll know is to test it in practice.'

'Why don't you, then? Test it, I mean?'

Leo stopped dead, causing Pumpernickel to cough in surprise and Marion to spin round. 'That,' he said, 'is a brilliant idea!'

141

'It was your suggestion.'

'Yes,' he said, 'but you took it to the next stage. That's why we're such a good team! You're right: we need a pilot scheme to see if a citizens' jury could effectively hold someone to account. The question is, who?'

They'd almost come to Park Lane, where they would part ways, Leo and Pumpernickel continuing to their office in Soho, Marion returning to her apartment for her next consultation.

'George Ramirez,' she said, 'would seem to be the obvious choice, don't you think?'

'Another brilliant idea,' Leo replied, 'but if I might say so, about as likely as getting President Trump to admit he is guilty of anything at all. OK, George was a great supporter of Sidney's campaign, but he's hardly going to volunteer to be questioned about suppressing Nancy Chen's report, and persuading the government to go slow on phasing out fossil fuels, is he? Not to mention the deaths of several people that could be laid at his door.'

Marion pecked him on the cheek. 'Let me have a word with my old friend Mehrnaz,' she said. 'She's the sister of Zarastro's founder and largest shareholder, as I may have mentioned. And she can be very persuasive.'

~ ~ ~

'I'm sorry, Malcolm,' Nathan said, leaning back in his chair with his hands behind his head so that people at the other tables in the visiting room could hear him if they chose to listen, 'but I'm very disappointed in you. Very.'

Malcolm fidgeted and looked even more crestfallen. PJ, his boss at work, was not pleased that the mission to intimidate Patsy Finch had ended in ignominy. He had put Malcolm on night duty, patrolling the perimeter of the depot, accompanied by a dog, in sub-zero temperatures that secured even the homeless a shelter for the night. Malcolm hadn't dared tell PJ that he'd confessed to the hard man who felled him – who must have been a cop – that he'd been sent to intimidate Patsy by Zarastro. To add to his woes, Gilda was furious with him, not only because he was on nights, but because he'd agreed to burgle Leo's office for the notebook. She told him, in her exotically broken English, that he was seriously stupid, because if he'd been arrested, he would have gone straight back to jail, and then what would happen to her? He tried to explain that when your shoulder's being dislocated and your fingers crushed, you agree to anything to stop the pain, but she didn't understand, or refused to try.

Now Nathan was giving him a hard time. There were occasions when Malcolm missed being in jail. Decisions were made for you, you just had to look after yourself. Outside, it was a lot more complicated, and unpredictable. Inside, everything was physical; in the real world, there were obligations, invisible ties that pulled him in different directions, expectations he was supposed to fulfil because of what he owed people. He seemed to be permanently paying off debts he didn't know how he'd incurred. It did his head in.

He flexed his muscles. At least they were under his control, though his shoulder was still tender. Nathan was now leaning forward and looking at him expectantly. Obviously he'd missed something.

'Sorry?' he said, jiggling his thighs.

'You don't listen, do you, Malcolm?' Nathan said.

'Sorry. I was just—'

'I was saying, we need a change of tactics. The objective remains the same, but it's taking too long to get there. I am partly to blame: I put too much faith in your ability to cause trouble.'

'I've done everything Zarastro asked. Is it my fault if this last one didn't turn out the way they wanted?'

'Yes, and no, Malcolm,' Nathan said. 'You got them to trust you to do their dirty work, which was the idea behind you getting a job there. But unfortunately it hasn't had the desired effect of rattling George's cage, which you know has always been the goal I had in mind. I underestimated his tendency to hide behind others, like he did with me. My bad. Being in here can sometimes warp the mind, but it's now clear to me what we should do. Go for the jugular!'

His eyes took on a glitter which Malcolm recognized with a sinking heart. That glitter meant he was going to have to push himself beyond, well beyond, his comfort zone. All those hours of exercise to put muscle on a body that had been that of a lanky teenager. All that training so that no one would mess with him, and for what? So that someone else he didn't know would die of a stab wound? He'd been blamed, as a teenager, for a stabbing he didn't do. He'd escaped the blame for organizing Larry Coombs' death, so far, anyway. Was he now going to be asked to kill someone who would probably be as well protected as any gangster or royal? Could he say no to Nathan?

'Mercedes,' Nathan said.

Malcolm looked confused. Was he talking about getaway cars?

'Mercedes is the name of George Ramirez's wife,' Nathan explained, speaking slowly and quietly as if to a dog or a slow-witted child. 'She is a Spanish lady of a lively disposition, very demanding, far too demanding for George, in fact, which is why he has that Maxine Ensor as a mistress. But George and Mercedes are a power couple;

on all public occasions they are inseparable. You are going to kidnap her.'

At first Malcolm's head flooded with relief that he wasn't being called upon to kill this woman. But the relief drained away immediately he began thinking about the implications.

'K-kid . . .?' he couldn't even bring himself to say the word out loud, not in front of all those prison officers. 'H-how? Why? Where would I – I can't keep her in my little room, Nathan!' Gilda's reaction wouldn't be worth thinking about.

'The "how" is simple,' Nathan said. 'You use your seductive charms. She is a fitness fanatic, you are a bodybuilder, you are made for one another. The "why" I would have thought was obvious. By forcibly removing her from George's presence, you are effectively cutting him in half, at least as far as his public appearances are concerned. Let's see how well he copes with that! I trust it will break him into little pieces, especially if we demand a healthy ransom for her safe return.'

Malcolm shook his head, more to clear it than to refuse to take on such a task. Once Nathan had got an idea into his shaven head, nobody could dig it out again. Malcolm had seen what had happened to people who'd tried. He shuddered.

'But even if I managed to get close enough–' he began, only to be interrupted by Nathan, whose growing enthusiasm made his eyes glitter even more dangerously.

'You find out which gym she goes to,' he said. 'That shouldn't be difficult: you ask George's driver. Then you turn up there, ripple your muscles to attract her attention, and offer to act as her personal trainer. How could she resist? You won't find her repulsive, if that's

145

what's worrying you. She's quite a looker, if you like that kind of thing.'

Malcolm wanted to say that was the last thing on his mind, that the whole idea was batshit crazy, that it would be easier, *was* easier, to kill someone than seduce them to order, and while he didn't like killing, this was another game altogether, calling for skills he didn't think he possessed. But he couldn't put the words together, and anyway Nathan wasn't listening.

'As for where you keep her,' he said, 'if you think your place is unsuitable, then find somewhere secure at work that only you have access to. There must be cellars or silos at that depot of yours that only get visited once in a blue moon. And who would think of looking for the chairman's wife on Zarastro property? It's perfect!'

Taking a deep breath, Malcolm opened his mouth to say, 'Nathan, I really can't—' when the buzzer went to indicate visiting time was over. Nathan was hustled away, firmly but respectfully.

As if he had known what Malcolm was thinking, he mouthed, 'Yes you can!' before the door clanged behind him.

~ ~ ~

Katy met Leo and Pumpernickel in the muddy, scrubby bit of garden dignified as Soho Square, which in winter was only used as a shortcut by well-wrapped-up workers hurrying to offices whose lights were already on though it was only mid-afternoon. Katy was pushing a buggy which contained her son Midge, so protected from the biting wind that he was almost invisible, though he did reach out a mittened hand in Pumpernickel's direction, who sportingly approached and allowed his fur to be pulled without protest.

'I've brought it,' Katy said, her face under her beanie pink from the cold. 'Helen said it's incredibly useful, and would love to see the rest, if there are any more. She sends you her best, by the way. I didn't tell her about the burglary.'

She dug around in the canvas bag draped across the back of the buggy and took out a small package which she handed to Leo as furtively as if they were doing a drug deal. He shoved it in an inside pocket, drew his coat tighter around him, and said, 'Only her best? Give her my love and tell her that if ever she wants a drink—'

'You know she's married to the senior partner?' Katy said hastily. She didn't mean to sound censorious, and she had no hang-ups about the sanctity of marriage, but the idea of someone of Leo's generation coming onto her strait-laced boss was offputtingly grubby. She busied herself tucking in the blanket around Midge to cover her embarrassment.

'Listen,' Leo said lightly, 'I'm in a relationship which, God willing, though I don't believe in Him, will see me out. But as a Jesuit friend of mine used to say, being on a diet doesn't stop you looking at the menu. All I meant—'

'I'm sorry,' Katy said, 'I wasn't criticizing. It's just with everything that's going on...'

'Forget it,' Leo said. 'So tell me, just how did this notebook make its way from my desk to your place and back again?'

'It's a long story.'

'Shall we grab a coffee? Get out of the wind?'

'I'd love to,' Katy said, 'but it's such a business, unwrapping Midge, trying to get him to drink something, wrapping him up again – and how many coffee places round here have room for buggies, let alone dogs? I adore my baby, but nobody warns you that you need to add half an hour to your schedule every time you go out with him, just to get him ready! And when your schedule's pretty full on...'

'Point taken. So talk fast. How come a nice girl like you is mixing with burglars?'

Midge wailed as Pumpernickel moved out of reach. 'Pumpy!' Leo said reproachfully. 'Be nice! He just wants to play. Give us a couple of minutes, and I promise you some of that fishy paste you like which, by the way, costs more than the finest smoked salmon, not that I begrudge you a treat.' He turned to Katy. 'You were saying, about the burglars?'

'He's not actually a burglar, my partner, Midge's dad. He's...I'm not sure what he does, to be honest. Something in recycling. But apart from being a great father, he's very passionate and committed, and if anyone is ready to take a risk for the cause, he's up for it.'

'Sounds too good to be true.'

'What do you mean?' Katy asked sharply.

'Just saying he seems to have all the virtues,' Leo said soothingly. 'Which is rare in our naughty world. Is he a tall, well-built, muscular type? Because if he was the burglar, we passed him on the stairs.'

'He's small and slim,' Katy said, 'and tough as a pit pony. And he didn't burgle your office. He organized it.'

'Did he now? How did he manage that?'

'He was with Patsy Finch—'

'I know Patsy. She got me stacking shelves.'

'—when she happened to be raided by a thug sent by Zarastro. Who William managed to trip up and pin down.'

'He includes martial arts in his list of skills?'

148

'I suppose so. Anyway, the guy confessed he'd been sent to warn Patsy to keep quiet about what she knew...'

'A confession extracted under torture doesn't count, you know.'

'William wouldn't *torture* anyone! He's one of the gentlest—'

'All the good ones are, in public. Carry on. How did the notebook come into it?'

'William said Patsy mentioned it. When she'd recovered from the shock and had a slug of gin.'

'She said I had the notebook? How did she know?'

'I've no idea,' Katy said. 'Maybe she was just...speculating. You know she has scary ideas about how Larry died, as well as Nancy Chen. She won't stick her head above the parapet in case it gets blown off, but when she's had a gin – and when she's confronted by a big scary guy who's pinned down on her carpet...'

'She comes up with another crazy idea that turns out to be right,' Leo said thoughtfully. 'Or maybe your William knows more than he lets on.'

'What are you talking about?'

'Just thinking aloud, Katy. Something I normally do with Pumpernickel. That's why we're such a good team. I'm sure William is very clever – and is obviously a man with great taste – but it would take a Sherlock Holmes to make a deductive leap and assume Larry's notebook was in my office. It just makes me think he might have other sources of information that enables him to put two and two together and come up with something more than three and less than five. But anyway, he persuades the guy on the floor – using, I am sure, nothing but his charm and the power of reason – to burgle my office and steal the notebook. Why does he then give it to you?'

149

'Because he thought it would help the cause, of course! And as I'm campaign secretary, as well as working with Helen building a case against Zarastro, he thought I was the best person to entrust with it. And I'm returning it to you, though I'm not sure that's such a good idea now.'

'We're on the same side, Katy.'

'So I thought,' Katy said acidly, bending to tuck in a bit of Midge's blanket that he'd kicked loose while excitedly playing with the dog. 'But the surest way of destroying a campaign is to sow doubt among its members. It's what they all do, isn't it, spread fake news when they can't think of anything else?'

'I'm not spreading fake news, Katy,' Leo said. 'I'm just injecting a small dose of scepticism to keep you healthy.'

'I don't need your scepticism!' she said angrily. 'Don't you think my life is hard enough, juggling a cause and a job and a baby? How can I do that without trusting the people closest to me? How is you being suspicious about William helpful?'

She grabbed the handles of the buggy, wrenched it around, and marched off towards the bright lights of Oxford Street. Pumpernickel shook himself, and looked at Leo, his eyes full of intelligence and sympathy.

'That went well,' Leo remarked ironically. 'You still want that fish paste?' The dog turned his head away and sniffed the air. 'I thought not,' Leo said. 'I'm not hungry either.'

Eight

Marion's friend Mehrnaz Faruq invited her and Leo to breakfast at The Wolseley in Piccadilly. Dogs were not allowed, so Pumpernickel was left in the flat with a ball specially designed to keep a pet entertained for hours. It had holes and hollows which Leo had spread with peanut butter. Having licked them out in well under two minutes, Pumpernickel went back to sleep.

Mehrnaz was an elegant woman in her mid-seventies who wore a Hermès scarf over beautifully styled grey hair, with sunglasses perched on top, though it was another grey day and the lights in the art deco restaurant were not particularly bright. She had ordered a black Americano and a plain croissant which she left lying on her plate while Marion, whose hair was dyed purple, tucked into a full English. Leo had asked for eggs Florentine and worried about leaving bits of spinach between his teeth. Their hollandaise was better than his, though he would be reluctant to admit it, and he was anyway more concerned about not dribbling egg yolk down his chin. It wasn't that Mehrnaz made him nervous, he didn't want to let Marion down.

'You remember Sister Annunciata?' Mehrnaz said. She had a musical drawl that made her sound exotic and faintly amused.

'The demon hockey player?' Marion said. 'She showed us how much better dope tasted if you smoked it in a pipe rather than a roll-up,' she explained to Leo.

'Your father spent all that money to have you trained in the use of illegal substances?' he said, patting his lips with his napkin. 'I'd've asked for a refund!'

151

'I was a disappointment to him anyway,' Marion said, 'but his mistress liked me. Or felt sorry for me, rather the way a greyhound feels sorry for a carthorse.'

'I would never compare you to a carthorse!' Mehrnaz exclaimed. 'They're great plodding things, are they not? And plodding was never your style. You were more like, I don't know, a grizzly bear. Friendly, inquisitive, always poking your nose in to see what was happening, and ready to rear up and fight if the occasion demanded it.'

'That sounds like my Marion,' Leo said proudly. 'A grizzly bear! Nice!'

'With sharp claws,' Mehrnaz said. 'One always had to be careful of the claws. Anyway, Sister Annunciata: you know she left the order, became the second, or possibly the third wife of a prince in Bhutan, I think it was – somewhere in the Himalayas, anyway – and had eight children. Eight! Lost her figure entirely, but is as happy as Larry. Takes a suite at The Dorchester every year and goes to the races. That's where I saw her last. But you seem happy, Marion, my dear, which is good to see.'

'Even though I only had the one child, whom I rarely set eyes on – last heard of doing good work in Gaza – I've lost my figure too,' Marion said cheerfully. 'Not that it was much to boast of in the first place.'

'Nonsense!' Leo said forcefully. 'To me you are a goddess!' Both women looked at him quizzically. He took refuge in his decaffeinated cappuccino.

'Leo is a romantic,' Marion said to her friend. 'And also an optimist who veers occasionally into the realms of fantasy, which can be fun, and shows commitment and courage, considering he constantly deals with the shitty sides of life.'

'I usually tremble on the edge of disappointment,' Leo said, before adding hastily, 'not with Marion, of course. She is the best thing that has happened to me in all my seventy-three years, and I'm proud to be her toyboy!'

Mehrnaz looked at Marion, who threw back her head and laughed. Mehrnaz permitted herself a thin smile. 'If it is not her you are disappointed with,' she said, 'what is it? Your work? Your sex life? The state of the world?'

'All of those,' Leo said candidly. 'I love my work, not as much as I love Marion, but I've been doing it for longer. We still have a sex life, I'm happy to say, though it's not something I would normally discuss over breakfast. As for the state of the world, that's the most disappointing thing of all, and the most baffling. For the first sixty or so years of my life we seemed to be making progress in the things that matter: tolerance, kindness, generosity, civility, even. But for the last ten, we've got stuck in reverse. How did that happen? Is it a virus that is going to go on spreading its poison until we come up with a vaccine? Don't you find that disappointing?'

'I don't see how you can be disappointed in a virus,' Mehrnaz said. 'It is a fact of life, like greed or haemorrhoids. You can try and shield yourself and those you love, but there will always be victims, will there not?'

'And those are the ones I try and help,' Leo said, 'and sometimes I don't succeed, which is disappointing. But I do occasionally succeed in surprising and overcoming my opponents, and that's more than enough to keep me going.'

'I seem to be hosting a breakfast of saints,' Mehrnaz said dryly. 'The two of you working to save the world, each in your different ways—'

'*Very* different,' Leo interrupted, 'and saintly isn't the word I'd use. I dig around the rubble of the law, and

153

try and find facts that will make an ugly thing look beautiful. Marion listens, and in some magical way gets people to accept their own ugliness and make beautiful use of it. She's a woman of infinite patience and wisdom, not to mention gorgeous; I'm an impatient and impetuous *alte kocker*. Or old fart, if your Yiddish isn't up to much.'

This time Mehrnaz actually laughed. 'I like him,' she said to Marion. 'He's certainly an improvement on that one you married. What was his name? Something very ordinary, like Harry. I never understood why you bothered, though the wedding breakfast at The Savoy was rather good.' She took a small bite of her croissant. Leo noticed with admiration that she did not make any crumbs.

'What happened to Harry?' he asked. 'Should I be jealous, or sorry for him?'

'He preferred being called Hal,' Marion said, mopping up the last of her egg yolk with a piece of fried bread. 'He was the first man I met who was taller than I was, could beat me at arm-wrestling, and was better than I was at playing poker. He was nice to my mother, and chatted away to her, ignoring the fact that her only response was a vague smile. He called my father "Sir" and drank Kümmel with him until Dad fell asleep. He gave my little brother Harold racing tips that enabled him to double his pocket money. My father was desperate to get me off his hands and offered a wedding at St George's, Hanover Square, and a generous dowry. On our wedding night Hal ate oysters, claiming they were aphrodisiac, instead of which they gave him diarrhoea. He claimed he worked in television, though it was never clear in what capacity, and he expected me to behave like the good wife our finishing school was supposed to turn out. To say we disappointed one another would be to put it mildly, but I did get pregnant and Angus has turned out rather well. Hal and I separated when Angus was four months old, and I haven't seen the old bastard since. I imagine he's dead, the way he drank. I'd say,' she concluded, putting her knife and fork together and addressing Leo, 'that you need feel neither jealous nor sorry. Possibly grateful, but that's entirely up to you, sweetie.' She patted his hand and smiled.

Mehrnaz gave an admiring shake of her head. 'You can see,' she said to Leo, 'why we all looked up to her.'

'Possibly because I was five foot ten when I was sixteen?' Marion said dryly.

'I love looking up to her,' Leo told Mehrnaz, 'and I am not a tall man. Though it makes no difference—'

'In bed?' Mehrnaz said. 'I am glad for the pair of you. Now, tell me what you want of that little shit George Ramirez. Though he has grown bigger over the years.'

Leo glanced at Marion, who gave him an encouraging nod. 'Is he,' he asked, 'the kind of shit who would account for himself in public?'

Mehrnaz refilled her coffee cup, took a sip, and wiped the lipstick off the rim with her finger. 'He likes nothing better,' she declared, 'than talking about himself. I never fully understood why my brother hired him, very soon after he set up Zarastro. He said George was a bright young engineer, and he needed such people to take the company forward, but I suspect it was one of those shady deals my brother is so good at. You give me a bit of your oilfield, and I'll hire your useless son or nephew that no one else will take on, that kind of thing.'

'But isn't George one of the most successful CEOs around?' Leo asked. 'As well as being incredibly rich. And nobody, saving your presence, Mehrnaz, becomes one of the super-rich by being Mr Nice Guy, do they?'

'Yet that is exactly what he claims to be,' Mehrnaz said. 'He can, and does, justify anything, and that's why my brother keeps him on. George has the same relationship to truth as a mouse does to a cat: it's something to be played with, tortured, then killed and abandoned. My brother is a shrewd operator, but he is honest about what he wants, and I'd like to think he has a certain moral sense. George wouldn't know a moral if it was presented to him in a box surrounded by chocolate truffles.'

'Yet he, and Zarastro, supported Sidney Playfair's accountability campaign, which was a very moral thing to do,' Leo said. 'And it was very nearly successful, too.'

'If only Mr Playfair hadn't unexpectedly died the night before he was due to present his bill,' Mehrnaz pointed out. 'If I were being charitable, I would call that fortuitous, wouldn't you?'

'Don't tell me you think George might have had something to do with it!' Leo exclaimed.

Mehrnaz looked inscrutable. 'I have no evidence,' she said, 'but it wouldn't surprise me. It's not, however, something he's going to testify publicly about. Unless he were to be charged with it, in which case he would find somebody else to blame.'

'What if there was an enquiry into his conduct?' Leo asked, pushing his plate aside. 'Would the company – would your brother – allow that to happen?'

'If George was found guilty of something that brought the company into disrepute, my brother would fire him, I have no doubt. Even though he has a soft spot for George's wife Mercedes. Who George treats abominably.'

'Say there was an enquiry, not into his personal behaviour, but into his dealings as CEO – an enquiry not led by a government-appointed judge, but an independent moderator. Let's say it was to establish whether or not the company, who are sponsoring this big clean air conference, are in fact ensuring they can go on extracting and exploiting fossil fuels for the foreseeable future. If the evidence for and against was aired in front of a jury, like a coroner's jury, and expert testimony was called upon to help them reach an informed verdict, might your brother be persuaded this was a good way of showing what clean hands Zarastro has got, and get George to appear and defend the company's activities?'

'If the enquiry took the form you're suggesting – which I've never heard of before—'

'The idea was in Sidney Playfair's bill. It would need enormous public pressure to bring it about. But it was Marion who suggested it would be worth showing whether or not it can work by setting up a pilot. She's not just a pretty face.'

'Not even!' Marion said cheerfully, spreading marmalade on a piece of toast.

'At school,' Mehrnaz said, 'we were taught to judge people by their actions, not their appearance. Which was sheer hypocrisy, as they spent an inordinate time on making us aware of how we looked, and pointing out our deficiencies. But they left Marion alone.'

'Because of her irresistible attraction and the sweetness of her nature,' Leo suggested.

'And the fact that I could beat everyone at arm-wrestling except the Mother Superior,' Marion said.

'She was always distressingly physical,' Mehrnaz sighed. 'Which is no doubt why she is so successful in getting into people's minds.'

'Seriously?' Leo said. 'She never bullies anyone, that I'm aware of.'

'It's because she has such confidence that people pluck up the confidence to unburden themselves to her. Is this accusation against Zarastro, Mr Wengrowski, taken seriously enough by those that matter to merit George demonstrating the company's innocence in front of this jury, or tribunal, or whatever you are hoping to set up?'

'If it wasn't, I wouldn't be sitting here enjoying a breakfast that is even better than the ones I prepare,' Leo said.

'Are you tempted by an almond croissant or a *pain aux raisins?*' Mehrnaz asked.

'Always,' Leo said, 'but I will show I have a will of iron and resist. I try to keep myself *svelte* so that Marion's eye will not stray towards someone younger and thinner.'

Mehrnaz turned to Marion. 'Are you thinking of straying?' she said.

'At my age?' Marion said. 'Don't be ridiculous!'

~ ~ ~

Marching in a demonstration surrounded by people who fill you with the courage to chant defiance at the police and hostile onlookers is usually fun, Katy thought. Walking slowly down Regent Street pushing Midge in a buggy was actually quite scary, even with William at her side looking tense and wary. All the placards saying 'Just Stop Oil' were no defence against angry motorists and jeering pedestrians. Enraging people made Katy feel small and vulnerable, not proud and virtuous. When you are convinced you have right on your side, you feel the streets belong to you. When you are a smallish group surrounded by hooting traffic, the atmosphere is bitter, the air tastes sour, the cold and the damp seep into your bones and chill the warmth of your protest, you feel like an intruder, and your instinct is to curl up to protect yourself, and your baby, against being jostled and kicked and spat at and told you should be strung up or sent back to where you came from. Which in Katy's case was Battersea.

'I hate this,' she confided to William. 'We should never have brought Midge.'

'You were the one who wanted to,' he said. 'He's alright. Gurning and gurgling like it's all for his benefit. Which in a way it is. We're doing this for him, aren't we?'

'But what if we get arrested? Who'll look after him? My mother won't: she doesn't approve of you, or me, or the things we believe in. My sister's got enough trouble—'

'Calm down!' William said forcefully. 'We're not going to get arrested. We're exercising our right to protest peacefully.'

'They've removed that right, haven't they?' Katy said bitterly. 'A guy got six months for "interfering with key national infrastructure", when all he was doing was walking slowly with a Just Stop Oil poster down his local high street!'

William shook his head. 'It's not going to happen to us, is it?' he said, waving derisively at a woman who threw an empty Red Bull can at him, and missed. 'Not with all the press and cameras here.'

'You think that's going to stop them? They'll arrest us, and I might get bail, because of Midge. They could make me wear an electronic tag, they could impose a curfew on me, they could restrict my freedom of movement, they could even prevent me from speaking to other activists, which would include you!'

'You're getting paranoid, Katy. I promise you, we won't be arrested.'

159

'How can you promise that, William?' Their group stopped moving as it came up against a wall of police officers in hi-vis jackets.

'I just know we're going to be alright. I wouldn't have agreed to Midge coming otherwise. As long as we keep it peaceful, we'll be fine. They don't want to risk looking like Russia or China, not with the clean air summit coming up. Trust me!'

'I do trust you,' Katy said, 'but I know what they're capable of. You can't even stand up in court and explain to a jury why you were protesting, not any more. One judge forbad the defendants from saying the words "climate change", "fuel poverty", or even mentioning the civil rights movement. And a woman was arrested for holding up a sign outside the court urging juries to decide according to their conscience! We're living in a quasi-fascist state already!'

'Isn't all that part of what we're protesting against?' William asked, as chants of 'Just Stop Oil' began in an attempt to drown out a police loudspeaker urging them to disperse. 'Why are we here, if not to stop them getting away with all that? All that work you do, all that planning, all that risky business of digging up suppressed reports and secret notebooks – what use is it if you just stay at home and hide behind your laptop?'

'I suppose you're right,' Katy said. 'It's just...having Midge along makes me frightened. For him, not for me. I never realized how much a baby relies on you. That's what's so scary.'

'You wanted him, Katy. I did suggest...you know...'

'I did want him!' Katy said, pushing back the baby's hood so he could see more clearly. 'He's exhausting, he can be a pain in the arse, there are times when I'm so tired I feel worse than a zombie, but I wouldn't change him, not for the world. It's the world we've got to change, isn't it, so he can go on being healthy and happy? Thank you, William: that's why we're here!'

He put his arm round her, and gave her a squeeze. 'That's my girl,' he said. 'Or shouldn't I say that? I don't want to sound patronising or proprietorial, do I?'

Katy gave him a friendly push. 'Should we chant?' she asked, as the group squashed together, swayed, and shifted under pressure from the police surrounding them.

'Can do,' William said unenthusiastically. 'By the way, what did you do with that notebook I stole for you?'

'Copied it and returned it to the solicitor whose desk you had burgled. Why?'

'Just wanted to be sure it wasn't entirely a waste of time and effort. I thought the bit where he reports on meetings Zarastro had with ministers would be a big help in building the case against them, didn't you?'

'You read it all, then?'

He nodded. 'Better than any true-life crime story I've ever come across,' he said. 'Watch out!' he added abruptly.

Some members of the group on their left were trying to break through the police cordon. In response, the police began arresting them and, when they went limp, carrying them away. This created a gap in their lines which other protesters tried to break through. William grabbed the buggy.

'What are you doing?' Katy asked anxiously. 'You said they weren't going to arrest us!'

'And they're not going to,' William said shortly. 'Follow me!'

The police had drawn their batons and were beating the demonstrators who were resisting arrest.

161

Several fell to the ground, one bleeding from a cut to the scalp. This was cheered by hostile members of the crowd, which the protesters tried to counter by raising the volume of their chant.

More police drew their batons and charged into the group. Katy heard herself screaming, but William grabbed her hand and zig-zagged towards a gaggle of baton-wielding officers, pushing the buggy ahead of him and dragging Katy behind. She heard the shouting and the chanting and the jeering and the whack of wood on bone and she closed her eyes while running, expecting a blow or a punch from someone, any one of the people they pushed aside.

It seemed like they ran for miles but when they stopped and William released her hand, the smell of fear and anger was replaced by the scent of bruised vegetables. She opened her eyes to find they were in Brewer Street Market, with traders and customers going about their business as if the protest was a world away.

Katy checked on Midge and picked him up as he started to grizzle now the excitement was over. 'How – how did that happen?' she asked William breathlessly.

'Didn't I tell you we wouldn't be arrested?' he said. 'You should trust me more! How about some avocadoes? Three for a pound!'

He strode off to make the purchase. Katy watched him as she soothed their baby. She was grateful for William's quick thinking, relieved to have escaped being pummelled or arrested, ashamed of her panic, and feeling guilty about her colleagues who were now being herded into police vans while nursing their injuries.

She was also bothered about how she and Midge and William had managed to escape arrest when others hadn't. When she thought about it, rocking her baby on her breast, how did William know the police line would be thinnest where he had charged at it, when the cops were massing in force everywhere else?

She decided to stop thinking about it. Doubt was destructive. She wasn't going to play that game. She gave him a big smile when he returned with a full brown paper bag.

'What?' he said.

'Nothing,' she replied.

~ ~ ~

Felix paced up and down the red-carpeted waiting room outside Mike McDonald's mayoral office while Jazz and Robin sat on chairs that were hard enough and uncomfortable enough to discourage people from lingering.

'Felix,' Robin said through compressed lips, 'in the name of the living Christ, will you stop it?'

Felix shook his dark hair, which he hadn't had cut since his breakdown, out of his eyes. 'Stop what?' he asked, puzzled.

Robin opened his mouth but Jazz swiftly intervened to keep the peace. 'You're wearing out the carpet,' she explained. 'And you're making me nervous. When I get nervous, I get bad-tempered. And when I'm bad-tempered, I break things. You don't want that to happen, do you, Felix? So sit the fuck down!'

Felix took the chair between Jazz and Robin. He started jiggling his knees. Jazz put a hand on his right knee, Robin put a hand on his left. The jiggling subsided, then Felix slumped forward with a groan, his hair covering his face.

'What are they *doing* in there?' he moaned. Then he reared up, shaking off their hands, and would have got

163

to his feet if Robin hadn't leaned over and given him a kiss. Felix looked surprised.

'What was that for?' he said.

'I don't know,' Robin admitted. 'It was either that, or strangling you.'

'Why would you want to strangle me?'

'Because,' Jazz said, 'you can be fucking irritating. Loveable too, of course.'

'And quite cute,' Robin said. 'The long hair suits you.'

'If you two want to have a quick snog,' Jazz said, 'don't mind me. I realize my mother's peculiar sense of morality has kept you from sharing a bed, and it's been way too cold for rumpy-pumpy on a park bench, but if you think a good grapple will relieve the tension, go right ahead. I'll turn away, though I can't promise I won't peek.'

Robin and Felix looked at each other, then burst into giggles. Felix took both their hands. 'I couldn't do it with you watching, Jasmine,' he said.

'We could try a threesome, I suppose,' Robin said.

'You're training to be a priest!' Felix said.

'So? The trinity is at the centre of everything!'

'Thanks, guys,' Jazz said, patting Felix's hand and placing it on his thigh, 'but I don't fancy it. Not here and now, anyway. How long is it since you've been running, Felix?'

'I don't know. Ages. Not since Grandad...' His face fell.

Robin stroked his cheek with the back of his hand. 'It's OK,' he said softly. 'That's behind you now.'

'Thanks to Marion,' Jazz said, 'and us, of course.'

Felix shot up, his fists clenched. 'It isn't!' he declared passionately. 'It's something I've got to carry on, to see through to the end. Isn't that why we're here?'

'We're here,' Robin said reasonably, 'to support you in handing on the baton, if you like. But once Ginny in there has persuaded Mr McDonald to pick it up, that's it. You're done. You've run your bit of the relay, you go and have a shower, you get on with the rest of your life. Isn't that what we agreed?'

'It isn't that simple!' Felix wailed. He took a step forward, changed his mind, turned around a couple of times, then scrubbed his scalp in frustration. 'I don't *want* to do it, but I have to, don't you see? It's kind of like a penance?'

'But you didn't do anything wrong,' Jazz said. 'I thought you'd accepted that, after all those sessions with Marion.'

'And besides,' Robin said, 'you're not a Catholic. You don't do penance and then it's all over. You seek forgiveness and understanding, and you start by being honest with yourself. You decided that you'd caused your grandfather's death because you wanted to punish me.'

'Whoa!' Jazz said. 'How did you work that one out?'

'Isn't it true?' Robin asked Felix. 'I betrayed you, you decided to play Jesus and take the punishment yourself. Only I'm not having you nailed to a cross on my account. I love you too much for that. Though the way you behave, you do make me want to give you a good scourging from time to time.'

'You're into S and M?' Jazz said. 'That, I never suspected. I'm strictly opposed to any violence in the bedroom. If that's what you get up to, find someone else for your threesome!'

165

'It was a figure of speech, Jazz,' Robin said, keeping his eyes on Felix. 'You must have come across those from time to time.'

'I'm not sure what love means,' Felix said, pushing back his hair so he could return Robin's gaze. 'My mother talks about it a lot, but she doesn't practice it much, at least as far as I'm concerned. Grandad loved me, and Granny, in her way, and I loved them back. Until I found out this terrible thing—'

'That was my fault,' Robin said. 'I did a terrible thing to you, and I made it worse by telling you the terrible thing you went and accused your grandfather of. But it didn't kill him. You didn't kill him. How many more times can I say I'm sorry?'

'Is love the same as forgiveness?' Felix asked seriously.

'Jesus thought so,' Robin said. 'And if it was good enough for him...'

'Jesus, guys!' Jazz exploded. 'I might just have to go out and find somewhere to be sick!'

'Don't worry, Jazz,' Felix said, still looking at Robin. 'I'll need to go for a run before I can think of shagging.'

The door to the mayoral office opened just as he finished his sentence. Not noticing, Robin said, 'Ready when you are.'

'Good to know, boys and girl,' said Ginny Larue crisply. 'Mike has agreed to take up the accountability campaign, and has hired me to help. That's if you're still interested?'

Robin and Felix drew close together and enveloped one another in a passionate hug. Jazz looked at Ginny and shrugged. 'That's love for you,' she said. 'How about a drink to celebrate?'

~ ~ ~

There was no doubt that Malcolm far outclassed the other men in the gym Mercedes Ramirez went to early every Friday morning. With a light sheen of deodorized sweat, his well-defined and not at all over-developed muscles gleamed as if they'd been oiled. He lifted weights with an elegance that gave no hint of the awkwardness he normally displayed, and the methodical way he did his reps even impressed the female trainer who normally looked after Mercedes, a sinuous, shapely, all-over-tanned woman in her early fifties who had invested a lot of money and effort into looking twenty years younger.

Her marriage to the extremely weal"hy a'd sleek businessman George was the subject of much discussion. Some said she was too demanding in bed, others that she constantly repudiated her husband's approaches, which had driven him into the arms of the woman with whom his name was linked in all the gossip columns, Maxine Ensor, who'd even been ennobled, thanks to George's influence, his charitable work and his generous donations to party funds.

'Who is that?' Mercedes casually enquired as she started on the treadmill.

'Name of Malcolm Beamish,' the trainer said. 'Been here a couple of times. Bit out of his class, this place, I'd've thought. Ex-con, I shouldn't wonder, judging by those tattoos.'

'I quite like tattoos,' Mercedes said, upping her pace a little. 'As long as they don't go overboard, like David Beckham.'

'You'd have him if he walked in here, wouldn't you, lovey? You quite like a bit of rough, I'm guessing.'

'Doesn't everyone?' Mercedes asked coolly. 'I've seen you with that girl who looks like a samples book of

167

what do you call it, ironmongery? How do you kiss someone with so many rings on her lips, nose and eyebrows?'

'It adds to the pleasure, lovey. You should try it some time. Going to do your warm-up now, before your weights?'

'I'll go next to that Malcolm, I think.'

'Don't go straining yourself, lovey. I'll come and stand by you.'

'I don't need a chaperone, thank you,' Mercedes said sharply. 'And I could do with a new personal trainer. The last one you recommended was useless.'

'Useless horizontally, you mean? I wouldn't pin too much faith in young Malcolm. He's a bodybuilder, you can tell, not just a fitness fanatic, and you know they often have disappointingly small dicks. Or so I've been told.'

'I see nothing wrong with him in that department,' Mercedes said, after a casual glance.

'Appearances can be deceptive, lovey. That may all be padding. Inspect before you buy, is my advice, not that you take much notice of what I say.'

'For good reasons,' Mercedes retorted.

'Just don't say I didn't warn you, lovey,' the trainer said. 'And I look forward to your report on Trust a Trader. Or will you go for Instagram?'

Mercedes made her way towards Malcom without deigning to reply.

~ ~ ~

Sadie Macouba burst into Leo's office in her usual whirlwind way. Pumpernickel sighed and covered his head with his paws. Leo gave her a welcoming smile.

'We are making progress!' he announced before she could speak. 'Larry's notebook was stolen by someone working for Zarastro—'

'You mean you have lost it?' Sadie said, sitting herself in a chair and drawing it close to his desk so he couldn't escape her gaze.

'Absolutely not!' Leo protested. 'It was returned.'

'How?'

'How what?'

'How was it returned? Santa Claus made a late delivery? And how come you lost it in the first place? I think you are a careless man, Mr Wengrowski.'

Pumpernickel sat up and growled at this slur on his partner. Sadie waved him down. 'You be quiet!' she commanded. 'You are just as bad. You think one sniff makes you the Hound of the Baskervilles? I think I am wasting my time on one old man and his dog!'

Leo sat up very straight. 'Mrs Macouba,' he said formally, 'if you wish to terminate our agreement, you are at liberty to do so. But let me just remind you of what we have achieved so far. The report you attempted to steal from this office is now part of a dossier of evidence that will confirm your foster son's suspicions about his employer Zarastro. I have tracked down one of the main sources of Larry's evidence, Patsy Finch—'

'Whose name was in his notebook, that I gave you, and you lost!'

Leo dismissed this with a wave of his hand. 'We have it back,' he said. 'Did I tell you Ms Finch thought Larry's death was suspicious?'

'Any fool can see it was suspicious! You think he stabbed himself to death?'

'Give me a break, Sadie,' Leo said, throwing himself back in his chair. 'Zip the lip for one moment, and let me tell you the story. Then, if you want to storm out, you're welcome, OK?'

Sadie opened her mouth to protest, but Pumpernickel stopped her with a short bark. She shot him a hostile glance, then shifted in her chair, clutching her bag as if it was a weapon, and nodded at Leo.

'Thank you,' Leo said. 'So Zarastro sent someone to keep our Patsy quiet. How do I know? Because the partner of a colleague of mine happened to be with Patsy when this guy burst in. The partner also happens to know a bit about martial arts. He overpowered the intruder, and got him to confess who sent him. What is more, he persuaded him to steal Larry's notebook from this office in return for not revealing what he'd learned.'

'How did he know the notebook was here?' Sadie demanded.

'A good question. I think his partner, the young lawyer – well, actually she's a paralegal, but who's counting? – this young woman I'm working with, I reckon she must have told him after I'd mentioned the fact to her. She knew Larry too, by the way, and liked him a lot.'

'Everyone liked him, but it didn't stop him getting himself killed. So you told this girl something secret, something the police don't know about, only you and me? And then you let it get stolen? You call this professional conduct?'

'Let me finish,' Leo said. 'My young colleague's partner, the one who does martial arts, he thought Larry's notebook would be seriously useful to the campaign committee of which he and Katy are both active members. The same committee Larry was on, you know what I'm saying?'

'If Larry was on it, he would have shared this information with them, right? If he trusted them, that is.'

'Why shouldn't he trust them?' Leo asked. 'Isn't that why he turned whistleblower, for the cause they were fighting for?'

'The way I see things,' Sadie said darkly, 'I don't trust nobody. Finish your story.'

'Whether or not he told the committee about those briefings Zarastro held for government ministers, I can see the advantage of having it in writing, can't you? I think my colleague's partner believed he was doing something good for the cause.'

'But you were going to share them with this girl anyway, right? Without even asking.'

'He – Mr Martial Arts – didn't know that at the time, did he? Anyway, there's a happy ending. He handed over the notebooks to Katy, and she restored them to me. We're going to use the information about those briefings to pile the pressure on Zarastro. We want to reveal how corrupt and compromised they are by getting them to appear in front of a special enquiry I'm trying to arrange. Katy and the practice she works with are concentrating on the corporate angle while I – Pumpernickel and I – investigate any possible connection they may have with Larry's death. They must already be rattled, if they send a *blivet* to menace Patsy!'

'A what did you say?'

'A *blivet*. Two pounds of shit in a one-pound bag.'

Sadie gave him a grudging smile. 'OK,' she said. 'Now you listen to me for a change.'

'I'm listening,' Leo said, leaning forward on his elbows to show he was serious.

'What if there was someone on that campaign committee who's leaking information?'

That so surprised Leo his elbows gave way and he nearly banged his chin on his desk. Pulling himself together, he said, 'What makes you think that?'

'I get messages,' Sadie said darkly. 'On Facebook. Threatening me with all sorts. Rape. Stabbing. Chopping me in little pieces. Sending me back where I came from. They don't know it's Bermondsey.'

She gave a mirthless laugh. Leo looked horrified. 'That's terrible!' he said. 'You should report it!'

'To the police? What use are they? They're not doing anything about Larry, so why would they bother with a black nurse with a big mouth and a bad temper?'

Leo grinned ruefully. 'I wouldn't argue with that,' he said. 'But what makes you think there's an informer?'

'They say they're watching me. They know what I'm up to, where I go, who I'm seeing. You got a mention, even.'

'I suppose I should be flattered. Nevertheless—'

'They know about the notebook.'

'They do? How?'

'Exactly,' Sadie said. 'I have something to say to you, I tell you in person. No phone call, no messaging, just you and me and that dog. He may not be loose-lipped, but you are.'

'I assure you—'

'You tell that girl, she tells her partner, who knows what he does with the information, except getting it stolen and then returned? And another thing.' She leaned closer to the desk. Pumpernickel crept closer to protect Leo. 'Larry thought there might be an informer on that committee. It's in the notebook I haven't shown you. And I'm not sure I should, when you go blabbing to all and sundry.'

172

Leo tapped his pencil on his desk while he thought about all this. Then he cleared his throat. 'Sadie,' he said, 'I have only told people I trust about Larry's notebook. I cannot believe they would misuse the information. I've lived a long time and, OK, I sometimes get things wrong, but I trust my instincts, and on the whole they've come good. I certainly trust Katy, but her partner? Never met him, so I can't judge. But you know what? I'm going to check him out. My granddaughter's a whizz on the internet: she and her clever friends find stuff in places I wouldn't know where to look, and don't want to know, in case it jeopardizes my licence to practice. Patsy Finch might also know something, and I have a friend, a veteran investigative journalist, who might have a pointer or two. But the most obvious person to ask about this guy is Katy herself. Why don't I start with her?'

He got out his phone, peered and poked at It, then put it to his ear. 'Voicemail,' he said, and, into the phone: 'Katy, it's Leo. Can you give me a call? Something interesting has just cropped up I'd like to talk to you about.'

After stabbing at the off button, he threw the phone down on his desk. 'I've always believed,' he said, 'in asking straight questions, 'cos they're most likely to lead to straight answers.'

'You reckon?' Sadie scoffed. 'How many straight answers you got for me? Not a one!'

'Give me a chance,' Leo pleaded. 'An investigation takes time. You must see enough operations where complications come up and the surgeon has to take steps that weren't in his, or her, mind when they started. This case - Larry's death, Nancy Chen's, even Sidney Playfair's - gets more interesting the more we go into it. Don't stop me now.'

173

Sadie looked at him and Pumpernickel, sitting side by side, their expressions pleading, their eyes full of sincerity.

'One more chance,' she said, getting up in one energetic movement. 'But keep me informed, OK? No more surprises.'

'Agreed,' Leo said, standing up. 'And the same goes for you too.'

Sadie tossed her head and went out, slamming the door.

'That reminds me, Pumpy,' Leo said. 'We must do something about that lock.'

~ ~ ~

Marion was playing a Mozart sonata on the piano when Leo and Pumpernickel arrived carrying leeks and a packet of puff pastry. They knew better than to interrupt, so they went into the kitchen and the first thing Leo did, before even pouring himself a glass of wine, was to organize the dog's dinner: kibble made of crushed insects mixed with half a tin of chicken and turkey and some leftover roast vegetables.

Pumpernickel was a dainty eater, unlike his owner, who could rarely resist hoovering up everything on his plate as quickly as possible, despite telling himself to chew everything twenty times and put down his knife and fork between mouthfuls. Leo's excuse was that he was a war baby, when you had to eat fast in case someone nicked your rations. He'd asked Marion if there was a way to cure this habit and reinforce his willpower, at least as far as eating was concerned. She'd said he could try hypnotherapy, but why bother at his age, when she liked him exactly as he was? Which was very pleasing, but his vanity, when he caught sight of himself naked, made him worry about his shape and the way his skin had loosened,

174

especially around his neck and ankles, settling around his feet like an old pair of socks he couldn't wriggle out of.

But, he told himself, he enjoyed cooking, especially for Marion, who appreciated his efforts, and what was so terrible about celebrating the pleasures they shared, when the world was turning to shit around them, despite the efforts each of them made, in their own way, to improve matters?

'Spiced leek and mushroom tart?' he said, as Marion came in and Pumpernickel, who did have willpower, interrupted his meal to greet her.

'Sounds delicious,' Marion said, pouring herself a glass of Mâcon-Villages from the fridge. Seeing Leo didn't have a glass, she poured him one too, and clinked hers against his before sprawling in one of the kitchen chairs. Pumpernickel returned to his dish and nibbled delicately at the kibble, which he only ate because it pleased Leo. Leo mixed Boursin with single cream until it was ready to be poured over the leeks and mushrooms. He added paprika, cayenne, and a squeeze of lemon, dipped a finger into it, licked it, and added a turn of the salt mill and three turns of pepper. Then he lined an oven tray with baking paper and rolled out the puff pastry to cover it.

'I have had,' Marion said, 'an obsessive detective inspector who kept rearranging the sculptures on my table. It nearly drove me demented. Thank God for Mozart!'

She took a hefty swallow of wine. Leo sliced the leeks and mushrooms thinly, then scattered them over the pastry and drizzled them with olive oil.

'Naturally,' he said, 'you discovered the cause of his obsession and sent him away with a spring in his step.' He poured the spiced cheese mixture over the vegetables and smoothed it out with a fork. Then he put it in the oven and joined Marion at the table.

175

'It was a she,' she said, 'and she thought it sprang from her first murder, which involved a particularly gruesome division of body parts. I'm glad, sweetie, we're not eating meat tonight!'

'I'll convert you yet,' Leo said, drinking his wine. 'But?'

'But what?'

'There's always a "but" or a "however", isn't there? If it wasn't the butchery, what caused the obsession?'

'Oh,' Marion said, 'the usual. Father abandoned mother when daughter was seven, and returned a few months later when his affair ended in tears. Daughter thought it was all her fault, and devised rituals to ensure her father stayed at home. She kept them private, which of course only added to the strain, and it came to a head when she screamed at a young sergeant for using her coffee mug. He was a high-flyer who'd been assigned to help with a serial killer, it was his first day, and he was so startled he dropped the mug and burnt himself quite badly. That was when the DI was referred to me. How's your day been?'

'So-so. We got shouted at by the woman who tried burgling our office, and she thinks, or her son who was stabbed thought, there's an informer in the climate campaign committee. Which wouldn't surprise me in the least, but where do you draw the line between healthy suspicion and paranoia?'

'Is that a rhetorical question?' Marion said, pouring herself more wine. She offered the bottle to Leo, but he declined, and secretly congratulated himself.

'Happy to talk about other things,' he said airily. 'Plenty of wars to choose from. Or politicians behaving like arseholes. Did you know climate change might mean Latin America won't be able to grow potatoes? We'll have to rely on corn or maize, as we can't even count on it being warm and wet enough to grow rice. Is there an opera that deals with crises like that?'

Marion sighed theatrically. 'You really want to talk about paranoia, don't you?' she said.

'I'd be very interested in your opinion,' Leo said. 'It would help me understand the case, or cases, I'm working on. That you encouraged me to take up.'

'How long will the pie be?'

Leo twisted round to look through the glass door of the oven. 'Another quarter of an hour?'

'Shouldn't take that long,' Marion said. 'It's all to do with perception. Your average paranoiac – if there is such a thing – feels thwarted, neglected, frustrated and generally ignored. They are not stupid, they're aware of the way the world works, but cumulative failures of ambition or achievement make them feel the world is against them, for reasons they can't explain. Because it's only human nature to seek for an explanation, to come up with a story that answers all their questions, they end up inventing a set of malign forces that are just beyond their control, that either need placating or destroying, depending on how strong they feel. This gives the paranoiac an enemy that can be responsible for anything from preventing them getting the promotion they deserve, to missing the bus they were hoping to catch. It's never their fault, it's always someone, or something, else. Then they find other people who are as disappointed as they are, and they join together and comfort themselves with the idea of a conspiracy: anyone they dislike or distrust becomes part of the plot to damage or destroy them. Of course they don't use actual facts to identify their opponents, instead they rely on myths and fantasies that quickly harden into prejudices. And as with any addiction, prejudice needs ever stronger doses to be satisfying. Paranoia feeds on itself, whereas

177

people who aren't paranoid gather evidence to deal with their suspicions. If there's no evidence, healthy people put the matter out of their minds, whereas paranoiacs insist the evidence has been suppressed, and that fattens their conspiracy theories. Will that do as a summary?'

'Wikipedia couldn't have put it better,' Leo said. Then he sniffed the air and got up to open the oven door. He inspected the pie, turned it round, and put it back in. 'Three minutes,' he said, leaning against the stove. 'By your definition Sadie, the whistleblower's foster mother, isn't paranoid. Nor am I. Am I?'

'You are many things,' Marion said, 'but paranoid isn't among them.'

'I'll take that as a compliment. So if I believe the climate change campaign is riddled with informers, that's not paranoia. We know surveillance relies heavily on insiders feeding information to the authorities, insiders who can interpret what they see on all those cameras. And who is the most likely person to be an informer in a group dedicated to challenging the system?'

Marion shrugged. 'Will my guess be any better than yours?' she asked.

'If it's the same,' Leo said, 'the prize is, we can eat!'

'OK,' Marion said. She rested her head on her hand in a parody impression of someone thinking deeply. 'An undercover cop?' she suggested.

'Bingo!' Leo said. 'Lay the table, and we're off!'

Nine

William got Midge up at his usual time, fed him, changed him, put him back in his cot and was quietly getting back into bed when he noticed Katy was awake and watching him.

'What?' he said.

'Nothing,' Katy said.

'Still worried that I don't burp him right? He's fine, you know. No colic or anything. He wasn't even sick on my shoulder, like he was yesterday. Which reminds me, I must put on a wash when I get back this evening.'

'I can do that.'

'I know you can, but so can I. You've got enough to do.' He gave her a kiss, and snuggled up to her. He closed his eyes, to show that he wasn't trying to persuade her to have sex. Unless she wanted it, of course. She didn't respond by wriggling closer to him, so he sighed gently. When that elicited no response, he opened his eyes and found her staring at him.

'Anything the matter?' he asked.

'Not really,' she said.

'Then go back to sleep. You're working on the Zarastro case later, aren't you?'

She turned on her back and stared at the ceiling.

'Can't sleep?' he said. 'You want to read? Or do something more exciting?'

She gave an irritated wiggle. 'Only asking,' he said.

She turned on her side to face him, her expression serious. 'How come you were at Patsy's when that guy broke in?' she said.

He propped himself up on one elbow. 'Pure chance,' he said, reaching out to play with a lock of her hair that had fallen over her eye. 'I told you, I was helping her home with her shopping. You know she gets these dizzy spells.'

'I didn't know,' Katy said, sweeping her hair out of his reach. 'She always seems so full of energy.'

'Bit of a front, I reckon,' William said. 'She doesn't want anyone taking pity on her or anything, but she's quite vulnerable. She comes on strong, but she's a bit of a worrier, she scares quite easily. That's why I gave her a hand. And she was grateful, as it turned out.'

'You had no idea that guy was coming to try and frighten her?'

'How could I possibly?'

'I don't know, William. It's just such an odd coincidence. Like us getting away from the demo when everyone else got arrested.'

'If you'd wanted to get arrested, you could have stayed. It was Midge I was worried about.'

'Me too.' She looked at him for a while without smiling, then suddenly kissed him on the nose.

'What was that for?' he said.

'Just me being silly,' she said, and turned her back on him. But her eyes remained open while he started to snore.

~ ~ ~

'Do you think that's silly?' Felix asked, fondling a small sculpture of a snorting bull.

'For wanting to talk to your grandmother and being scared of what she might say? Not at all!' Marion said heartily. 'A frank conversation can only be helpful, as long as you're honest. You want her to understand why what happened hit you so hard, and you want to share your grief with her. She loved your grandfather as much as you did, from what you've told me. I think it can only add to the healing process.'

'It might make it worse,' Felix said sombrely. 'Robin and Jasmine want to keep me away from the campaign because they think it will be too painful. But what if Granny didn't know about Grandad blackmailing George Ramirez? You've shown me how hurtful honesty can be, and I don't want to add to her grief. Or,' he said, suddenly banging down the bull on the arm of his chair, 'what if she *did* know? I couldn't bear that!'

'When you were a boy,' Marion said, pouring herself a glass of water, 'did you ever do something you knew was wrong, and keep it to yourself?'

Felix thought about this, and said, 'You mean, like when Timmy Barrett taught me how to masturbate?'

'Did you think that was wrong?'

'*I* didn't,' Felix said simply. 'I thought it was lovely. I put a chair under the handle of my bedroom door to stop anyone coming in, and we took off our clothes. Timmy showed me what to do, and then my mum rattled the doorknob and we got dressed ever so quickly.'

'What did your mum say?'

'She was cross because she couldn't get something from my wardrobe – she kept dresses there that she didn't have room for in hers – and she said she knew we'd been doing something wrong because we were all red-faced, and if it was what she thought it was, did we know it would make us go blind? And then she laughed and went out and I asked Timmy if it was true and he said my mum was weird and he went home and we never did it again. Not together, I mean, but I did it by myself lots of times after that and it felt terrific. And I've never had to wear glasses.'

'Did you tell anybody else?' Marion asked.

181

'I told a boy called Mick Higham, who was a bit spotty though he had nice legs. We went swimming together and he invited me for a walk behind the changing rooms when no one else was about and suggested we play a game called "Naughty Fleas" where your hands jumped around pinching bits of your body and ended up on your cock. And he asked if I knew what to do after that and I told him I knew 'cos I'd done it with Timmy. Mick wore glasses and I asked if that was because of playing with himself and he said his mum and his gran and his sister all wore glasses and he didn't think they played with themselves, so the answer was no. And I felt much better after that, so we played "Naughty Fleas" a few times but then I told him we had to stop.'

'Why?'

'I got bored. There were other boys, bigger boys with better legs, which made it more exciting. Why are you asking about all this?'

'Because I wanted to know if there was a time when telling the truth made you feel better rather than worse, and obviously there was. You can be very honest with yourself, about yourself, and that should give you the courage you need to be honest with your grandmother.'

'I can be honest with her about myself,' Felix said. 'She knows I'm gay, that's never been a problem. Unlike Mum, who has a thing about it.'

'Why do you think that is?'

Felix shrugged. 'She has things about lots of subjects. Giles, her partner, thinks it's because of my real father – apparently he's one of those Greeks who has no time for gays, though their culture is full of them, isn't it? But Granny's fine with it. Is she fine about Grandad being a blackmailer? Or about me knowing about it? I really don't know.'

'She's a head teacher, isn't she?' Felix nodded. 'I would imagine there are very few things that would surprise her about people,' Marion continued. 'You might find she's stronger than you think.'

Felix put the bull back on her table and folded his arms. 'What if she isn't?' he asked. 'What if she goes all to pieces?'

'You'll be there to comfort her, won't you?' Marion said. 'You have your strengths too, don't forget. Look at the progress we've made!'

Felix slowly uncrossed his arms, then smiled. 'We have, haven't we?' he said. 'Even Robin remarked on it!'

'*Even* Robin?' Marion echoed. 'Did he have his doubts?'

'He doubts everything,' Felix said fondly. 'That's why he's reading theology.'

~ ~ ~

'What do you mean, you can't tell me?' Leo demanded crossly as he sat opposite Dennis at their usual table. 'I've just bought you a drink!'

Pumpernickel shook his head reproachfully and retreated under the table. Dennis poured himself a generous measure of wine from his carafe. 'Do you think my expertise is so easily purchased?' he demanded rhetorically. 'How would it look to my extensive contacts in the worlds of crime and policing if it came to light that I was vouchsafing confidential information to a lawyer, especially a lawyer of such dubious repute?'

'When we were young,' Leo countered, 'you were the one with the dubious reputation. I should cover Pumpy's ears before I talk of the orgies you used to organize that made the little gatherings in our basement flat look like a *kaffeeklatsch*. Luckily my dog doesn't go in for gossip.'

183

'Have you not noticed,' Dennis asked, drinking and then patting his lips delicately, 'that the more outrageous the behaviour of celebrated senior citizens, the more the public admires them? So if you think a bit of sordid blackmail will prise any secrets from my hermetically sealed lips—'

'How about I organize a Scrabble evening with Marion? And Susan, of course? She likes my cooking.'

A gleam appeared in Dennis's eyes. 'When?' he demanded.

Leo sipped his spritzer. 'Oh, maybe next Friday?' he said casually. 'Of course I'll have to check with Marion first.'

'And we play by Arbuthnot house rules?'

'The ones that allow you to use proper names you have just invented? If you like. Isn't Susan bored with you cheating outrageously in order to win?'

'How could life with me ever be boring? Susan has been fortunate enough to have enjoyed half a century of unalloyed bliss, to which our numerous children will bear witness. If you were capable of offering the delightful Marion a scintilla of the joy I have bestowed on Susan – though joy is not a quality I normally associate with you...'

'I make Marion laugh!' Leo protested. 'A lot, as it happens!'

'At your pathetic attempts at humour? Or at your general incompetence?'

'In return for my generous hospitality...'

Dennis held up a warning hand. 'You will kindly avoid making cassoulet,' he said. 'The wind factor was unendurable. Even the cat, who, like you, is now hard of hearing, abandoned our bedroom believing an earthquake was imminent.'

'I will make latkes,' Leo said. 'Potato cakes, lightly fried.'

'I am not, as you know, particularly interested in food,' Dennis said, squinting through his glass at the grey sky outside. Leo managed to restrain himself from making a comment, though he heard Pumpernickel snuffle under the table. 'It is the quality of the liquid refreshment that engages me,' Dennis continued, 'and as I recall Marion has a good cellar to add to her panoply of virtues. I imagine some of it was inherited from her father.'

'She drank all that years ago,' Leo said. 'Naturally she has excellent taste, in men as well as wine. An eye for a good vintage, you might say. Now can we talk about undercover cops?'

Dennis sighed, drank more wine, put down his glass, examined his fingernails, and said, 'By the very nature of their work they are difficult to identify. That, even someone as dense as you are must realize, is why they're chosen. Their abilities must include impersonating a character with a credible background, and remaining in character at all times, especially under extreme provocation. They must be sufficiently grounded to inspire the confidence of people who are naturally suspicious, and sufficiently strong-minded to suppress or ignore the real lives they have left behind, to which they will return when they have exhausted their usefulness. They have to have a day job that stands up to scrutiny, and which affords them a plausible way of passing on information and receiving orders. And they have to pretend to espouse attitudes that would be anathema to members of the police service, as well as turning attitude to action when the occasion demands it.'

'Yeah, yeah,' Leo said impatiently, 'but how do I find out which member of the campaign committee is

185

leaking information to the cops? Somewhere among the trillion bits of data they have on all of us, there must be a note of which cop is working to undermine which cause?'

Dennis picked up his glass and twiddled it around before taking a gulp. 'That,' he said eventually, 'is information I am not privy to.'

'What?' Leo said incredulously. 'How come? The world's most lauded crime reporter, according to you, can't identify a grass?'

'I have exposed many in my time,' Dennis said, 'including the notorious Nantwich nark who fathered three children on the leader of an extreme nationalist cell, and abandoned his long-suffering wife and mother of two teenagers to go to New Zealand and foment anti-immigrant feeling. But they have tightened up security since then, at least in the Met. The people who would happily talk to me have retired or been fired. I am still told secrets, but they tend to be fed to me rather than me ferreting them out.

'I sometimes wonder,' he added, pouring himself more wine, 'for how long I can carry on. Of course you have never done a proper day's work in your life, being self-employed as well as self-indulgent, but those of us who labour in the salt mines of the information business find the work back-breakingly hard, and getting harder. You would think, with the internet and social media and all those dubious websites claiming to reveal information that is supposedly kept secure and secret, that anyone could find anything they wanted if they knew where to look. But as with television programmes, more only means being swamped by more rubbish. Fake news is as common as the fiction you see on reality shows. Identifying the truth is harder now than it has ever been; the pollution of lies is as corrosive and destructive as any cloud of carbon dioxide.

If I had any faith in the younger generation's ability to separate fact from fiction, I would give up gladly. But I don't, so I soldier on. You might say I owe it to the world.'

He emptied his glass and banged it down. 'So you can't help me?' Leo said unsympathetically. 'All that flannel, and you're no use!'

'Any campaign committee worth its salt,' Dennis retorted, 'will suspect all information of being leaked, and every newcomer of being an informer. It's what the security services rely upon: that the energies of those committed to the cause will be dissipated and diffused by sowing doubt and dissension. What should make them more careful only makes them more paranoid.'

'Well, at least Marion doesn't think I'm paranoid,' Leo said. 'And it's obvious you don't know who these informers are, even though you have accepted my drinks and invitation. Which means you are no help to me.' He finished his drink, looked at his watch, and pushed back his chair.

'The most obvious way to identify an informer,' Dennis remarked casually, emptying the last of the carafe into his glass, 'is to select the one you suspect, feed them a titbit of information you have invented, and see if it comes out. But of course the obvious would never occur to you. There will still be Scrabble next Friday with the fair Marion?'

'Hmf,' Leo said thoughtfully, as Pumpernickel scrambled out to join him. 'I'll let you know.'

~ ~ ~

Malcolm was patrolling the perimeter on the other side of the depot from the one where the protesters usually gathered when he noticed a set of steps littered with cigarette ends and the odd used condom. The steps led to a basement with a locked door and a grimy window.

187

Malcolm peered in and could see only rubbish: old cardboard boxes spilling ancient plastic packing and the entrails of electrical equipment that had long been superseded. He judged the place was in the same area as the up-to-date gym Zarastro provided for its employees to work off the tensions of being under constant attack from kids trying to shut down their activities. There must be an internal door that gave access to it, and Malcolm went in by the next entrance to take a look.

He remembered Nathan telling him to find a place where he could do the unthinkable and imprison Mercedes. Carrying out Nathan's orders, however difficult and unwelcome, gave Malcolm a purpose, a sense of order in his disorganized life. For as long as he could remember, people had told him what to do, given him tasks which seemed pointless, criticized the way he had done them, then demanded he do more of them. Nathan was the only person, apart from his late father, who had given him explanations, sketching a pattern into which his efforts fitted, training and equipping him for the tasks he had in mind, and instilling confidence that he would succeed. However reluctant he was, Malcom still wanted to please Nathan. As with his girlfriend Gilda, he felt he owed it to him, to them both, to succeed. He'd succeeded in finding the gym Mercedes used, and managed to attract her attention. Now a chance discovery might enable him to take the next step in Nathan's programme. He was about to check this out when his phone vibrated.

His boss PJ summoned him to his office. Immediately.

~ ~ ~

Katy paced Leo's office in agitation. Pumpernickel watched sympathetically. Leo sat at his desk, waiting for her to calm down.

'Listen,' he said, 'just because you love someone doesn't mean they won't hurt you. What you do—'

Katy whirled round to face him. 'This is all your fault!' she blazed. 'Everything was fine till I met you! No wonder Helen won't see any more of you!'

'Is that what she's said? What have I done to upset her?'

'It's *me* you've upset! I can't look at-at the father of my baby without wondering if anything he says is true! You're like some poisonous Iago—'

'You should hear my sister Becky on the subject of *Othello*,' Leo said. 'Boy, does she have it in for him for being a vain, credulous, sexist fool! She once did an all-woman production which, I must admit, put it in a very different light.'

'Fuck *Othello*!' Katy said. 'What am I going to do?'

'Well,' Leo said, 'here's what I suggest. You feed him a fact we've made up and see if it comes back. Like Iago and Cassio, if you like. You tell William, if that's his real name—'

'It's the name Midge and I know him by!'

'OK, so you tell him, I don't know, how about I've found, among Nancy Chen's papers, notes about George demanding the government prosecute her for, let's say fraud or misuse of company funds. He wants her reputation trashed and for her to be deported. And Zarastro might worry that Larry Coombs had found out about these messages, and want him disposed of too. If the messages were genuine, not invented by me.'

'And if I tell him, tell William all this, what do you reckon he'll do?' Katy demanded.

'Mention where I keep it, in the safe behind the Warhol, and maybe he or the people he's working for will send someone to get it. Everyone and their mother seems

189

happy to burgle my office, why should your William be any different? Or maybe the cops – assuming that's who employs him – will be a bit more subtle and get in a denial before the news goes public.'

'It's the kind of thing they do all the time,' Katy said bitterly.

'Exactly,' Leo said. 'Only this time, you'll know who supplied them with the information.'

~ ~ ~

'You may be a useless tosser,' PJ told Malcolm, stirring sugar he wasn't supposed to have into his china mug of coffee, 'no, correction, you *are* a useless tosser, but I've got a job for you that may just about be within your capabilities, limited though those are. Are you listening?'

'Yes, PJ,' Malcolm said dully.

'We're getting a visit from the top brass. Mr Ramirez wants to take the opportunity to boost the morale of our poor beleaguered drivers, and also to reason, in front of a carefully chosen set of journos, with that rabble in front of our gates. He will explain to them, in words of one syllable, that Zarastro is one hundred per cent committed to the green revolution, but that until that happy day dawns, we will still need oil to stop little old ladies dying from hypothermia. Clear?'

'Yes, PJ. Mr Ramirez is coming here himself?'

'Isn't that what I just said? What is more, he is bringing Mrs Ramirez. Not to mention the local MP, the Minister for Climate Change, and various odds and sods who will want their arses licked. All for the benefit of the media.' He drank some coffee, grimaced, and stirred more sugar into it.

'Naturally,' he continued, 'I will have my best men, and women, out in front ensuring that the peasants behave themselves. You, naturally, will not be joining them.'

He glanced at Malcom to gauge his reaction. 'What will I be doing, PJ?' Malcolm asked simply. PJ sighed. There was little point in needling someone if they didn't react.

'You,' he said, 'will be accompanying my PA as she shows Mrs Ramirez around the facilities the company has so generously provided. And you will ensure that no trouble ensues. Do you think you can manage that?'

'Yes, PJ,' Malcolm replied dutifully. A small flicker of excitement beat within him. Things seemed to be aligning to serve his purpose, or the purpose Nathan had in mind for him. Maybe he would be able to carry out the job, despite all his misgivings.

'When is all this happening, PJ?' he asked.

PJ glanced at his watch. 'In about half an hour,' he said. 'They're on their way. Get yourself a clean hi-vis jacket. Try to stay out of shot when the photographers take pictures of Mrs Ramirez, but if they insist on snapping you, make fucking sure you smile.'

~ ~ ~

'We won't be here for long,' George Ramirez said to his wife in the back of one of the company's Range Rovers, which offered more protection than the Bentley he usually rode around in. 'You'll be back in time for cocktails or whatever.'

'I'm not drinking till the end of the month, George,' Mercedes said, 'but you probably didn't notice. I'm doing dry January, remember?'

'Whatever for?' George said. 'Are you ill?'

'I try to take care of myself. You want your wife to look like that cheap tart you go around with?'

'Max? She's not very happy with me at the moment.'

'Even after you got her made a lady lord? What more does she want?'

George sighed. 'You always said you didn't want me to accept a peerage. It was against your republican principles, you said.'

'It is! Why be impressed by a bunch of old people who bought their way into a crumbling building to flounce around in fancy dress? It would demean you to be one of them!'

'Should I take that as a compliment?'

Mercedes flicked a bit of fluff from the short black skirt that framed her shapely legs. 'We are still married, George,' she said. 'For better or worse.'

'What about for richer or poorer?'

'You think I married you because of that? You were always the one who cared about money, not me! You had nothing – you were nothing – when we met! I could have done a lot better, and you know it!'

'I do,' George agreed. 'Some people say I don't deserve you, which is wrong, because I do, but I would miss not having you around.'

'You'd have your lady lord.'

'She's useful as a mistress,' George said, 'but a mistress isn't the same as a wife. And old Faruq likes you. He's not keen on Maxine.'

'Is that why I'm important to you, George? Because the big boss likes me?'

'Let's just say it helps.'

'You think he cares about me that much?'

'In a fatherly kind of way, yes. He can be quite sentimental at times.'

'No one could ever accuse you of being sentimental, George.'

'That's true. If I show any sign of it, you can shoot me.'

'If someone else hasn't done so first.'

'I'm well protected, Mercedes.'

'And I haven't got a gun, George,' Mercedes said.' So you're safe. For the moment.'

They were now within sight of the depot, where police and security guards in high-vis jackets outnumbered a huddle of protesters holding placards. They provided a flash of colour against a cold grey sky and the ugly concrete bulk of the processing plant. When they saw the procession of Range Rovers with darkened windows, the protesters waved their banners. Reporters and TV crews readied their equipment to record the inevitable clash. It was like a dance where everyone knew the steps but was waiting for the music to start.

'When I first met you,' Mercedes said, 'I would have been among those protesters. And you would have joined me, if only to get me into bed.'

'Probably,' George said. 'And afterwards I would have told you it was a waste of time because they're never going to beat us. We are organized, they are not.'

Mercedes leaned back as missiles thrown by the seething crowd surrounding them hit the car. 'They may surprise you, George,' she said. 'I used to surprise you, once. Remember?'

'I remember,' George said, with a grin that was more self-satisfied than sad.

Mercedes sighed. The driver came round to open the door. She did up her jacket, straightened her shoulders, put on a big smile, and stepped out to face the cameras.

~ ~ ~

William was feeding Midge when Katy came back from her meeting with Leo.

'Hey,' he said.

'Hey,' Katy said. She went to kiss Midge but he screwed up his face and waved his fists around in that uncoordinated way babies have when they don't have the words to protest.

'Good meeting?' William asked, spooning apple mush into Midge's open mouth.

'Oh yes,' Katy said, flopping on the sofa. Watching William with their son, she didn't want to think he could be betraying her, and the cause. She liked him, his fierce concentration and commitment, his conviction, his body. Maybe she even loved him. Not the way she loved Midge, which was an all-consuming passion to protect her child, despite the irritation and lack of sleep involved; for William, her feelings were less visceral and more practical: she was grateful for his presence, for his help, for his taking a share of the parental burden that most men, certainly her own father, would have avoided. For being her partner in everything that mattered.

She had to force herself to see his ugly side. You can always look at someone you like and find fault, either physical – a spot, a crooked tooth, a dirty fingernail – or mental, such as their attitude to a TV show, or a certain politician, or veganism. The snorting laugh you found endearing can grate, the habit of tucking lank hair behind an ear can become maddening. Which is when you turn and snap at them, for no serious reason.

William suddenly sneezed, loudly enough to startle Midge into a little cry. Katy shot up and grabbed the boy to soothe him. 'It was just a sneeze,' William said.

194

'You frightened him,' Katy said crossly, pacing up and down. Then, over her shoulder, she said, 'Did you know Zarastro wanted Nancy Chen – the one who wrote that suppressed report – to be prosecuted and deported, to destroy her reputation?'

'Really?' William said. 'Do you want to finish feeding him? There's two spoonfuls left.' He relinquished his place next to the seat they hooked over the back of a chair, which they also used when they took Midge in the car. Katy sat down with the baby on her lap, and reached out for his food.

'Poor Larry found notes to the Home Secretary,' she said, 'asking what evidence they would need to have Nancy thrown out. Can you imagine?'

William merely shrugged. 'He'll get his food all over you,' he warned. 'Have this tea towel. It could do with a wash anyway.' Katy took it from him. How could a man who cared about such details be a traitor? She shuddered. Midge, sensing her unease, started squirming and fussing. She calmed him with food. William began to tidy up.

'I'll do that,' Katy said sullenly. She was irritated by his lack of reaction to what she'd told him. She tried again, half-heartedly.

'The lawyer I'm working with, Leo Wengrowski – he's actually got those notes to the Home Secretary. They're going to make Zarastro's insistence they're the good guys look like rubbish, aren't they?'

'If the notes are genuine,' William said, running the water in the sink to get it hot.

'Leo says they're kosher,' Katy persisted. William had his back to them. 'He's got them in his safe, among the papers Nancy left him that he hadn't bothered with until all this came up. It's an old-fashioned safe,' she added, 'hidden behind a Warhol print he got from a grateful client.'

'Well,' William said, clattering dishes, 'if the details could be checked against the ministerial diaries of the time, I guess that could be significant.'

'You reckon?'

'I reckon. Damn, we've run out of washing-up liquid. Tell you what, I'll nip round the corner, pick some up, and get us a pizza for tea. Or do you have a meeting?'

'Pizza sounds great,' Katy said, concentrating fiercely on getting the baby to finish the last spoonful. William grabbed his phone and went out before Midge could complain. Katy didn't know whether to be relieved or sad.

~ ~ ~

Malcolm located the neglected basement storeroom while pretending to hunt for a new jacket. It was in the older part of the complex that was little used, separated from the block that housed the gym and the games room and showers by a grubby stretch of broken concrete disfigured by rubble and weeds. The storeroom door was made of rusty steel and the key was in the lock. Malcolm had a quick look inside. It was dusty and dirty and smelled of oil and damp and mouse droppings. It wouldn't be comfortable, but she wouldn't be there for long, would she? He had seen the way she'd eyed his body, and the few words they'd exchanged about private training made him confident – reasonably confident – that he could persuade her to go off the beaten track for a quick fumble. He could lock her in, but then what would he do? Everyone would know he was the last person she'd been seen with: if she disappeared for any length of time, he'd be the first one they'd question. If he refused to answer, they'd arrest him, and then what would happen to Gilda?

Then he had a brainwave. It was Nathan's plan: as soon as Malcolm had got Mercedes safe, he'd call Nathan, who always had a phone to which the screws turned a blind eye. He'd suggest Nathan issue a warning to Mr Ramirez. Look what could happen to your wife, the warning would say, if you don't do...whatever Nathan wanted Mr Ramirez to do, your wife won't be so lucky next time.

It was the technique PJ employed. Malcolm was the advance guard, the hustle with muscle sent to frighten people into compliance. If that didn't work, violence followed. Malcolm thought about Patsy, and the failure of his mission there. She was a nice lady, and he hoped nothing bad would happen to her. He certainly didn't want to hurt Mercedes, who was a very nice lady indeed.

He hurried over to the gym block where he was supposed to be meeting her.

~ ~ ~

'*I* can't go, boss,' DC Alan McNeill, aka William Flanagan, said on the phone to his handler outside the convenience store round the corner from Katy's Battersea flat. 'Katy will immediately know the information came from me. She's not stupid.'

'I guess you're right,' DI Pringle said thoughtfully. 'You've already organized one burglary at Wengrowski's. Any more, and he might start complaining about police harassment. We'll move to Plan B.'

'You have a Plan B, boss?'

'Everyone has a Plan B, Alan. Everyone with ambition, that is. We will take the wind from their sails.'

'Don't we need to know that the messages exist before we rubbish them?'

'No. We will turn her into a heroine.'

'Who, Katy?'

'You're a bit besotted by Katy, aren't you, Alan?'

He turned away before a neighbour coming out of the shop recognized him. 'I wouldn't say besotted,' he muttered. 'I like her. We've had a child together, remember?'

'A child you're going to have to abandon, sooner rather than later. Better not let yourself get too attached, Alan. We don't want you going native.'

'No danger of that, boss. They trust me, that's what matters. Katy tells me everything.'

'And she doesn't suspect?'

'No way! Giving her that notebook I got Malcolm to nick was a stroke of genius, if I say so myself.'

'It's certainly proved useful in letting us know what they're focussing on. Plan B will steal their thunder.'

'How, boss? I gotta rush – I was in the middle of washing up.'

'I could do with you at my house. Jack still thinks it's women's work and leaves it for me even when I come in late. He'll make me something to eat but says washing pots keeps me grounded.'

'I'd've thought, with his salary and yours, you could afford a dishwasher, boss. He's a super, after all, isn't he?'

'We've got one, but Jack says we can't put the pans in because the coating comes off, and that's bad for the environment. We do our bit to combat climate change, you know.'

'Good for you, boss. So who are you going to turn into a heroine?'

'Nancy Chen, of course. We'll say she was ahead of her time, and it was a tragedy, not only what happened to her, but that her views on the effects of fossil fuels were ignored for so long.'

'I thought Mr Ramirez ordered her report to be suppressed, boss.'

'We say it was kept from him by underlings anxious to protect their jobs and future. A failure in communication, Alan. Mistakes were made. Lessons will be learned. That kind of thing.'

'You think anyone's going to believe that, boss?'

'Of course they will, Alan. They'll believe anything if you say it often enough, with enough conviction!'

~ ~ ~

The photographers tried to get Mercedes to show what she could do with the weights in the depot's gym, and she obliged, stripping off her jacket which she handed to Malcolm with a smile. In a tightly-fitting sleeveless top that revealed muscled arms of which Madonna would have been proud, she went through a routine with dumbbells that had them shouting for more until the PA reminded them that refreshments awaited them upstairs.

Mercedes told the PA she would follow them shortly. She and Malcolm were left on their own. He offered to wrap her jacket around her; she suggested he take his off. He was wearing a shirt of fleecy cotton which she swiftly unbuttoned and ran her hands over the pecs straining through his skimpy singlet. One hand strayed down his jogging bottoms and lingered on the growing bulge of his credentials. He hoarsely suggested they go somewhere more private, but she demurred, saying she wanted to see how he used the equipment provided. The rest of the company would be listening to her husband telling them how much he appreciated their efforts; she assured Malcolm she would appreciate his. Especially if he stripped so he was unencumbered when lifting the heavy stuff.

He shrugged off his jogging bottoms and took a grip on the barbells. He squatted, strained and raised them above his head, every sinew of every muscle standing out to perfection. Mercedes admired his calves, his thighs, his abs and his erection, which she insisted on handling while he still held the weights above his head. He warned her away, but she ignored his warning and knelt to examine it more closely. He felt his hold slipping and tried to twist away from her, but the weights evaded his grasp and caught her on the temple. She fell to the floor and the weights crashed down beside her. They rolled a little distance, but Mercedes didn't. Her head was at the centre of a pool of bright blood that crept out over the wooden floor it had cost the company so much to instal, dulling as it claimed the parquet as its own.

Malcolm had seen a lot of blood in his time. He'd been present at two stabbings, when guts had been spilled, and blood was as common as snot in prison. But he'd never seen a dead woman, let alone one who, a moment before, had had her still-open mouth around his penis. He backed away as her blood advanced on him. Who should he call first, security, emergency services, or Nathan?

PJ, as head of security, would sack him on the spot. The cops would arrest him, given his record. And Nathan? He'd wanted to make George Ramirez suffer, but by having his wife kidnapped, not killed. Nathan would blame Malcolm, though it wasn't his fault. None of this was his fault, and yet he'd probably end up back in jail. Where Nathan, or someone like him, would make Malcolm do more things he didn't want to do, and make sure he was the one who paid the penalty. He couldn't let that happen, not again.

He pulled up his shorts, snatched his phone before it got drowned in the still-advancing rust-coloured tide, and called Leo.

Ten

In a bar near the YMCA where Robin stayed when he was in London, Jazz sucked loudly on a margarita that had come with a straw as well as a little umbrella. Robin stared gloomily at a pint of Guinness.

'Drink up!' Jazz encouraged him. 'It's happy hour!'

'He no longer trusts me, does he?' Robin said. 'And who can blame him?'

'Just because he's gone to see his grandmother...'

'I should have gone with him! He's still so...vulnerable!'

'Maybe this is something he has to do alone,' Jazz said. 'A sort of penance for having that row with Sidney and not being able to make it up with him. What with him being dead and all?'

They both drank in silence, which Jazz rapidly broke. Like her grandfather Leo, she preferred noise to quiet. 'I quite like being alone with my grandmother,' she said, 'even if she is in a home. I can talk to her about anything and she either smiles vaguely or comes out with something completely different. It puts it all in perspective, you know? When there's other people there, you make conversation across her; if it's just her and me, I can include her. When you don't know what the other person's thinking, it makes you answer your own questions, and I think that's a good thing, don't you?'

'Felix's granny is as sharp as a tack,' Robin said. 'What if she makes him worse? I should have insisted on accompanying him.' He grabbed his glass and emptied it, as if he was preparing to do something important.

'I think we have to trust him,' Jazz said. 'That's what therapy is all about, trusting yourself.' She looked at her watch. 'Felix has got Marion, you've got me and Guinness. At least for another twenty minutes: I'm having supper with Gramps. Plenty of time for one more. Two, even.' She waved at the barman.

'Go on, then,' Robin said sadly. 'Felix doesn't want me, you've got your family...'

'Will you for fuck's sake stop feeling sorry for yourself?' Jazz exploded. The barman approached. In a flash, Jazz put on her sweetest smile and ordered another round. Then she hissed at Robin, 'It's always about you, isn't it? If you can't restrain yourself from buggering anybody who'll give you the time of day—'

'You can't talk!' Robin protested. 'You have a different lover for every day of the week!'

Jazz giggled. 'That's not *quite* true,' she said. 'I don't have anyone the night before my essay's due. And I'm making proper use of my time at university by exploring all available options. I don't claim to be madly in love, the way you and Felix do!'

Their drinks arrived. Jazz waved a card at the barman, who tapped it on a machine and asked if she wanted a receipt. She shook her head and thanked him, then picked up her glass. 'I'd drink to love,' she said, 'if I knew what it was.'

'I'll tell you what it is,' Robin said, touching his glass to hers. 'It's not just someone you fancy, though of course that's part of it. It's finding someone who makes you look at things differently. Someone you want to go exploring with. Someone who makes you feel stronger even though you want to protect and take care of them. Someone who can drive you mad one minute and who makes you laugh the next. Someone who brightens the world when you're with them and leaves it duller when you're not. Someone you think you know and who then surprises you. Someone—'

'Whoa!' Jazz said. 'Felix is all those things, seriously?'

'Yes,' Robin said simply. 'He is. And I screwed it all up by having a fling with a guy who couldn't stop talking about all the brave things he was doing until I had to, as you so charmingly put it, bugger him to shut him up!'

'I love Felix too,' Jazz said, 'but in a completely different way. I love it that he cares so much, about his causes and his numbers and his cross-country running. I love the way he can be ridiculously serious and then giggle like a baby. I love it that he doesn't try to make people like him, or care what they say about him. I love him for forgiving you and his grandfather for pissing him off.'

'I'm not sure,' Robin said, 'he has forgiven me. Or Sidney, come to that. I wish I knew what to do to prove he can rely on me.'

'You could try not picking someone up on your way back to the hostel,' Jazz said tartly.

'Jasmine!'

'Just kidding.' She sucked at her drink, loudly and thoughtfully. 'There's the accountability campaign,' she said, 'but you don't - we don't - want him to get too tangled up in that, not in his final year.'

'It contributed to his breakdown,' Robin said. 'But then, so did I. And his grandfather.'

'If only you - we - could prove Sidney was poisoned...'

'They haven't finished their tests, have they? Or if they have, they're not releasing the details.'

'What about the guy you had an affair with?'

'Larry Coombs? What about him?'

'According to Gramps, the cops still think his death was a homophobic robbery. What if you proved them wrong?'

'How is that going to make Felix trust me again?'

'It would show you cared. About justice, about combatting prejudice, about inadequate policing, about accountability, if you like.'

'Y-e-e-s-s,' Robin said doubtfully.

'It would show you're not just studying religion, you're putting its precepts into practice. Righting a great wrong to earn forgiveness. Doing penance by going beyond your comfort zone. Instead of moaning, investigating.'

'But—'

Jazz looked at her watch and drained her drink. 'You move in gay circles,' she said, slipping off her bar stool and picking up the rucksack she always carried. 'Maybe someone knows what really happened, and has been reluctant to come forward because they thought no one would believe them. In fact,' she said, getting more excited as she shouldered her rucksack, 'your guy – what was he called again?'

'Larry,' Robin said.

'He could be the link between Zarastro and Sidney! He was going to blow the whistle on Zarastro, wasn't he, and he went to Sidney about it, maybe a year ago? And Sidney, instead of helping him expose Zarastro, got them to finance his accountability campaign, which is what so upset Felix when you told him. So if you – we, all of us – find out who killed Larry, we'll be killing all sorts of birds with one stone! Not, I admit, the most appropriate of metaphors, but still...'

'That's all very well, Jazz,' Robin said, 'but even if I come across someone who knows what actually

205

happened to Larry, rather than the predictable speculation that all the members of his campaign committee go in for, how am I going to persuade the police to take it seriously?'

'Find something my grandfather can use,' Jazz said, 'and he'll take care of the cops. Maybe you can get a gay one to talk without using his truncheon? Got to go: see you tomorrow!'

'I might join Felix in Yorkshire tomorrow. I have a feeling he might need me.'

'Find out what you can about Larry first, then you'll really be Mr Popular!' Jazz said, banging her way out of the bar. Robin mournfully turned back to his Guinness.

As he drank, he remembered a prison chaplain he had met on a retreat he had attended. The chaplain was a Guinness drinker too. Robin got out his phone. Jazz had a point. It was better to do something about the wrong that had been done to Larry than dwell on the wrong he, Robin, had done to Felix. The prison chaplain was a start. He was gay, but Robin wouldn't sleep with him – he was determined to behave himself. Even without sex, they could have a seriously useful conversation.

~ ~ ~

Malcolm called Nathan eventually, at Leo's insistence, though Nathan didn't know that. Nathan hid the phone he'd been using inside his mattress. The screws knew it was there but never did a search without warning him first. A rare smile played around Nathan's sallow features. For once, Malcolm had exceeded his expectations. He had accidentally achieved what Nathan had been planning for years, and knocked away one of the pillars that kept George Ramirez in position. Having to do without the woman he relied on would give George a taste of the pain, the loss, the grief and the punishment Nathan had suffered ever since he had been set up to take the blame for a tragedy – multiple tragedies – that weren't his fault. Well, maybe Nancy's death was a *little* down to him, but she shouldn't have left him in the first place, should she? It had certainly earned him brownie points at Zarastro, and put him in charge of one of their companies when he was still under thirty. And he'd run it successfully until that stupid truck driver had panicked and left a container load of illegal immigrants to die. For which George Ramirez had ensured he, Nathan, had got the blame.

His smile disappeared. What was the best way to exploit this? And why didn't he feel more elated about it? It was the goal that had kept him going, the thin fuse of resentment that would one day lead to an explosive revenge. Now that moment had arrived, not quite how he'd imagined it, but undoubtedly an achievement that should have had him punching the air in triumph. Yet he felt flat. The feeling you get when you're cooling down after an orgasm. Was that it? A small spurt of pleasure before you started clearing up the mess?

Malcolm had seemed weirdly calm when he called. He'd been arrested, of course, but he'd got hold of a lawyer, the one who'd wanted Nathan to talk about Nancy, and the lawyer had him released. Obviously Mercedes' death was an unfortunate accident, like the one that happened to Nancy, not to mention the illegals. But how could he, Nathan, enjoy his triumph if he couldn't claim the credit for arranging it all? Which obviously he couldn't do without adding to the sentence he was already serving.

George would grieve for his wife, but there was the danger that his loss would only make people sorry for him. Pacing his cell, Nathan persuaded himself that the way to punish George properly would be to make him appear responsible for his wife's death. Which, of course, he was: his infidelities, his deviousness, his exploitation of her as the glamorous face of Zarastro while he pulled strings to ensure that no government would ever do anything that would harm the company's profits – was it surprising that Mercedes, known to be a woman of passion and principle, sought satisfaction elsewhere?

George drove his wife into Malcolm's arms. And if Malcolm's muscles had given way under the strain, whose fault was that?

It was a story of sex, muscles, revenge and the super-rich. The public would love it, but who would write it? And who would be brave enough to publish, on the evidence of a serving prisoner, a story that attacked someone as powerful as George Ramirez, who could afford very powerful lawyers?

Thinking about lawyers brought Leo to mind. He must have good connections, or he wouldn't have lasted so long. It was worth a little chat, anyway. He'd helped Malcolm, why shouldn't he help Nathan too, when his story was so much more sensational?

OK, the last time they'd met, Nathan had told Leo he wouldn't see him again, but things had changed. He dug out his phone, and called Malcolm, to get Leo's number.

The first time, it wouldn't connect.

The second time, it rang and rang without going to voicemail.

The third time, it told him the number wasn't recognized.

What he didn't know was, Leo had told Malcolm to get rid of his phone.

~ ~ ~

Leo and Marion had already started on their dim sum when Jazz arrived at their favourite Chinese restaurant in Queensway.

'I'm so sorry,' Jazz said, tossing her rucksack onto the fourth chair at their little table, 'I was with Robin, and lost all count of time. He's still worried about Felix.'

'We couldn't wait,' Leo said, a little sourly, 'and punctuality's never been your strong point, has it? I blame—'

'Mum,' Jazz blithely interrupted. 'She's always on time, and you can't blame me for rebelling, can you, Gramps? You'd be disappointed if I didn't!'

'It doesn't matter,' Marion said, pouring Jazz white wine. 'We've ordered enough for four, like we usually do, the food is so good here, and if there's anything you want, just ask. We end up with a doggy bag, and Pumpy has learned to love beef with mushrooms.'

'Why is Robin worried?' Leo asked, grabbing the last vegetarian dumpling before anyone else could do so. 'Marion's done a brilliant job on Felix. He's going to see his grandmother—'

'And I promised Mum I'd go and see mine,' Jazz said, using her chopsticks expertly to convey a slippery prawn and garlic dumpling to her mouth. She chewed on it, poured herself some jasmine tea, drank it, and said, innocently, 'You could come too, Gramps. Mum says it's been ages...'

'It hasn't been that long,' Leo said, his defensive tone giving way to a smile of pleasure as the waiter began bringing enough dishes to cover the entire table. 'And anyway,' he continued, helping himself to noodles, 'she never remembers who I am. Last time she decided I was a vicar and said she turned away Jehovah's Witnesses by

209

claiming to be Jewish. I must try it some time. It might be one of the few benefits of losing your foreskin.'

'How are you, Jazz?' Marion said, helping herself to sea bass with ginger. 'It's lovely to see you, which is what your grandfather meant to say, only his hunger took priority.'

'I am being very restrained,' Leo protested, piling up mushrooms and aubergine and sweetcorn and bean shoots. He plunged in while Jazz filled a pancake with crispy duck and plum sauce.

'I know you can't talk about Felix's personal problems,' she said to Marion, 'but I told Robin that finding out who killed Larry Coombs would be a great way of doing penance for having been unfaithful. Was that a stupid thing to do? It was after three margaritas.'

'Robin's nice enough,' Leo said, reaching out for some fried bean curd, 'and he seems to care about Felix, though not enough to keep his *shmeckel* in check. But Larry's mum Sadie Macouba is going to take a lot of persuading that Robin is one of the good guys—'

'She was asking me, sweetie,' Marion said gently, filling her porcelain teacup. 'I don't think it's a stupid idea at all. Undertaking a difficult and delicate task, maybe even putting yourself in danger, is a good way of showing someone you've wronged how much you care for them. Even if Felix may be preoccupied with other concerns, I'm sure it will register with him.'

'And what's he going to find that we haven't already looked at?' Leo asked, wiping mushroom sauce off his chin and reaching for his wine glass. 'I'll bet you a bowl of lychees that all he'll come up with is what the police have concluded, that Larry died as a result of a homophobic attack by hooligans.'

210

'You don't move in the gay circles Robin does, Gramps,' Jazz said.

'Ain't that the truth?' Leo said. 'I was saving buggery for my old age, till I had a colonoscopy, which more than satisfied my curiosity, thank you. Seeing your own intestine live on screen as they shove a camera up your *tuchus*—'

'Eeeuw, Gramps!' Jazz protested. 'Not while we're eating noodles!'

'Sorry,' Leo said. 'So let's talk about something else. What is Robin going to do with a degree in theology? Become a bishop?'

'I'm willing to bet, sweetie,' Marion said, tackling some scallops, 'that he'll go into something like banking or a hedge fund. They love people who bring a completely different perspective to the grisly business of making money. I get clients all the time who come to me convinced they have wrestled with their principles, and lost.'

'How do you cure them?' Jazz asked, while picking at the sea bass with ginger that Marion pushed towards her. Leo didn't interfere. He didn't eat anything with a face.

'I don't *cure* them,' Marion said. 'I help them reorder their priorities. Are they scrabbling for wealth because they want to roar down Sloane Street in a Lamborghini, or because they need to support their aged parents, or because it gives them the power to make a difference through philanthropy? If you examine your motives for engaging in the work you do, it helps you decide whether it's worth carrying on, or turning to something else.'

211

Jazz paused eating long enough to drink more wine. 'But if you take someone like Gramps,' she began, only to be interrupted by both her hosts.

'I carry on working because people still come to me who've been screwed by the system and have nowhere else to turn,' he said. 'Simple!'

'And though I avoid analysing your grandfather,' Marion said, 'I'd say his motives are absolutely clear. He's out to right wrongs, and however often he gets knocked down, he always bounces back.'

'That's a good thing?' Jazz asked ironically.

'Can you think of a better epigraph?' Leo asked. 'You can put that on my tombstone. Or, as I intend to be cremated, have it engraved on my urn. If there's room. Now, is it alright if I finish the aubergine?'

~ ~ ~

The prison chaplain managed to persuade Robin that his memory would work so much better if they went to bed. Robin wrestled briefly with his conscience and decided that if the truth about how Larry Coombs died was going to heal his relationship with Felix, then the quickest way to get it was to do as the chaplain was begging him. Felix need never know about it, and besides it was just a one-night stand, a venial sin, not a mortal one.

The chaplain knew Nathan Flowers. He knew Malcolm Beamish. He had talked to Malcolm both inside prison and after his release. Malcolm had trusted him enough to pour out his troubles, on the understanding they would go no further. But just as confession had relieved Malcolm, the chaplain also needed relief. And Robin offered it, both in the physical and the theological sense.

The chaplain talked. About how Nathan had taken Malcolm under his wing, because they were both, in

Nathan's view, victims who had been framed for murders they didn't commit. About how Nathan had groomed Malcolm – there was no other word for it – to be the instrument of Nathan's revenge against the person who had framed him, George Ramirez of Zarastro. How Malcolm was encouraged to build himself up, physically as well as mentally, so that he would be hired as a security guard on Zarastro's 'Rehab rather than recidivism' scheme. How Nathan told Malcolm to take on the dodgy tasks his bosses would set him to gain their confidence. Such as silencing an employee called Larry Coombs who was threatening to turn whistleblower.

Robin kept quiet about his own relationship with Larry because he didn't want to interrupt the chaplain's flow. He knew that Larry liked to go running at night across Hampstead Heath, but he was unaware parts of the Heath were also used by gangs of youths, both men and women, to experiment with drugs, sex and violence.

Malcolm had told the chaplain he was welcomed by one such gang because of his own (unearned and undeserved) reputation as an ex-con who had been (unjustly) convicted of killing a boy in the woods above High Wycombe. The night Larry was killed, Malcolm confessed that he had passed around some coke which his boss at Zarastro had supplied him with, and got the gang all pumped up to kill. When Larry ran by at his usual time, the gang brought him down. They all had knives, of course, and they used them. Malcolm had told them to bugger off after they'd killed him, and he took Larry's trainers so it would look like a robbery. There was only one witness, according to Larry, but he'd never come forward, and Malcolm was never questioned. That was all the chaplain knew, as they hadn't met again.

Robin found this tragic story rather moving, and was convinced Felix would too. It might also make him feel better about his grandfather. Even if Sidney had taken up Larry's case, it wouldn't have altered his grisly fate. Robin emailed what he had learned to Leo and Jazz, said a prayer for Larry's soul, and went back to bed feeling quite excited about setting off for Yorkshire in the morning.

Eleven

The death of Mercedes Ramirez was described as a tragic accident, which immediately made Dennis suspicious, especially as his police contacts were unable to give him any details. He had almost finished his first carafe of Beaujolais when Leo and Pumpernickel arrived in a state of suppressed excitement. Leo ordered drinks and put them on his own tab without even questioning whose round it was.

'Boy, do I have a story for you!' Leo said.

Dennis rolled his eyes, refilled his glass, and said, 'Astonish me!'

Pumpernickel gave a short, quiet bark. Leo apologized and opened a bag of unsalted nuts for him. 'Enjoy!' he said, putting them on the floor next to the usual bowl of water. 'Now,' he continued, turning to Dennis, 'the late Mrs Ramirez—'

'If her death was natural,' Dennis snorted, 'I am the Thin Man!' He swallowed half a goblet of wine to prove his point.

'Exactly!' Leo said. 'For once, we agree! *L'Chaim!*' And he clinked his glass against his friend's.

'On what, precisely, do we agree?' Dennis demanded. 'Your investigative skills make Inspector Clouseau look like a genius, and as you invariably jump to the wrong conclusion—'

'You remember that report you witnessed me opening? The one drawn up by a former client of mine.'

'Dr Nancy Chen,' Dennis said impatiently.

'You *do* remember!'

'My memory for names is legendary. What about her? You thought her report had been suppressed, I pointed out (a) that it would not be surprising, (b) that it was within the company's right to do so, and (c) that without proof of any kind—'

'But I have proof!' Leo said triumphantly. 'From the man who died uncovering it, who wasn't the victim of a random homophobic attack at all. You can make up for shamefully accepting the police version of events by printing the truth: his murder was arranged by Zarastro!'

Dennis looked at him sceptically. 'Oh yes?' he said. 'On what evidence?'

'Of a police chaplain,' Leo said triumphantly. 'And of a client of mine who was given the job of arranging it, and was never charged!'

He waited for Dennis's reaction. Pumpernickel poked his head out from under the table to see what would happen. Dennis puffed up his cheeks, then blew out enough air to fill a party balloon. The force of his blast fluttered the order slips on the bar behind Leo, who fortified himself with a sip of his wine. Pumpernickel returned to his nuts.

'And what, exactly, does this have to do with Mercedes Ramirez?' Dennis demanded.

'Her death may have been an accident, but responsibility lies with her husband George. His affair with Lady Ensor—'

'Which the whole world knows about,' Dennis said.

'But they don't know that he had the author of the suppressed report killed. They don't know that he pinned the blame for the deaths of those illegals he was exploiting on the guy he had promoted for killing Nancy Chen. They don't know it was on his orders that Larry Coombs was murdered. The person they got to organize that – my unfortunate client, Malcolm Beamish – was ordered by his cellmate, Nathan Flowers, to seduce Mercedes Ramirez. It was all part of Nathan's long-term plan to revenge himself on Mercedes' husband George. Mercedes found Malcolm irresistible, which unfortunately resulted in her accidental death. But the man ultimately responsible for all those bodies is none other than George Ramirez!'

'All of which is highly dramatic,' Dennis said, 'but if all you have is the evidence of convicted criminals—'

'There's more,' Leo said, emptying his glass to refresh his vocal chords. 'The *real* real story, revealed to me by the mother of the dead whistleblower, whose notebooks the police never even looked for, is this: George and Zarastro have steadily been watering down the government's commitment to clean air, through secret meetings and the sort of bribes politicians are unable to resist – you know, trips in private jets to unspoilt places, or tickets to Centre Court.'

Dennis was silent as he helped himself to more wine. Eventually he said, 'You have the notebooks?'

'I do,' Leo said. 'One of them, anyway.'

Dennis put his glass down without drinking from it, which was unusual. 'Well,' he said grudgingly, 'I dare say I could make something of that. Improper behaviour, both personal and professional. A number of deaths...'

'You can use the story on one condition,' Leo said.

'A condition?' Dennis echoed, in a voice that could have cracked ice cubes.

'One you will approve of,' Leo said bravely. 'You call for a special enquiry into Zarastro's relationship with the government. An enquiry of the type Sidney Playfair suggested, that gives a citizens' jury the opportunity to hold the company's bosses to account.'

217

'The enquiry would be a whitewash,' Dennis said contemptuously.

'Not if it was led by an independent moderator, in front of a jury who would be tasked with deciding what actually happened. A narrative verdict, we call it. Not deciding on guilt or innocence, just with establishing the truth. Like a coroner's inquest, only with live issues. And lots of bodies.'

Dennis sat back, swirling the wine around his glass. Then he said, 'I thought that accountability bill was dead and buried.'

'Not at all,' Leo said. 'Mayor Mike McDonald is going to revive it.'

'A popular figure,' Dennis conceded, 'and one outside the Westminster bubble. So your intention, fuelled by the confession of criminals, is to bypass the legal edifice in which you are an insignificant pebble, and attempt to indict, in a court that doesn't yet exist, a panjandrum beloved by princes and politicians?'

Pumpernickel put his head on Leo's knee to give him courage. 'That's one way of putting it,' Leo admitted.

Dennis poured himself more wine and gazed at Leo over the top of his glass. 'If these were normal times,' he said eventually, 'I would regard such a proposition in the way I regard most proposals of yours: risible, ridiculous and resistant to reason. But these are not normal times. We are governed by people as corrupt as they are inept, we are destroying our planet, and civilized discourse has given way to civil war. Plus I need a page one story to silence the jackals who constantly snap at my heels. Is Scrabble still on for Friday?'

'If I say yes, will you do it?'

'I will certainly investigate further. But you had better be prepared for a drubbing.'

218

'Last time we allowed you to get away with "Jerzy" with a zed.'

'A well-known name in Poland,' Dennis said. 'Drink up!'

~ ~ ~

Ginny Larue organized a launch at the House of Lords for Mike McDonald to announce he was going to take up the campaign for accountability that had been starved of support, direction and publicity since Sidney Playfair's death.

'You're wasting your time,' Maxine Ensor said, coming up to them as they looked around for people to persuade. 'You're never going to get the financial support you got from George. I'm still not sure why he sponsored it in the first place – I told him it would never pass into law – but now he's a grieving widower you can bugger off home and stop flogging a very dead horse!'

'Nice to see you too, Lady Ensor,' Ginny said confidently. 'Have you met Mike McDonald?'

'I've known Mike,' Maxine said, waving her glass around for a refill, 'since before you were born, young lady. We were elected the same year, and paired quite often, didn't we, Mike? We were younger and prettier then, but he did the sensible thing and got out of the Commons before I did. Still dyeing your eyebrows, I see, Michael. They always were your best feature.'

'At least I haven't had Botox, Max,' Mike said pleasantly. 'I'm surprised you can still smile. Tits are looking good, though. Just as well you spend a lot of time on your back.'

Ginny tried not to look startled at this very personal exchange. Maxine laughed. 'Ah, I've missed you,' she said. 'We had a better class of insult way back then, didn't we? Everything's gone to pot since. I can't tell you

219

how boring it is in the Other Place. Like an old people's home without the therapy and singalongs.'

'Food's only so-so, I hear,' Mike said. 'Nothing that requires serious chewing.'

Maxine drank some more. 'You're wasted in the provinces, you know,' she said. 'Is it true what they're saying, that you're using Sidney's stupid campaign to stage a comeback?'

'He's going to see it become law,' Ginny said, 'and make sure you lot don't cut its balls off. Aren't you, Mike?' The grown-ups ignored her, or that's how it felt. She tried again.

'Sidney always insisted it wasn't just about him, didn't he? Even you would grant him that, wouldn't you, Lady Ensor? Despite your row at that reception I never wanted him to go to.'

Maxine turned on her with a thunderous expression. 'I don't know what you're talking about,' she snapped.

Mike raised his suspiciously dark eyebrows questioningly. 'Row?' he said. 'Maxine? Surely not!'

'I wasn't even there,' Maxine said.

'How can you say that?' Ginny protested. 'I was with Sidney when you attacked him!'

'I was attending a debate in the Lords,' Maxine insisted. 'My views on the Accountability Bill are well known.'

'But you knew he had the numbers to get it passed,' Mike said. 'What did you do, threaten him? Blackmail him? Warn him of dire consequences that would affect his entire family if he persisted? I know you of old, Max, remember? I wouldn't put it past you to try and seduce him if it would stop the vote taking place!'

'I'd have to be blind drunk to seduce an old fart like Sidney Playfair!' Maxine retorted.

'I'm sure that could be arranged,' Mike said tartly.

'I tell you, I wasn't even there!'

'But you were, Max – Lady Ensor,' Ginny said. 'I was at Sidney's side, trying to get him to leave because he was late for a constituents' surgery and had to finalize his speech for the rally. And you tore into him...'

'Have you got any witnesses? Was anyone else around?'

'Well – no, apart from me,' Ginny said, taken aback. 'We were on our way out, he'd said his goodbyes, everyone else was still milling about.'

'Exactly!' Maxine said triumphantly. 'This is typical of your tactics, isn't it? You invent an attack to make your leader look like a beleaguered hero, whereas in fact nobody was taking any notice of him. It's all smoke and mirrors!'

'Come on, Max,' Mike said reasonably. 'I wasn't there, but everyone thought his bill was going to pass its Second Reading. You never could let go, could you? I can imagine you, eyeball to eyeball with Sidney, frothing at the mouth and giving him hell. You can be a tough opponent when you've got the bit between your teeth. And you have a mean right hook! I remember when you slugged that fat old Tory who pinched your bum.' He turned to Ginny. 'What did she do?' he asked. 'Challenge him to a fight? Pistols at dawn?'

'I seem to remember she gave him a push,' Ginny said.

'Impossible!' Maxine said. 'I deny absolutely that any such meeting took place. Ms Larue is making it up, just as she made up the supposed benefits of that ridiculous bill that would destroy the constitution and bring the business and the politics of our great country to a grinding halt! Sidney's death fortunately made people see sense, but I had nothing to do with it! I gave a tribute at his memorial, for Christ's sake! And without George's backing that stupid campaign would never have come to the gullible public's attention. It will be a waste of effort trying to revive it, Mike McDonald: don't say you haven't been warned!'

Mike raised his glass to her. 'I love it when you get all vehement, Max,' he said affably. 'You make me all the more determined to see an accountability bill gets on the statute book. And it will, even without Zarastro's backing. As a matter of fact, we've decided to avoid being tainted or compromised by corporate sponsorship, and we're going for crowdfunding. It's come on a lot since Sidney started: people just don't trust big corporations any more. You're the one backing a dead horse, Max. We're going for democracy in action!'

Maxine turned away so sharply she almost broke a heel. Mike emptied his glass and refused the offer of a refill.

'Right,' he said, 'I think we're done here, don't you? Unless you're desperate for another tired canapé, shall we get some fresh air?'

~ ~ ~

Robin walked the two miles from the station to the Playfairs' cottage on the edge of the Yorkshire moors. There was rain in the wind that buffeted him, and rather than huddling inside his raincoat he raised his head and felt he was being cleansed. He was intent on showing Felix how much he loved him, and felt his decision to join him in this remote northern village, as well as his wet hair, would be certain proof of his devotion. He wasn't going to make the same mistake as before, and blurt out an admission of a tiny infidelity. Sex wasn't the only thing that bound them together: what mattered was that they both cared about the same things, campaigned for the same causes, mocked the same poseurs, liked the same music, both Albinoni and Blur.

He rehearsed what he would say. About missing Felix, about feeling bad at letting him face his grandmother alone, about giving him space while wanting him to know he was there for him. He envisaged cuddles, maybe even a quickie, as Mrs Playfair was broad-minded as well as fearsome, followed by tea and hot buttered toast around a wood-burning stove.

He was not expecting Beth Playfair to open the door with a frown, look him up and down with an expression that was more irritated than welcoming, and say, grudgingly, 'Oh, it's you. You can go out and find the little bugger. He's been gone for ages.'

'What do you mean, Mrs Playfair?' Robin said anxiously, shaking the rain from his hair. 'Where's Felix?'

'Somewhere out there,' Beth said, waving a hand towards the sodden vastness of the moors. 'He came to me with some cock-and-bull story about Sidney blackmailing George Ramirez, and then he babbled about him being poisoned! They should never have let him out of the Warneford: the boy is completely deluded!'

She allowed him into the draughty little hall of a cottage that was a maze of poky dark rooms, low ceilings, small windows and mysterious staircases. Robin shrugged off the shoulder bag into which he'd hastily shoved a few clothes and the *Confessions* of St Augustine, and said, 'He's been under the care of a therapist with a worldwide reputation. He was a million times better – just like his normal self, in fact. She felt – Dr Fitzwalter – that he was

223

ready to come and see you. The things he - we've - discovered about your late husband—'

'Are complete fantasies!' Beth snapped. 'I know my grandson, Robert—'

'It's Robin.'

'Robin, then. I know Felix as well as, probably better than, anyone else: we brought him up, as I'm sure you're aware. In his formative years, before his mother decided she might after all have room for him in her life. He was always an odd child, withdrawn, solitary, on the spectrum, in my opinion, but who isn't, these days? Of course I'm not blaming him - his early life was quite traumatic - but we tried to offer him stability. And I'd like to think we succeeded: he did get a scholarship to Balliol, after all. But he always had wild ideas, and though he and Sidney had the occasional row, which usually happens between people who love one another, as I'm sure you know...'

Robin nodded vigorously. He knew.

'I never thought he would accuse Sidney of being a blackmailer! And then to tell me, in that lordly way you Oxford people put on, that he's forgiven him! I could have slapped him, though I am vehemently opposed to corporal punishment.'

Robin felt the need to defend Felix. That was why he'd made the long journey, after all. 'There is evidence—' he began.

'Can you produce it?' Beth demanded, in that head-teacherly voice that strikes terror into grown-up colleagues as well as any child within a hundred-metre radius.

Robin shivered inside his raincoat. He swallowed. 'From what I understand—' he said.

'You can't, can you? Nor could Felix. Some nonsense about a whistleblower who was killed before he could reveal the so-called details.'

'That whistleblower,' Robin said with as much firmness as he could muster, 'was called Larry Coombs, and I knew and trusted him. He told me, and I told Felix, that he made Sidney aware that Zarastro suppressed a critical internal report on the company's activities. The author of the report was killed in dubious circumstances which looks like an arranged murder. So was the whistleblower, who tried to get your husband to expose what was going on. Instead of which, we believe Sidney went to Zarastro, to George Ramirez, and threatened to expose his part in suppressing the truth if he didn't support the campaign for accountability, which was then floundering for lack of funds. Mr Ramirez obliged...'

'Because he believed in Sidney, and in accountability!'

'I suppose it depends how you look at it. And I didn't come here to attack you, Mrs Playfair.'

'Of course you wouldn't dream of attacking a grieving widow, would you?' Beth said bitterly. 'You came because of your intimate relationship with my grandson, which naturally leads you to back up his lies!'

'I assure you, Mrs Playfair—'

'This always happens, doesn't it! Sidney was a man of principle who resigned from the shadow front bench when its spineless leader went back on all his promises. That's why he set up the accountability campaign, so that politicians would stop making pledges they had no intention of keeping, and be answerable to a regulator and a citizens' jury if they broke their word. He devoted himself to it body and soul – you could say he gave his life for it – and just as he was about to see what he'd worked for come

225

to pass, he was snatched away. But not before his only grandson, whom he loved dearly, accused him, thanks to information *you* supplied him with, of blackmail! That would be enough to kill a weaker man, but now Felix arrives here babbling about some Korean poison no one's heard of! Have they lowered standards at Oxford so much that you can seriously expect a rational person to believe such nonsense?'

Robin took a deep breath. 'How did Felix react?' he asked.

'He went for a run, of course!' Beth said. 'Just like his mother, I'm sorry to say. Neither of them can face the consequences of their own irresponsibility. I tried – for years I've tried, believe me! I thought I'd got somewhere with Felix, but obviously I failed. You have no idea how painful it is to have someone you've loved and cared for turn on you and attack the one person in your life you knew you could always rely on! Forty-one years Sidney and I were married! He may not have been perfect, but we were just beginning to enter calmer waters. If his bill had been passed—'

'Mrs Playfair,' Robin interrupted, 'when did Felix leave?'

'I don't know exactly,' Beth said. 'He didn't have any breakfast.'

'And you've no idea which way he went?'

'He has the whole of the moors to choose from. But he's like a dog: he'll come back in the end. He always has before.' She blew her nose on a large cotton handkerchief she then tucked into the sleeve of her cardigan. If she felt doubt, or remorse, or even fear, Robin thought, she knew how to hide it.

'I'll see if I can find him,' he said, 'though I'm not a runner like he is. And I didn't really bring the right clothes...'

'Plenty of waterproofs you can borrow,' Beth said, turning practical. 'And take a whistle, as well as your phone. I don't suppose he's come to any harm – he knows this part of the world pretty well, he's been coming here ever since he was a boy – but if he's had a fall or sprained his ankle...'

'Just point me to the waterproofs, and I'll get going,' Robin said, with a confidence he didn't feel. What greater proof of love could there be than searching for a distraught Felix in the pissing rain? He could only imagine what the poor boy was suffering: he'd mustered the courage to confront his grandmother with the truth about her beloved husband, and she had thrown it back at him. He'd come to offer forgiveness, understanding and comfort, and she'd rejected all three. Robin pushed aside visions of Felix lying in a heap of gorse or brambles, his lovely body torn and twisted, those long legs broken or bleeding. He would wrap him in his arms until the warmth returned to his body, he would bind his wounds, he would assure him he was loved, admired and believed. But first he had to find him.

~ ~ ~

'Who the hell are you working for?' Katy demanded the moment the man she knew as William came into the flat. She wanted to shout, but Midge was having his mid-morning nap. She felt hot and cold, a fire of fury welling up inside her, tamped down by dread of the consequences of his betrayal, her shame and astonishment that she had been duped, that she had allowed herself to be so stupid.

227

He looked taken aback, but she realized what a good actor he was. It tarnished everything, corroding and crumbling her convictions right down to the core. The cause they had worked together on; what were her efforts worth if they were founded on a lie? The child they had together – surely his innocence would be corrupted?

William, or whatever his name was, took off the beanie he wore to keep his shaven head warm and twisted it in his hands. Katy noticed, and mistrusted, his every gesture. It was as if he was auditioning under a spotlight that magnified every fault. How could she have loved a man with such square, spatulate fingers? Those hands that had caressed her face and body so often, so expertly she shivered to think about it, what dirt did they dig in?

'What brought this on?' he said lightly. He threw himself down negligently on the sofa, at the other end from her, his legs spread wide, one arm along the back, within touching distance. She shrank further away. Her own legs were trembling, she wasn't sure she had the strength to get up and go to another chair. She despised herself for feeling so weak. She hated personal confrontation. You can fight, and chant, and argue for a cause, but when it came to yourself, to the person you thought you were, a person in whom you no longer had confidence, the words of accusation you want to use sound empty. Hollow. Pointless.

'You haven't answered my question,' she said dully. She felt stolid. Bunged-up. A useless lump. Of course he had never loved her. She couldn't love herself.

'You know I work in a recycling centre,' he said. His other hand, the one furthest from her, flapped the beanie on the arm of the sofa. Tap. Tap. Tap. A sign of nerves? Or menace?

'You don't,' she said, keeping her head down and her voice low, though she felt at any minute it would burst out in one long scream. She wanted it to, she wanted to vomit out the poison he had made her swallow, to cover him in a sulphurous stream of burning lava.

'All right,' he said, as if humouring her in a teasing game, 'where do you think I work, then?'

She raised her head slowly, to look him in the eye. He was smiling. That crooked-toothed smile that was so inviting and so repellent.

'Are you a cop?' she said. It wasn't meant to be a question. It should have been an accusation, hurled like a thunderbolt that would strike him between the eyes and make him disappear in a sheet of cleansing flame.

He shook his head slowly, but the smile remained. 'Katy, Katy,' he said. 'How could you even *think* such a thing?'

She cleared her throat. She needed a glass of water, but she wasn't going to move. If anyone was moving, he was.

'I want you out of here,' she said thickly. 'Now. Right now. Before he wakes up.'

'Katy...' He stretched out towards her. She wrapped her arms around herself protectively.

'Don't,' she said.

'You think I'm going to attack you?'

'Just go. Please. Now.'

'I'd never hurt you, Katy. I love you. I love the son we made together. Just give me one reason—'

Something clicked in Katy's brain that caused her tongue to unknot itself. 'That story,' she said.

'What story?'

229

'The one about Ramirez asking the Home Secretary to have Nancy Chen deported...'

'Which he's now acknowledged was a dreadful mistake. Just like those in charge of the Post Office, covering everything up, denying the truth even though people were ruined, several died, through no fault of their own. Ramirez is now saying he takes responsibility, that it was an appalling failure of communications, that lessons will be learned. Do you believe that bullshit? I don't!'

His passion brought a glow to his normally pale face. Katy had always been impressed by it. His eyes were round with sincerity and conviction.

'Is your name even William?' she said suddenly.

The tiniest flicker crossed his face, like the light that shows you a security alarm is working. Panic? Doubt? Fear? It emboldened her. She had always been someone who took the initiative, the first to volunteer, the person in a protest who stepped forward to confront their opponents, the police, the press. This man, whatever he was called, had undermined her confidence, made a mockery of her certainties, winded her courage. She could either collapse, or fight back. Hand him, and whoever he worked for, a victory, and become yet another casualty of the system, the object not of pity but derision, a dupe, or worse, a traitor who would be shunned by everyone she held dear, a woman who could not be trusted, a collaborator.

Or she could expose him, expel him, amputate him and quickly cauterize the wound, confessing to her colleagues that she had been wrong. She would have to earn back their trust. Some would be pitiless, pretending they'd always had doubts, hinting that they would never have fallen for his artificial charm, or been persuaded by his fake passion. Some would be sisterly, saying we all make mistakes, undercut by the implication that only a birdbrain would make a mistake as huge as Katy's. A mistake that would always feel as painful as a phantom limb.

She sat up. She rearranged her arms, crossing them across her chest in defiance, not as protection. 'I invented that story,' she said.

His eyes slid away from hers, then came back, duller, dimmer, with a hint of desperation. 'Why would you do that?' he asked simply. 'What's *wrong* with you, Katy?'

He was trying to put the blame on her. When you're backed into a corner, you either crumple or come out fighting. Predictable. Patronising. Pathetic.

'You are,' she said.

'What have I done? Did I forget to tuck Tata in when I left for my early shift?' Tata was the name of their son's favourite toy. 'Or was it last night's pizza? I know you're not that keen on olives. Are they giving you a hard time at the office? Because I honestly don't know why you're suddenly turning against me like this. I thought...I thought we loved each other.'

That little word. The cause, Katy thought grimly, of more trouble than religion, that created more problems than sex and politics combined. An IED you didn't realize you'd trodden on until it blew you up.

'You told your minders,' she said wearily. In the aftermath of an explosion the dazed survivors wander round picking up the pieces. 'It must have been you, it couldn't have been anyone else. We made it up, about Ramirez begging the government to have Nancy deported. You passed it on, and what happens? Within hours a story comes out with Ramirez confessing he was wrong about Nancy and he's truly sorry. Then, very conveniently, his

231

wife dies and everyone starts feeling sorry for him. Whoever employs you, I've got to admit they're good at twisting things around. So are you. Will you please leave now?'

He looked down and picked, with those spatulate fingers, at a stain on his jeans. He sighed. 'You've got me all wrong,' he said. 'But I can see, the mood you're in, it's no good explaining.'

He suddenly heaved himself upright, startling Katy but not frightening her: it was like a whale breaching the waves, making a show of taking a breath. She didn't even raise her head, just nodding to acknowledge it was over.

He hesitated, looking down on her. 'Katy,' he said, 'let me try—'

She put up her hand, palm facing outwards, to stop and silence him. He picked up his beanie, turned and left, closing the door softly behind him. It was ghostly quiet in the flat. The noon shadows slowly adjusted to his absence. Then Midge started to cry.

~ ~ ~

Robin was so wet, despite the waterproofs, that he decided Felix must have sought shelter. No one could run for very long in weather like this, on terrain like this, with gorse and brambles tearing at your boots, tripping on ruts and stones and stepping in sheep shit. He imagined Felix fuelled by anger and disappointment for a mile or two, then realizing it was pointless carrying on. He wouldn't go back, not immediately - he'd want to punish his grandmother by giving her cause for worry, in which he'd succeeded - but he wasn't foolish enough to punish himself for too long. His sessions with Marion had purged him of such craziness. Felix was quite sensible, in his own eccentric way.

Cresting a hill, Robin saw the outbuildings of a farm halfway down the next valley. A tractor was moving sluggishly around a yard, behind which was a farmhouse. It looked like the only habitation for miles. Robin was sure, with the conviction of a lover, a very wet one, that Felix had stopped there. He tried calling him on his phone, but Felix's was turned off. Robin suppressed his irritation. He was on a mission. He would not fail. He trudged towards the tractor. As he got nearer, he could see it was shifting manure. Of course it was.

~ ~ ~

Malcolm sat, massive and fidgeting, on a chair in front of Leo's desk. Pumpernickel regarded him sympathetically from his basket. Leo was waving his arms around a lot. He thought he was being patient, but Pumpernickel knew otherwise.

'They've bailed you, right?' Leo said. 'You do as I suggest, I reckon they'll drop the charges. Zarastro have kept the details out of the media, which is all to your advantage. Unless one of your security guard buddies wants to make a few bob by selling the story.'

'PJ won't let that happen,' Malcolm said. 'I bet he'll fire me as soon as this is over.'

'So?' Leo said. 'Plenty of jobs for a boy built like you!'

'Not if I have a criminal record. Unless they have a special scheme like Zarastro.'

'So you do a bit of burglary,' Leo said. 'I knew it was you last time, by the way, with that notebook. At least you didn't make as much mess as the *ganef* before you.'

'I was made to do it,' Malcolm said sullenly. 'I tried not to do any damage. Even though you couldn't help Gilda.'

'Dealing with the Home Office,' Leo said, 'is like fighting a bunch of clowns in a hall of mirrors. You think you know who you're up against, then they disappear and up pops someone else. But she's still here, your Gilda, right?'

'Under the radar. But if I go to jail...'

'If you listen, you won't go anywhere,' Leo said. 'We do a deal—'

'But Nathan said—'

Leo held up his hand. 'Just stop right there. You do realize it's Nathan who dropped you in the shit, right?'

Malcolm shifted uncomfortably in his chair, which creaked in protest. 'I'm not a grass,' he said eventually.

'But you want to stay out of jail, right? For Gilda's sake, if not your own.'

'We had a plan, well, Nathan did. It didn't include anyone dying, though.'

Leo sighed. To calm himself down, he turned round to look at the yoga class taking place in the room on the other side of the street. People of his age had squeezed themselves into Lycra that failed to flatten their lumps and bumps. But that didn't stop them twisting their arthritic bodies into positions that were absurdly graceful. One or two even looked as if they were enjoying it. If I had time, Leo thought, I might give it a go. Though thank God I don't. He turned back to his client.

'My partner Marion is a therapist,' he said. 'A very good one. Maybe you should talk to her. I can deal with your fuck-ups with the law. But a fucked-up mind, you need someone like her.'

Malcolm looked puzzled, then hostile. 'Are you saying I'm away with the fairies?' he demanded.

Leo spread his hands in a placatory gesture. Pumpernickel gave a warning bark.

'Honestly?' Leo said. 'You're no crazier than most of my clients. But I'd say, going strictly by the facts, that you can't see that you're the victim here. And as Marion might suggest, though we keep our professional lives strictly separate, you have to learn to help yourself before you can help anyone else. Anyone like Gilda, for example.'

'Leave her out of this!'

'I'm trying to. It's you I'm talking about. You've built yourself an impressive body, but inside that, you're still a little boy, aren't you? A little boy who does what other people tell him, because left to himself, he's not sure what to do.'

Malcolm's expression darkened. He leaned forward and grabbed the front of Leo's blue shirt, one that brought out the colour of his eyes. Pumpernickel shot to his feet and tugged at Malcolm's leather jacket, trying to pull him away from Leo. Malcolm swatted him away with his free hand, but the dog snarled and wouldn't let go.

'It's alright, Pumpy,' Leo said, in a voice that was surprisingly calm, considering his chest and windpipe were constricted. 'He's not going to do anything crazy, are you, Malcolm?' He managed to look Malcolm in the eye. Malcolm shook his own head as if to clear it, then opened his fist and released Leo, who sank back in his chair.

'This shirt,' he said conversationally, smoothing its surface, 'I got in Jermyn Street. Two for eighty quid. A bargain. Not.' Pumpernickel gave a short bark and returned to his basket. He picked up his yak stick and gnawed it loudly while keeping his eyes on Malcolm, warning him what might happen if he misbehaved again.

'Sorry,' Malcolm muttered.

Leo shrugged. 'No harm done,' he said. 'You didn't even rip off a button. Are you ready to listen to me now?'

Malcolm looked down at his hands, examining them as if they belonged to someone else. 'My dad,' he said slowly, 'he's dead now, of course...'

'My condolences,' Leo said automatically. Malcolm nodded.

'He said, you don't always have to be a hero. This was after I'd got done for murder.'

'The gang thing, in High Wycombe?' Leo said. 'I read your file.'

'Yeah,' Malcolm said. 'How I met Nathan. Dad told me to keep my head down. Nose clean, all that sort of thing. But when he died...' His voice tailed away.

Leo said, to fill the silence, 'Nathan stepped in?'

Malcolm nodded, still gazing at his fingers. 'He got me training,' he said. 'Taught me all sorts. To look after myself. Make sure no one messed with me.'

'Or with Nathan, presumably,' Leo said.

Malcolm raised his head to look at him. 'Nobody messes with Nathan,' he said. 'Nobody, not even the governor. People still tried to mess with me, though. Nathan wanted me to listen to my killer instinct. Trouble is, I'm not sure I ever had it.' He dropped his head again. 'I never told him that. I didn't want to let him down.'

'So what did he get you to do?' Leo asked softly.

Malcolm threw himself back in his chair and blew out his cheeks. 'It was what *they* got me to do. At Zarastro,' he said. 'Take care of stuff.'

'Like Larry Coombs?' Malcolm nodded. 'You didn't have anything to do with Sidney Playfair, by any chance?' Leo ventured.

236

'Who?'

'Forget it. And it was Nathan who got you tangled up, if you'll forgive the expression, with Mercedes Ramirez?'

Malcolm blew out his cheeks again. Pumpernickel growled. Leo tossed him a treat. 'It's OK,' he said. 'A painful experience the boy's been through.'

'PJ, the head of security, he told me to look after her,' Malcolm said.

'And before that?' Malcolm stayed silent. Leo leaned forward. 'I'll tell you what I think,' he said. 'Nathan wanted something to happen to Mercedes in order to get at her husband. You know, of course, because you're not stupid, that George was the guy who made sure Nathan was blamed for the deaths of those illegals.' He paused. Malcolm gave the slightest of nods.

'So Nathan wanted revenge. A not unnatural desire, considering he'll be in jail till he qualifies for a bus pass, while old George continues to make money and friends in high places, and enjoys having affairs with high-class floozies like Maxine Ensor. You know what I'm saying?'

Malcolm once more bobbed his head. 'I'm guessing Nathan wanted everyone to believe that George was responsible for his wife's...accident,' Leo continued. 'But the trouble is, old George is never going to be brought to trial. At least not in a court of law.'

Malcolm put his head in his hands. 'What do you mean?' he said in a muffled voice.

'The plan is, we get him to account for himself in front of a citizens' jury,' Leo said. 'It'll be a different kind of trial from the one your friend Nathan might have been hoping for, but some skilful questioning should reveal everything he's been up to. At least it'll stop everyone

237

feeling sorry for him as a grieving widower. A death for which, at the moment, you are being held responsible.'

Malcolm jerked his head up. 'It was an accident!' he protested. 'OK, Nathan did want me to kidnap her...' He stopped, and put his hands over his mouth. Leo gave him a warm, encouraging smile.

'That's what I figured,' he said. 'That's all I need, to keep you out of jail.'

'No, no,' Malcolm said. 'I couldn't – I wouldn't – Nathan would...'

'Kill you?' Leo suggested. 'Not if you don't go back inside. Just think about it, OK? Think of what your dad said. Think of Gilda. Think, maybe, of yourself, for a change?'

Pumpernickel got up and went over to Malcolm, not nuzzling or nudging him, but just standing near enough to be petted if he agreed. Malcolm hesitated for a long time, then he put out his hand and began playing with the dog's ears. Leo nodded. Pumpy made a noise that was almost a purr.

~ ~ ~

Robin picked his way across the muddy and shit-stained farmyard and, nodded on by the surly man on the tractor, opened the back door to the house. He stood, dripping onto worn flagstones, in a dark, cobwebbed hallway that felt even colder and damper than outside. Once-whitewashed walls were stained with the mud from boots and tattered jackets that drooped forlornly on battered pegs. There was a pervasive smell of wet dog, though nothing barked, in welcome or otherwise.

'Hello?' he said uncertainly. 'Felix?' He found a light switch and jiggled it, but the bulb had obviously gone. He kicked off his boots, hung up his raincoat, pushed open the nearest door, and found himself in a tack room littered with mouldering harnesses, hanging like the ghosts of long-dead horses. He backed out and tried the next door. This led to a kitchen, long and narrow, with most of the space taken up by a wooden table big enough to seat twelve, and dressers full of chipped china. The light from the grimy windows was obscured by blackened pans hanging from a contraption on pulleys that was once used for drying clothes. At least there was a bit of warmth from the ancient solid-fuel range that took up most of the end wall.

'Anyone here?' Robin said hopefully. Receiving no answer, and feeling nervous about what he might tread on in his stockinged feet, he advanced to the stove. It was hot to his touch, which gave him hope and courage. He thought he heard a noise coming from further inside the house. Looking round, he discovered a dark wooden door with an old-fashioned iron latch. When he opened it, he was confronted with a wooden staircase, uncarpeted, with worn treads and an old wooden handrail that looked unreliable. There were murmurings from above. Robin took a couple of steps up and was about to call out again, but his foot slipped, and he had to grab the handrail to stop himself falling. It wobbled dangerously in the iron hoops that pinned it to the wall, so he concentrated on mounting the steep twisting staircase without doing himself a damage.

He reached the safety of a carpeted hall and paused to get his breath back. Then he heard voices. He advanced along a dark corridor – the farmer was economical about lighting – until he arrived at a door at the end of the passage that was open a crack. It was obviously a bathroom: he could hear giggles and splashing.

239

Not wishing to intrude, he stood with his back to it, and said, 'Excuse me?'

The giggling stopped. Then a voice said, 'Robin?'

Robin pushed the door open. In the middle of a fair-sized room, under a high ceiling of blackened beams and plaster, an ancient white enamel bath stood on iron clawed feet. In the bath were two young men. One was well-built and wiry, with the kind of muscles that come from hard physical work rather than time in a gym. The other was Felix.

~ ~ ~

'I've never had a negroni,' Ginny Larue said, sipping a vodka-and-tonic on the top floor of one of the many Georgian Soho townhouses turned into 'exclusive' clubs that allowed anyone in with enough money, provided they didn't wear a tie.

'You don't know what you're missing,' Leo said. 'It was what I seduced Marion with. You want a try?' He held out his glass. 'Not, you understand, that I have any designs on your person. I am a happily settled and totally faithful lover who counts his blessings on a regular basis. And anyway, you have Mike Macdonald to contend with.'

'True,' Ginny said coquettishly. She took a sip of Leo's drink, made a face, and handed it back. 'Too sweet,' she explained, 'and far too fashionable.' She put on a breathy American voice. 'I like my drinks the way I like my men: clear, clean and dry.'

'Good to know,' Leo commented. 'though you didn't get to the best bit, which is bitter. So, you and Mike: how's it going? The funding must be rolling in if you're buying drinks in a dive like this!'

'You know he's going to stand as an Independent?' Ginny said. 'We're making three pledges: constitutional reform, including the electoral system;

240

introducing a wealth tax; and of course holding politicians accountable. He should win by a landslide.'

'I should live so long,' Leo said. 'Proper accountability: that should really make a difference.'

'That's one of the things I wanted to talk to you about,' Ginny said.

'Sidney's idea about the citizens' jury,' Leo said, 'is looking good. Dennis's article has certainly had a powerful effect. All credit to the old walrus: I never thought he'd be such an effective advocate for...what do we call it? Restorative justice? He's even promised to report on its hearings. I don't see how Zarastro can escape putting George on the stand to give evidence, however sorry people are about the death of his wife.'

'Never mind about George,' Ginny said. 'What about Maxine Ensor?'

'What about her?'

Ginny glanced around to make sure no one was listening, but they were all practising their shmoozing techniques or pretending to be busy on their phones. Nevertheless Ginny lowered her voice.

'I think she killed him,' she said.

Leo fiddled with his hearing aids. 'Sorry,' he said. 'I always forget to adjust these to party mode. I thought you said—'

'I did,' Ginny said. 'You heard right. The thing is, you see, she couldn't bear the thought Sidney was going to get the bill through. She hates losing.'

Leo took a sip of his negroni, put the glass down, and leaned forward. 'OK,' he said quietly. 'She had motive. What about means, and opportunity? Aren't the cops still looking into the poison thing?'

Ginny nodded. 'Minseng, yes. From what the scientists are saying, it's a Korean version of Novichok. I reckon Maxine got hold of some, and administered it at the APPG reception on the afternoon of the day he died. She pushed him, you see – and now she denies even being there!'

'Wait, wait, wait,' Leo said. 'She pushed him? In front of witnesses?'

'It was just me and Sidney. But I can swear—'

'I hate to damp down a nice bit of speculation,' Leo said, 'and I'd love to believe you, especially as you're buying the drinks, but without corroborative evidence...'

'I've checked Hansard. She claimed, in front of me and Mike, that she contributed to a House of Lords debate that day. But there's no mention of her making any such contribution. And Hansard never lies!'

Leo picked up his drink, swirled it around thoughtfully, then emptied it. 'And how would she get hold of this Minseng?' he asked, putting his glass down. 'Presumably it's not something you can ask for in an Asian pharmacy. She's a peer of the realm and a public figure. Not to mention the long-term lover of our old friend George Ramirez.'

'She'll dump him once he's been dumped by Zarastro,' Ginny said, signalling to a waiter for another round. 'What I wondered is, could you get your friend Dennis to write about her being a suspect?'

Leo shook his head sorrowfully. 'He wouldn't do it without evidence that can stand up,' he said. 'I know him.'

'She's quite capable of violence, you know! Mike remembered her slugging an MP she claimed had assaulted her!'

'That won't be enough for Dennis,' Leo said firmly. 'Why don't you go to him with your evidence? He has a high opinion of you.'

'And I of him,' Ginny said, 'but he might think I'm just doing it to smooth the way for Mike.'

'Aren't you?' Leo said.

'Partly,' Ginny admitted, 'but also because, if she is a killer, she should be brought to justice. You're a lawyer: isn't that what you believe?'

'The big question is "if",' Leo said. 'I have to say that, negronis or no negronis, I find it hard to believe Lady Ensor would kill a political opponent, and then pay him a fulsome tribute at his memorial. Few people hold Parliament in high esteem these days, but has it really fallen that low?'

'You'd be surprised,' Ginny said darkly, as their fresh drinks arrived.

'Then it's about time we had a new crop of MPs who'll clear things up,' Leo said, picking up his glass. 'You want to win, you want to do it cleanly. Isn't that what Sidney stood for?'

'Until he got killed,' Ginny said. 'And why should Maxine get away with murder?'

Leo sighed. 'You could always go to the police with your theory,' he said. 'But...' He made a seesawing motion with his free hand indicating his doubtfulness.

'They'd take it more seriously if it came from someone like you or Dennis, wouldn't they?' Ginny pleaded.

'I'm an optimist, as you know,' Leo said cheerfully, sipping his drink, 'but even an optimist full of negronis needs more something than a supposition to make a case!'

'But if Max didn't kill Sidney,' Ginny wailed, 'who did?'

'That,' Leo said, clinking his glass against hers, 'is still to be decided!'

~ ~ ~

'I used your name today,' Leo said, as he was brushing his teeth. 'And not in vain, either. Worked like a charm.'

Marion dried her face vigorously with her towel and emerged even ruddier than usual. 'Should I charge you?' she asked jovially.

'I should take commission! Actually,' he continued, making way for her at the basin, and pulling on the T-shirt he slept in. He never wore pants or pyjama bottoms in bed, because he liked feeling the skin of Marion's legs, and was optimistically ready for any eventuality. 'Actually, you'd find Malcolm an interesting patient. His mother is a manic chiropodist – or podiatrist, they now call them – who was accused of abusing a patient, which led to his family moving to High Wycombe. Malcolm was an only child, gangly and lonely, and he tried to make friends with the wrong people. Long story short, he was egged on to stab a rival gang member and jailed for manslaughter. Which is where he met Nathan Flowers.'

He looked in the mirror over Marion's shoulder and ran his fingers through his hair. Then, still talking, he padded into the adjoining bedroom, turned off the electric blanket, and hopped into bed while Marion finished cleaning her teeth.

'Nathan was also doing time – a long time, thirty years – for manslaughter. Naturally he insisted he was innocent. He came to see me once, before he was jailed, because he'd been the boyfriend of my client Nancy Chen...'

'Where is this going, sweetie?' Marion enquired, climbing into bed beside him. She didn't need an electric blanket because she always felt hot. 'I mean, it's all very interesting, but I'd quite like to finish my book.'

'I'll talk quicker,' Leo said, unabashed. 'So Nathan grooms Malcolm to be his instrument of revenge. Gets him to bulk up his body so he can get a job as a security guard at Zarastro who, among other philanthropic gestures, run a scheme to employ ex-prisoners. They get him to do some of their dirty work, which includes silencing the whistleblower Larry Coombs.'

'The one whose mother ransacked your office?' Marion said, picking up her book, a police procedural set in Oxford.

'That's the one,' Leo said. 'You do listen!'

'Always,' Marion said, settling back against the pillows and opening the book. 'What's more, I can listen and read at the same time. It's another of my many skills.' She settled her glasses on her nose. 'Go on,' she said. 'The unfortunate Malcolm was being exploited by all and sundry, it seems.'

'You got it in one! Is it any wonder I love you?' He kissed her chastely on the cheek. She smiled and nodded, her eyes on her book. 'OK,' Leo continued, 'then Nathan puts his plan to punish George Ramirez into operation. He holds George responsible for getting him jailed in the first place.'

'For the manslaughter of illegal immigrants,' Marion said, turning a page.

'How did you know?'

'You must have told me.'

'Did I? That would be after I went to see Nathan in jail, and accused him of killing his ex-girlfriend. He refused to talk to me after that, which I reckon is as good as a confession. Anyway, you can understand why he holds George Ramirez responsible for everything – all the deaths that have happened under George's watch, including his own wife's. And thanks to my persuasive skills, Dennis saw

245

it that way too. As well as Zarastro's corporate malfeasance.'

'He wrote a powerful article,' Marion said, turning a page. 'It might actually force the government to hold an enquiry.'

'Not just any old enquiry. The pilot scheme for a citizens' jury that you suggested!'

'If you make it happen, sweetie – you and Dennis – then the credit is yours, not mine.' She turned another page.

'In return,' Leo said, rather more quickly than usual, 'I promised we'd have Dennis and Susan over for a game of Scrabble. Is Friday alright?'

'Do we have to let him win?' Marion asked without looking up.

''Fraid so,' Leo said, letting out a relieved breath. 'It's you he wants to impress.'

'The things we do for love!' Marion sighed, turning another page. 'And where does all this leave young Malcolm?'

'Well,' said Leo triumphantly, 'I applied another of your techniques. I persuaded him to be true to himself and not always be the fall guy. Turns out that's what his late father said too. And it worked!'

Marion turned to look at him, and slid her glasses down her nose. 'What's he going to do?' she asked.

'You probably don't know, because the details were kept out of the media, that Mercedes Ramirez died trying to seduce our Malcolm. Who will naturally be the prime suspect if her death is ruled suspicious rather than accidental. Fingers crossed he'll sign a statement saying that Nathan put him up to it. Naturally he doesn't want to be a grass, but he has a girlfriend, an illegal I tried to help, and God knows what will happen to her if he goes back to jail.'

Marion looked at him unsmiling, then shook her head very slightly before returning to her book.

'What?' Leo asked anxiously. 'Is that so wrong?'

'Not at all,' Marion said.

'But?'

'But nothing.'

'Marion, look at me,' Leo begged. 'I know when you're not happy. I can tell by what you're not saying. The easiest part about being in love is saying you're sorry. Putting it right is the hard part. If I've done something wrong, tell me how I correct it. You want me to go on bended knee, even though we're in bed? I'll throw back the duvet—'

She turned towards him. There was, he was relieved to see, a smile on her face. 'Don't mess up the bedclothes,' she said. 'You've done what you thought was right for the best possible reasons. You don't have to apologize for that.'

'I know what the "but" is,' Leo said. 'You wouldn't have done it like that. You wouldn't have cajoled—'

'Blackmailed,' Marion interrupted.

'That's maybe a bit strong. Can we settle on "persuaded"?'

'I would have preferred it if he had persuaded himself, not have you do it on his behalf. But that's because I'm a therapist and you're a lawyer.'

'That's exactly what I said to him! My very words were, "I can deal with your legal fuck-ups, but if you have a fucked-up mind"...'

Marion gave a grim smile. 'Not the language I would use,' she said.

'But it's true, no? And the truth makes you free!'

Marion put her bookmark in where she'd stopped reading, and closed the book. 'Not always,' she said. 'The truth can wound, the wound can go septic, it can cause untold damage.'

'But lies,' Leo said firmly, 'especially the lies you tell yourself, the damage they cause can be fatal!'

'Also true,' Marion said, putting her book on her bedside table and turning off her light. 'Everything's a compromise, isn't it? When there's a battle between instinct and intellect, I always back instinct. Your instincts are different from mine, that's all.'

Twelve

Jazz was trying to mediate between Felix and Robin, and had chosen the London Zoo as neutral territory, using their student concessions. They sat on a bench inside the reptile house, as it was warm and relatively empty. Robin was still sulking.

'I don't understand,' Felix said, for the umpteenth time. 'You did it, and I forgave you.'

'I travelled all the way to Yorkshire.' Robin repeated.

'I never asked you to!'

'Boys, boys!' Jazz admonished. 'You love each other. You've both had flings. It's not such a big deal!'

'Not to you, maybe,' Robin retorted, 'but neither of us go on the pull the way you do!'

Felix watched an enormous python, as inanimate as the bare branch around which it was draped, slowly open one eye. Its forked tongue flickered briefly to taste the air, then Felix thought it winked at him. He cleared his throat and said, brusquely, as if taking up a conversation the others had dropped, 'Anyway, Edwin invited me to move in with them.'

Both Robin and Jazz started speaking at once.

'Edwin? You mean the boy who—?'

'The farmer's brother? How could you possibly—?'

'What would you do all day?' Jazz demanded.

'What would your grandmother say?' Robin asked.

'Marion was wrong about her,' Felix said. 'Granny refuses to believe that Grandad blackmailed Mr Ramirez. She thinks I'm a little crazy for even thinking such a thing, and if they prove Grandad was poisoned, she won't accept he could have compromised himself in any way. Everything's black or white with her. I begin to see why Mum stays away from her as much as possible.'

'But Felix,' Robin burst out, 'your mum's bonkers!'

Jazz started to protest, but Felix just nodded. 'Maybe,' he said, with a tight little smile, 'that's where I get it from.'

Robin reached out a hand, then withdrew it. 'You're one of the sanest people I know,' he said earnestly. 'You have your mad moments—'

'Everyone does!' Jazz interrupted. 'You did too!'

'And I confessed it,' Robin said sadly. 'Sometimes I wish I hadn't. If I'd kept quiet, would we be sitting here now?'

'We are where we are,' Jazz said confidently. 'That's what Gramps would say.'

'That's pretty obvious,' Felix commented, 'and not particularly helpful.'

'A useless tautology,' Robin agreed.

'OK,' Jazz said, 'forget it. The important question is, where do we go from here? Felix has his Finals coming up—'

'What does a degree matter,' Felix asked, 'when I could live in the middle of the moors and go running whenever I liked?'

Robin opened his mouth but Jazz put a restraining hand on his arm. 'You think they'd let you?' she said. 'I had a thing with a farmer in my first year. His family owned thousands of acres in Scotland, they lived in a crumbling castle that was never warm and never dry, even though they burnt whole tree trunks on an open fire. They expected Dermot, who was the youngest son, to get up before dawn to milk the grouse or whatever they kept, they lived on porridge, which was lukewarm and lumpy, they made me spend all day stalking some flatulent stag in a permanent drizzle, there was never enough water for a hot bath, and they were stingy with the supermarket scotch. Is that what you want? Because it's what you'd get, minus the castle!'

'Edwin can skin a hare,' Felix said proudly.

'You're a vegetarian,' Jazz observed.

'Yes, well, alright. But my point is...'

'The point is,' Jazz said warmly, 'Edwin may be lovely, but so is Robin. He can be a drama queen and a pain in the arse, he's not the most faithful lover in the world, but you know he loves you because he's been there for you all through this whole crisis that nearly killed you. And so have I. He may not be as pretty or as muscly as Edwin, and Port Meadow may not be as wild as Haworth or wherever those lunatic Brontes wandered about, but you've got things to do down here that you couldn't do up there. Hasn't he, Robin?' She gave Robin a nudge.

'Definitely,' Robin said. 'There's the campaign to combat the climate crisis.'

'That's your thing, not mine,' Felix said.

'The accountability campaign's very much your thing,' Robin retorted, 'and maybe we were wrong to tell you to forget about it now. You're involved whether you like it or not, and you can't turn your back on it just because of a family argument! And I know I'm not the most responsible of people, but the history of theology, the whole point of it, is that you try to do the right thing, but you keep stumbling, tripping over distractions you should learn to avoid. And whether or not God forgives you, you have to carry on down the right path, because otherwise you get caught up in the brambles. If we can forgive each other, that's like having, I don't know...'

'Secateurs?' Jazz suggested. 'Isn't that what you use to cut through brambles?'

'Shut up, Jasmine,' Robin said, looking soulfully at Felix.

'Yes, shut up, Jazz,' Felix echoed, returning his gaze.

'They want me to shut up?' Jazz said, addressing the python, who'd opened its eyes. 'Happy to oblige. I don't even expect gratitude. A cup of coffee would be nice. A drink, even better. You think I should leave them to it? If they go into a clinch, don't blame me. I dare say you've seen all sorts of encounters on this bench. Humans are only animals, dressed to kill, aren't they? We shouldn't be shocked by their behaviour.'

Felix and Robin were now holding hands. Jazz got up. 'Just tell them I'll be in the cafeteria,' she said loudly to the python. She winked at it. It definitely winked back.

~ ~ ~

Leo thought he was really getting somewhere with Malcolm, and Pumpernickel agreed, but then Sadie Macouba burst into the office making her usual commotion.

'Sadie!' Leo said warmly. 'Great timing! This is Malcolm, and he can tell you exactly how Larry died.'

Sadie looked Malcolm up and down, critically. 'Why would I trust a man like that?' she asked. 'Big body, tiny brain, that's what the doctors say.' She plumped herself down in the chair next to Malcolm's and gazed at him challengingly. 'Well?' she said. 'What you got to say for yourself?'

'Nothing wrong with my brain,' Malcolm muttered.

Leo hastily intervened. 'Why don't you tell Mrs Macouba,' he suggested, 'about Nathan, and PJ, and what you were asked to do?'

'Who you worked for, boy?' Sadie demanded.

'Zarastro,' he mumbled.

'Same as my Larry. You knew him?'

'Yeah, sort of,' Malcom admitted, avoiding her eyes.

'What department you work for?'

'Security.'

'Then you never come across him. He was in research. Very clever, my Larry. Are you clever? You don't look it!'

Pumpernickel put his head between his paws. Leo said, 'Give the boy a break, Sadie!'

'What for? He and Larry wouldn't have met.'

'He joined those protesters!' Malcolm was goaded into saying.

''Cos he knew what was right!' Sadie said. '*I* taught him! You should have joined them too, if you knew right from wrong!'

'Bunch of weirdoes,' Malcolm said, under his breath.

Sadie heard, and leaned forward. 'You calling my Larry a weirdo? A pervert like you?'

'I'm not a—'

'Malcolm,' Leo said hastily, 'was told by his boss, a Mr P J Rotherwick, the head of security and George Ramirez's go-to guy when there's dirty work to be done, to make sure Larry was taken care of. Right, Malcolm?'

Malcolm gave a reluctant nod. Sadie didn't say anything, but she made a seething noise like a kettle about to boil.

'Malcolm got in with a north London gang,' Leo continued, 'who welcomed someone with his reputation. He was,' Leo added before Sadie could interrupt, 'jailed for a stabbing he didn't commit. And he didn't actually stab your Larry. It was on the Heath, the gang was high, Larry ran by wearing a flash new pair of trainers...'

'He never spent money on himself,' Sadie said. 'Except for that.'

'Which is what attracted the gang's attention—'

'You sound exactly like the police,' Sadie interrupted. 'You saying it was all Larry's fault, just for taking a bit of exercise in the shoes he was so proud of. That's not the true story, not at all!'

'The true story,' Leo insisted, 'is that Larry's death was what you might call a contract killing. Ordered by Zarastro, possibly by old George himself – it'll be one of the questions put to him during the tribunal, you can be sure of that. George's right-hand man, P J Rotherwick, pushed Malcolm into arranging the hit. We're not saying he was blameless, we're saying he was given no choice in the matter, because of his past. He was groomed to be a killer, Sadie, by someone he met in prison, someone with an even bigger grudge against Zarastro than you have, or Larry had. The guy who groomed him – his name is Nathan Flowers – wanted to bring down George Ramirez by revealing his role in silencing people who tried, as Larry nobly tried, to expose the harm the company was doing. Unfortunately for Nathan, the fatal accident that killed Mrs Ramirez – Malcolm was there, he can give you a blow-by-blow account.'

'What do I care about the wife?' Sadie exploded. 'Does Ramirez feel the same pain I feel about Larry? If so, I'm glad!'

'Exactly!' Leo said triumphantly. 'That was what Nathan was hoping, but George has been turning it all around. He's playing for sympathy, but we're going to get justice! Truth and reconciliation, Sadie, that's what we're aiming for! If it was good enough for Archbishop Desmond Tutu...'

Sadie sprang out of her chair. Standing next to Malcolm, who shrank back in his seat, she barely came up to his shoulder, but she was a fireball of fury. 'Tutu?' she spat. 'Don't give me no Tutu! You think bringing me together with the Incredible Hulk here's going to make me feel better? Here's what I think of him, and you!'

She fumbled in her handbag and brought out a small phial. She waved it in Leo's and Malcolm's faces. 'You know what this is?' she said. 'One drop of this, and you'll die, as you deserve to. Not immediately, not like my poor Larry, bleeding out while his shoes are stripped from him. No, one drop of this on your skin and you'll have an hour or two, no more, and I'll be out of here and gone!'

She shook the phial at Malcolm, who pushed back his chair so violently he fell over, and lay sprawled on the floor, before curling up in the foetal position, trying to make his bulky body as small as possible.

Leo got up slowly behind his desk, holding up both his hands, palms facing forward in a gesture that was both submissive and peaceable. His voice was calm, reassuring, almost jokey.

'You think killing an *alte kocker* like me's going to make you feel better?' he asked. 'You won't even benefit from the insurance which, now I think about it, is probably out of date. Unless what you've got in there is just moisturiser, and you're trying to frighten us. At which, I have to say, you're not doing such a bad job.'

Sadie shook the phial at him, like a shaman about to administer ritual magic. 'Minseng, is it?' Leo continued conversationally. Surprised, she nodded. 'Where'd you get that, then?' Leo enquired. 'Don't tell me you number Korean toxicologists among your friends and admirers?'

'Dr Chun Lee Pak doesn't know I've got it,' Sadie said. 'But he boasted about it so much when he was drunk, what did he expect? And it works, I can tell you that. It works, alright!'

'Tested it on poor old Sidney, did you?' Leo asked. 'You know they've identified it, don't you? I'd put it back where you found it, if I were you. Unless you fancy being in jail, which I really don't think you'd enjoy. With your attitude, you're not going to be Miss Popular, not with the class of prisoners you'd find yourself with.'

Sadie made an explosive noise that sounded like something between a swear word and a sneeze. Which is when Pumpernickel chose to make his move. He had watched the goings-on from his basket without making a sound, and now he exchanged a rapid glance with Leo and leapt at Sadie, sinking his teeth into her arm. Leo was sufficiently prepared to grab the phial from her hand before she dropped it.

Sadie and the dog grappled with each other, Pumpernickel growling and retaining his hold as Sadie shouted and tried to shake him off. Their struggle gave Malcolm time to scrabble to his feet. He enveloped Sadie in a hug from which there was no escape, however hard she kicked and struggled. Leo sank back into his chair and examined the phial cautiously. Then he got out his phone and dialled Emergency Services.

~ ~ ~

Katy had Midge in a backpack as she marched, surrounded by her friends and colleagues, with hundreds of thousands of protesters demanding that Zarastro answer to a citizens' jury over the allegations against it. Katy felt surrounded by warmth and love, especially among campaigners supporting Mike Macdonald's new Voice of the People Party who, thanks to crowdfunding, were expected to be a significant force after the forthcoming elections.

Midge's first complete sentence was, 'Tata come on march, Mummy?' Katy was very proud of him.

~ ~ ~

'I'm really sorry, Alan,' DC McNeill's minder said, 'but you're going to have to stand trial. The Federation will provide you with a lawyer, of course, but the new commissioner is keen to show that our undercover ops don't involve taking advantage of the target by, well, getting them pregnant.'

'But you knew about Katy and Midge!' Alan protested. 'You encouraged it! You said—'

DI Pringle held up a warning hand. 'I think you must have misunderstood,' she said firmly. 'You had operational discretion: if you abused it, you must take the consequences. We will only earn back the public's trust if we take responsibility for our actions and are honest enough to own up to our mistakes. That's the new thinking.'

'What good is that going to do me?' Alan asked bitterly. He tossed back the shot of scotch his boss had bought him, on expenses, and washed it down with some beer. They were in a pub in Ladbroke Grove next to a betting shop, and the bar was crowded with people celebrating their successes or drowning their failures.

'Linda won't let me see Evie,' Alan continued, 'and you know what? That Clive is wearing my leather bomber jacket Linda and me bought in the Portobello Road. Stealing a man's wife is one thing, but stealing his clothes?'

'You'll get compensation, Alan,' DI Pringle said soothingly. 'I'll put in a word.'

'Like you were going to put in a word about my promotion? Lot of good that did!'

'Yes, well, you weren't exactly ready for the exam, were you, Alan? All over the place, you were!'

'How would you feel, ma'am, if you were given your marching orders not once, but twice, in a single day? But you don't have anybody to tell you what to do, do you? Of course you don't!' He drained his beer and banged the glass down with sufficient force to turn heads.

'That will do, Alan,' DI Pringle said quietly but forcefully. 'You're in enough trouble as it is, without facing a disciplinary charge.'

Alan gave a bark of laughter. 'All I did was obey orders,' he said. 'That's going to be my defence.'

'I think you'll find,' DI Pringle said, gathering her things together in order to leave, 'that won't be much help to you. You put yourself forward for the job, you knew what it involved. How you carried it out was entirely down to you, and the fact that it ended in failure is not going to reflect very well on your qualities as an officer.'

'Oh, is it my fault the government collapsed before the summit took place? You said nobody would listen to Katy's lot, but the government had to know what they were up to just in case. Well, people did listen,

258

didn't they? The government collapsed, nobody believes the other lot are going to do anything different, so they won't vote for them either, which means the Voice of the People are going to take charge, and they'll hold you accountable as well as me, ma'am! What will you do then?'

DI Pringle slid off her barstool with elegance. 'I'm sorry for you, Alan,' she said. 'You've been undercover for so long, you can't tell truth from fiction. Which is why the security services are shifting their reliance from human to digital intelligence. At least an algorithm can't get someone pregnant.'

Alan tried to interrupt her, but she carried on regardless. 'I performed my role to the best of my abilities, Alan, but if my operatives let me down, am I to blame? If I have made mistakes, I will acknowledge them, because I am always ready to embrace change. That's something you're not good at, I'm afraid, but you're going to have to learn, Alan, and fast, because if you don't, I can't help you.'

'You're not going to help me anyway, are you, ma'am, not really?'

'I will if you let me, Alan. But you know what they say: adapt, or die!'

She swept out in a click of Manolos. A man further down the bar leaned over to Alan. 'There's a horse called that running in the four thirty,' he said. 'Think it's worth a punt?'

'Why not, my friend?' Alan said resignedly. 'What can you lose?'

~ ~ ~

The screws raided Nathan's cell without warning him, and confiscated his phone. When he protested, they threatened to rough him up a little. He didn't resist, but

259

lay on his bunk until the officer he regarded as his special friend, Don Briggs, came to check up on him.

'What's happening, Briggsy?' Nathan asked. 'What have I done to deserve this? Haven't I always treated everyone right, kept my nose clean?'

Briggsy looked uncomfortable. 'It's not you, Nathan,' he said eventually. 'it's the new governor. No more turning of blind eyes. Any officer found to be complicit in criminal activity faces instant dismissal.'

'There won't be anyone left, Briggsy! We'll have to look after ourselves!'

'You'd think so,' Briggsy said, ''cept there's a new bonus scheme. She's magicked some money from somewhere, and they're all falling over themselves. Terrible, it is. No scruples, most of them.'

'But you're better off with me than any bonus scheme, Briggsy! Didn't I get your wife the moisturiser you couldn't afford? Not to mention the VR headset for your little boy?'

'Yeah, and he loved it, Nathan, until he broke a finger whacking a baseball out of the stand without realizing he was right up against his wardrobe. You should have heard him yell! Those kits should come with a safety warning!'

'Yes, yes, Briggsy,' Nathan said testily, 'but that's not my fault, is it? Why have my privileges been withdrawn?'

The guard looked round, then came in and pushed the cell door to. He pulled Nathan's chair up to his bunk, and sat on it cautiously. 'Remember that pillow-biter of a padre?' he said darkly.

'You shouldn't call him that,' Nathan said reprovingly. 'He was alright, the chaplain. Quite keen on young Malcolm, of course, especially when we'd got him into shape, but I made sure it didn't lead to anything.'

'That's where you're wrong,' Briggsy said, trying to keep the satisfaction out of his voice. 'He's only gone and talked about what you put Malcolm up to. And somehow that information got to that lawyer who came to see you, the one you took against. Only then you changed your mind, and that didn't do you much good did it?'

'If you mean that whole story about the unfortunate Mrs Ramirez, whose death was entirely her husband's responsibility...'

Briggsy shook his head sadly. 'No chance, Nathan,' he said. 'That lawyer's saying you groomed young Malcolm to do stuff that he didn't want to do. Like getting onto the Zarastro scheme for ex-cons and carrying out their dirty work.'

Nathan sat up and swung his legs off the bunk to face Briggsy. 'First of all,' he said, 'who trusts lawyers? No one, that's who. Secondly, what Malcolm did when he was employed by Zarastro had nothing to do with me.'

'Not according to the chaplain, if I must call him that.'

'What does he know?'

'What Malcolm told him, apparently. About you saying it was all to get your own back on George Ramirez.'

'I just wanted the truth to come out, that's all! They're going to hold an enquiry, aren't they? At least George won't be able to wriggle out of that!'

The guard got up from his chair and replaced it carefully at the little table. 'The truth will emerge about what you did too, Nathan,' he said. 'And I'm sorry to say, you're not exactly going to come out of it looking all that innocent.'

Nathan stared at him for a long while. Then he got up very suddenly, grabbed Briggsy by the throat, and began strangling him. Briggsy used his alarm, and within seconds three guards rushed to the cell. It took half a dozen of them to subdue Nathan's fury.

~ ~ ~

ARE CITIZENS' JURIES THE FUTURE OF JUSTICE?

By the World's Most Fearless Crime Reporter, Dennis Arbuthnot

I have attended many trials in my long career. I have sat through many enquiries. And I have to say I have never seen anything quite like the event that has just concluded after several days in a featureless committee room in Whitehall.

We never give enough praise to our juries. People chosen at random, of all ages and backgrounds, abandon their normal routines, leave their loved ones and their everyday concerns, put aside their prejudices, and listen patiently as terrible facts are recounted. They are not paid for their time, except for expenses; they did not volunteer, but they fulfil, without complaint, their civic duty.

This particular jury's heavy task was not to decide whether someone was guilty or innocent. It was to cut through the fog of lies, fake facts and evasions to uncover the truth: was one of the world's leading and most profitable companies breaking its word when it claimed, in a relentless and expensive campaign which was impossible to avoid, to support the government's promise to usher in an era of clean air? Or was it secretly undermining the government's proposals to improve the

262

environment – supposedly for our benefit, and the benefit of our children and our grandchildren – by ensuring nothing that could harm the company's profits would see the light of day?

We are all, sadly, used to the actions of global companies that put profit before people. We are so jaded by the greed of corporate bosses that all we do is shrug and grumble. However outrageous their actions, we let them pass because we think there is nothing we can do.

Not any more.

Not after the verdict of the heroic citizens' jury that was convened, for the first time in our history, to hold to account the people who run our daily lives. The people we put in charge, who then betray our trust. The people who promise us the world, and think they can get away with destroying it. The people who enrich themselves at our expense without regard to the simple things we care about. Unfashionable but enduring things like honour, dignity, honesty and truth.

I thought I was unshockable.

I have seen people acquitted of horrendous crimes because they could afford expensive lawyers. I have seen innocent people sent to jail because they couldn't.

But never have I seen a jury listen so intently while expert witnesses, questioned politely by lawyers who were courteously moderated by the presiding officer, testified to the involvement of George Ramirez, the CEO of Zarastro, in shameful cover-ups, appalling murders, and the bare-faced bribery of our elected representatives in order to benefit his shareholders.

The same jury listened impassively as Mr Ramirez admitted to the cover-ups, apologized to the families of those involved, and said that mistakes had been made and lessons learned. If they were familiar with such confessions, it did not show on the jurors' honest faces.

When Mr Ramirez denied that he had ever been involved in ordering the killing of employees who threatened to reveal the truth behind his activities, the jury did not believe him. Nor did they believe him when he said private meetings with ministry officials and members of influential parliamentary committees was normal business practice, to ensure these important people had a full grasp of the facts.

They listened carefully to all the evidence, and came to their own conclusions.

They were not asked whether they considered Mr Ramirez guilty or innocent.

They were not asked to decide what penalty he might be required to pay.

They were asked to separate the facts from the fiction, and their verdicts were clear. They did not believe Mr Ramirez's denials. They believed the cover-ups took place. Thanks to the confession of a convicted prisoner that I was the first to report, they believed Mr Ramirez was complicit in at least two unlawful killings, those of scientist Nancy Chen and whistleblower Larry Coombs. And they believed the company engaged in corrupt practices to bring about changes in government policy.

The government has acknowledged its failings by calling a general election. Can Mr Ramirez survive as head of a company whose activities have been deemed unlawful by a jury of impartial citizens?

Only time will tell. But things will never be the same again.

~ ~ ~

'X-O-R-G-O-Z!' Dennis said triumphantly.
'That's not a real word,' Leo objected.

'Nonsense! We agreed we're allowed proper names. He's a well-known Greek footballer. Or politician, or long-forgotten classical hero. Anyway, I get ninety-seven, with the triple letter and double word score. Should the rest of you decide my lead is unassailable, I will accept your surrender with all the grace at my command. I am never one to crow, but if you wanted to salute my success with another libation from that excellent bottle of Pomerol, I would not demur.'

'Susan,' Leo said to Dennis's wife, a thin, brisk, no-nonsense woman with white hair cut in a neat bob and rimless spectacles she took off to reveal very blue eyes, 'I don't know how you do it. If I were a cardinal, I'd vote for you as Pope. Whatever, your sainthood is assured.' He filled Dennis's and Marion's wine glasses and offered to do the same for Susan, but she put her hand over her glass.

'No more,' she said. 'It gives me wind. Would you have a mint tea, or is that an awful bore?'

'I'll make you one,' Marion said, getting up from the round table in the living room which had been cleared of its usual books and papers and was now dominated by the Scrabble board. The remains of three English cheeses – Yarg, Shropshire Blue and Single Gloucester – were on a wooden platter that had been pushed to one side. The table was large enough to accommodate used plates and cutlery as well as bottles and glasses. Marion picked up a couple of empties. Pumpernickel, who'd been lying quietly between the twin sofas that faced one another where the fireplace had once been, got to his feet and ambled over to the table to see if there were any crumbs of cheese that needed his attention.

'Does anyone else want anything while I'm up?' Marion enquired. 'I know you don't drink coffee after dinner, Dennis...'

'Because, dear lady, my body is a temple,' Dennis said expansively.

'More of a cathedral, dear, I'd say,' Susan volunteered. 'And one that is beginning to show signs of wear and tear.'

Leo snorted with laughter. 'The upkeep must be horrendous!' he said.

'Everyone loves the mystery behind a noble ruin,' Marion commented, 'but I'd say we're all in pretty good shape, at least if you judge by outward appearances. I'll get us a tea, Susan. And I think that's the last of the Pomerol, but we do have an excellent single malt from Wales...'

'I would prefer to stick to the grape, dear lady,' Dennis said. 'My needs are simple: good wine in good company.'

'Those potato cakes were lovely, Leo,' Susan said, 'and your paprika chicken. Even Dennis had a second helping, which he never does at home. But then I am rather a plain cook. When you've got four children – or five, if you count Dennis – you concentrate on quantity, not quality.'

'And I,' Dennis said with dignity, 'eat very little, as it happens. I come from a large-boned family.'

'Me too,' Marion said firmly, before Leo could comment. 'On my father's side, anyway. I wish I could have taken after my mother, who had the bones of a sparrow.'

'I love you just the way you are,' Leo said, meaning it. Pumpernickel looked up from snuffling round the cheese platter and growled his agreement.

'My brother Harold's the same,' Marion continued, patting the dog absent-mindedly, 'and he looks better in a skirt than I do.'

'Does he wear them often?' Dennis enquired.

'Where does he get them from?' Susan asked. 'You'd think it was easy, with so many outsize people around, but unless you have them made...'

'At least you did not use the politically incorrect word "fat", Susan,' Dennis said severely. 'It is not employed in polite society, nor is it an epithet I would apply to myself.'

'*I* wouldn't call you fat,' Leo said. 'Well-covered, maybe; generously proportioned; sturdily built...' Pumpernickel uttered a short warning bark. 'OK!' Leo said, throwing up his hands. 'So I'll stop digging!'

'Good idea, sweetie,' Marion said. 'And I have a feeling I have a bottle of Armagnac that a client gave me to celebrate the millennium. I'll see what I can find.' She went out, and the dog followed her.

'Do you boys want to fart and tell dirty jokes?' Susan asked. 'I can easily go and join Marion in the kitchen.'

'God forbid, Susan!' Leo said. 'First of all, we're not chauvinist pigs, as we used to call them. Secondly, we see each other practically every weekday, and tend to talk shop when we're not trading childish insults. Did he tell you he was thinking of retiring, before the great scoop that has made him once again a writer to revere?'

'What do you mean, "once again"?' Dennis demanded. 'My reputation as a crusading journalist has endured for at least half a century, and time has only burnished it! As for retiring...'

Marion appeared with a tray on which there were two mugs of mint tea with the bags still in, a bottle of vintage Armagnac, and four old-fashioned brandy balloons. Pumpernickel trotted behind her, so as not to miss anything.

'I thought you might like a sniff of this, Susan,' Marion said. 'You don't have to drink it, but if all you want to do is inhale, there's nothing better than my father's brandy balloons. And I so rarely get the chance to use them.'

'I'll give it a go,' Susan said cheerfully. 'Dennis has been talking about giving up writing because nobody wants stories that are properly researched and decently written. But I've heard it so often before, I take no notice!'

'It was our cook here – or should I dignify him with the title of chef? – thank you, dear lady,' Dennis said to Marion, accepting the drink she offered him, 'it was my old friend Leo who was maundering on about throwing in the towel.'

'I was?' Leo said. 'When?'

'You do it so often it's possible that, with your declining faculties, you are no longer aware of it. Do you not recall bemoaning your lack of achievement, not only on a personal level – always excepting,' he added gallantly, 'your relationship with the fair Marion, which I still find inexplicable, considering you are hardly the catch a woman of her qualities deserves...'

'When are you going to come to the point, dear?' Susan asked. 'Or have you forgotten it? It happens,' she explained, 'at his age. His brain is marinated, though it never seems to interfere with his writing. Can this be as delicious as it smells?' She swirled her glass around, took a sip and smacked her lips. 'It can!' she said.

'I was coming to the point, Susan,' Dennis said, sounding wounded, 'and my brain may be marinated, but that has flavoured rather than softened it. I was about to say that our friend Leo's ambitions and expectations in the spheres of the law, and even more in politics, have invariably met with disappointment. And while I naturally defer to Marion's psychological expertise, I would maintain that the pain and frustration this causes might sap the determination of most sensible people to carry on ploughing so barren a farrow. Not that anyone could dignify Leo with the adjective "sensible"!'

Leo opened his mouth, but Marion intervened. 'The reason you two remain such good friends,' she said, 'is that you are both quite similar.' This gave rise to a clamour of protest from both men; it took a sharp bark from Pumpernickel to restore order.

'Not physically,' Marion continued, unperturbed, 'not even in your viewpoints: Leo sees the best in people, Dennis sees the worst. But in the roles you have chosen to play, you both strive to do the right thing: to expose injustice, to see the bad guys caught and punished and their victims compensated. I bet you even agree on who the bad guys are, though you may quibble over the few good ones who are still standing. Does what I'm saying make sense?'

'This Armagnac makes sense of everything,' Susan said happily. 'Should we drink to justice?'

'I suppose,' her husband said, 'we could agree on that. Though it all depends...'

'To justice, Dennis!' Leo said, touching his glass to his friend's before doing the same to Susan's and Marion's. 'And you don't always have to have the last word!'

If you enjoyed *Dead Honest*, why not give *Dead Rich* a try? Here's the opening:

'The first victim was strangled,' Leo said.

'And the second was stabbed,' Rita said. 'I know.'

'And the third was pushed onto the live rail at Baker Street station. You don't see a connection here? Seriously?'

Pumpernickel, Leo's black poodle, shook his shaggy head. He was used to his master's impatience, but he was uneasy when he got tetchy. It was probably the new hearing aids getting on his nerves. Pumpy was not sure they were much of an improvement, but then he had no problem hearing things, even though he was the same age as Leo, and had more hair.

The three of them were in Leo's office two floors above a Chinese grocery in London's Soho. Pumpy had never known any other workplace in the ten years they'd been together, though Leo had been there for even longer, since quitting a City office of corporate lawyers to set up on his own. There were two rooms: the larger one, where they were now, overlooked a yoga studio on the opposite side of the street which Leo usually kept his back to. When he turned to look, he often remained gazing for a long time, and had to be recalled with a short bark, delivered from the beanbag at the side of his desk, which faced an Andy Warhol portrait of Marilyn Monroe. Leo frequently boasted this was given to him by a client in lieu of a fee, and it was large enough to cover an old-fashioned wall safe. There were three wooden chairs with arms for visitors, set on a Persian carpet that was worn in a way that added distinction rather than shabbiness.

On one of the chairs, nearest to Pumpernickel's beanbag, sat Rita Farr, a woman quite a lot younger than Leo but who treated him as an equal, which indicated to Pumpy that she wasn't a client. He thought she smelt of police, and he was almost right. She was a former CID detective who had been forced to retire or face being sacked for what the tribunal described as misconduct, though Rita knew she was being scapegoated for messing up an investigation that wasn't at all her fault.

Rita was the kind of human Pumpy appreciated: she didn't give him a perfunctory pat and then ignore him; she treated him with respect, stroking his ears and then tickling behind them when he showed he enjoyed it. She had strong fingers on a strong body, a face that must have been attractive or Leo wouldn't have paid it so much attention, a mane of straight blonde hair that was loosely tied back, and a clear firm voice without any harshness.

Leo drank the fresh coffee he'd made in the machine that was kept in the smaller office next door, where his secretary had worked when he'd had a secretary, but who needed one these days when computers did everything? He noted Rita had only sipped hers, and wondered if he should ask if there was anything wrong with it, but he didn't want to make her feel he was fussing over her. Technically she was working for him – or rather, for his client whose money was paying for her services – and Leo was keen to make the most of the situation. In all the years he'd been practising, he'd got advice and information from a variety of sources, some more kosher than others, but he'd never employed a security consultant before. His client, Emily Jackson, was a young Canadian who had inherited millions and was intent on giving most of it away. She lived in London and had arranged for a panel, randomly chosen to represent all sections of the UK

271

community, to decide who her money should go to. Three members of this panel had already been killed. Which was when Rita was hired.

9 781068 333316